JESUS' SILENT YEARS

Dear Slovia

VOLUME 4

May all your homecomings be glorious!

Homecoming

VANCE SHEPPERSON

Vance

Homecoming (Jesus' Silent Years, volume 4)
Copyright © 2021 by Vance Shepperson

ISBN's:
978-1-7344471-8-7 (e-book)
978-1-7344471-9-4 (audiobook)

Published by Carpenter's Son, Nashville, TN

Publisher's Note

This is a work of fiction. Names, characters, places, and incidents either are the product of the author's imagination or are used fictitiously, and any resemblance to actual persons, living or dead, events, or locales is entirely coincidental.

Printed in the United States of America.

Cover and interior illustrations by Dorine Deen

To my encourager and life companion, Bethyl Joy.

There are so many other things Jesus did. If they were all written down, each of them, one by one, I can't imagine a world big enough to hold such a library.

John 21:25

LIST OF MAJOR CHARACTERS
IN VOLUME FOUR

Abby, Slow's blood sister from the same mother and father, Ahab, Dhiban's chief rabbi

Ahab, Dhiban's chief rabbi

Caligula, Germanicus' younger son, one of Tiberius' lovers, 3rd emperor of Rome

Claudia, daughter to Tribune Gaius and Livena, granddaughter of Caesar Augustus

Crispus, Samaritan terrorist, demon-harassed, all-around bad guy

Deborah, Jesus' youngest sibling

El Abba, God the Father in Hebrew Scriptures

Emil, Ahab's older son

Ester, Slow, Leah, and Abby's Jewish-Moabite mother

Esther, Rav Moshe's wife

Gemellus, Drusus' grandson, Germanicus' oldest son, adopted by Tiberius

Gomaria, Go, sister to Leah, wife of Laz, name changed to Slow by Jesus

James, Jesus next youngest brother, three years younger

John, also called John the Baptist, Jesus' second cousin

Jesus, also called: Jesus bar Joseph, Messiah, Jesus of Nazareth

Jude, Jesus' middle brother, after James, before Justus

Julius, Jesus' childhood friend from Egypt, son of Egyptian Prefect

Justus, Jesus' youngest brother

Laz, called Lazarus, Jesus' close friend, husband of Gomaria

Leah, daughter of Achan, sister to Gomaria, or Go; wife to Rabbus, mother to Gabe

Livena, wife to Tribune Gaius, illegitimate daughter of Augustus, Claudia's mother

Livia, wife to Caesar Augustus, also known as Augusta

Maltesa, known also as Maltie, husband to Rastus, rich merchant in Jericho

Mary, wife to Ehud, daughter of Hez and Beta, sister to Martha and Laz

Mary, Jesus' mother, daughter of Eli, a scribe

Martha, wife to Mordi, daughter of Hez and Beta, sister to Mary and Laz

Miriam, Jesus younger sister

Mordi, Martha's husband; Laz's brother-in-law

Moshe, called Rav, Jesus' teacher from age eight to twenty-eight

Rastus, healed murder-thief-leper, married to Maltesa, older half-brother to Zacchaeus

Roy, El Roi, proprietor of Rahab's, wise man, disguised incarnation of God the Father

Tiberius, adopted son of Augustus, birth son of Augusta (or Livia), 2nd Roman emperor

Zacchaeus, tax collector in Jericho, husband to Esmeralda, younger half-brother to Rastus

Zayan, younger son to Ahab

You can find most of these people inside you. But only if you stretch your imagination.

TABLE OF CONTENTS

PREFACE

Homecoming is the final novel in the series, Jesus' Silent Years.
The previous three volumes,
Foundations, Parable, and Journey,
followed Jesus from age 13 to 26.
When this book opens, Jesus is twenty-six years old.
He lives within Castle Rozafa, located in Scodra,
the capital city of Illyria (modern-day Albania).
The young Messiah is in a bad fix.
He suffers with plague and famine.
The castle is under siege by enemies.
Everyone is starving or been killed by plague.
Enemies threaten to break through, torture, and kill whoever's left alive.
Two cousins, Gemellus and Caligula, feud.
Which of them will succeed Tiberius as next emperor of the Roman empire?

1

WINDY

The night before his assassination, Gemellus reclined at table across from his Uncle Tiberius, cousin Claudia, and Jesus. Caligula sat beside Tiberius, massaging his neck. Servants brought their one meal for the day, slippers shush-shushing into the cavernous banquet hall.

Gemellus looked at what they'd placed in front of him—a hot, open-faced ham and onion sandwich, dripping with horseradish garnish, a side of deviled eggs, and a Caesar salad. Iced herb tea, sweetened with honey and topped with mint leaves, was to the right of his plate.

He blinked. What remained on the table was a bowl of thin gruel with a lonely carrot peel floating on the top. Everyone else's place setting held a similar bowl and the same soup.

Decades of incense were heavy in the air, floating down from the wall tapestries or off the oriental carpets, mingling with the stink of unwashed bodies. The massive stone fireplace, smudged by many fires, was big enough to baste a brace of boars—or alternately, a good-sized giraffe with his head up the flue. But tonight, nothing; it was dark and empty.

Gemellus sipped his soup from a silver spoon. He re-capped, "the siege has already lasted a year, Uncle. Pox and battle have decimated two-thirds of our army. The only remaining meat inside the castle is human, and those corpses are worthless. Eating poxed people poxes people—so, we burn them. We live with the smell of roasted flesh in the air. Our stomachs remind us daily that living dogs are better than dead lions."

Tiberius had lost a third of his body weight during the last year of siege. He said, "I've never thought I'd eat my citizens. But now, I'm melting to sticks. I've taken to hoping a non-poxed Roman will die so we can roast him and stay alive another day."

Gemellus flicked his eyes off his emaciated uncle. He examined his worn caligae and tightened a strap on his right foot. "Uncle, I'll lead a sortie through the sewage tunnel tonight. It's a new moon, dark, and a storm is brewing. We'll slip their knot and inform Grandmother. She'll send fresh troops and crush this rebellion."

Tiberius *thought*, no chance of success there. Mother is punishing me for choosing the Seer over her. He *said*, "As the gods will. But I'd rather you stay beside me. I can lose lesser people, but you're my appointed heir. You're irreplaceable, unique."

Gemellus replied, "Unique means alone, Uncle."

Tiberius shook his head. "The course you suggest is dangerous. Our enemies crouch at the door, rain or shine, waiting to strike us."

Gemellus agreed. "All we do is catapult the poxed that we don't burn over the wall. Our enemies do the same. Weaponized corpses fly by each other, going opposite ways. Meanwhile, we starve, and our enemies feast."

He paused. "Uncle, why hasn't Grandmother sent reinforcements from Rome?"

Tiberius stalled, crafting yet another lie. Gemellus caught the flux of shadows from this torn man, his mentor, and the leader he honored. He levered himself to a standing position and leaned over his uncle. "Goodbye, my liege lord. The gods call to me. *Amor fati*." [1]

He abruptly strode out a stone-arched doorway into the shadowy halls.

Caligula remained, reclining beside Tiberius. He stroked his uncle's arm lightly. He was a different piece of work than Gemellus—sexy boy-toy, practiced admirer, and secret usurper. He turned his head away from this conversation between his older uncle-lover and his rival. A smile hung in the air, evil's afterglow.

Caligula stood and excused himself. He trotted away through a shadowy doorway, different from the one his cousin, Gemellus, had taken. He needed a water closet, and quick. Preserved from pox, he'd been plagued by an irritable bowel. His ambition strained north. His body drained south.

He glided in and out of shadows, one wall torch to the next. Squatting over the toilet hole, he multi-tasked, releasing his bowels while scribbling a note. He tied the message to a rock inside a blue velvet drawstring bag. He made his way alone through a curtain of rain pouring across the marsh below and to the east. Lightning forked down and rolled across this gassy swamp in a ball before splintering into white-hot whips, sizzling, then nothing more.

Caligula flicked a glance at the banquet room above, checking for prying eyes. Creamy light poured out the lunettes, but no curious eyes stared down at him. He tossed the rock over the wall toward a solitary, old-growth cypress tree. Rock rolled downhill. Sound of scampering feet briefly hushed the tree frogs and cicadas. Rushlight flared, extinguished. Message, delivered.

Back in the ballroom, the emperor's bodyguard, Rabbus, stalked the room's perimeter. He looked behind draperies, popped open doors, hand on his dagger. He had become almost mute after his toddler son had died of starvation and his body was sent to the kitchen. Rabbus *understood* that all non-plague corpses were to be used to feed the living. But after the idea was made flesh, Rabbus couldn't digest this new learning. He entered a sad, silent year with a rock of unresolved grief stuck in his gut.

While Rabbus guarded himself from sadness, Jesus and Claudia huddled in a tight triangle with Tiberius over fat, umber candles whose flames danced in contrary breezes.

Tiberius said, "God-man, it's only a matter of days before these savages are up and over the western wall's ramp. Seer, tell me what to do." [2]

I hovered around, over, and within Son. Could he remain One with Father and I, or would he dither into rescues We had not given him to do? I brooded like a mother hen, nesting love and limits into him. Just as Jesus was about to engage with the emperor, I nudged a 'no' into him.

Jesus said, "Sire, if it pleases you, I'll consult Father in the night hours. You and I will talk in the morning." Jesus once again was available and responsive to Father's voice delivered with My breath. He took my wind in his lungs, in and out, syncing my breath with his and Father's heartbeat with his own.

Claudia, the friend Jesus loved, also responded to my promptings. She, too, was teachable and because of that, reachable for kingdom purposes. What moved Son moved her.

Jesus had passed *this* test. But could he continue to keep his mind and heart on point? The emperor's pressured presence was a short sword of desperation. Claudia's net of longing and love was an entirely different thing. We'd provided both as a gauntlet to train our growing Messiah into maturity.

Jesus and Claudia got up, leaning on each other for support, heading for the infirmary. Tiberius watched them go with heavy-lidded eyes. He examined the empty bowls in front of him, wiped the last bit of gravy smear from Jesus' bowl, and sucked it off his finger.

Truth was, he was famished for a seared steak, cooked rare, with a bloody core.

2

CLAUDIA

Jesus and I began our slow shamble back to the infirmary. We leaned heavy on each other, each holding the other up. I mentally reviewed what I'd gotten from journeying with Jesus— shipwrecked twice, betrayed by my grandmother, exiled for over a year, poxed, starved, and sieged. A sane person might have second thoughts about this romance.

Yesterday I'd drawn up my courage and looked in a mirror for the first time in six months. Gaunt, sunken eyes, pox craters deep enough to park a chariot. Pasty white skin, hair dull and patchy, body emaciated. My neck, armpits, and groin screamed at me from pox buboes on the mend—tiny, fire-red volcanoes, oozing yellow pus. All told, a dazzling candidate for a play I could write where I'd star as Illyria's first beauty queen.

Jesus had told me, "Be proud of each of your scars, warrior woman. Avoid scars, and then you get to live a useless life before you arrive safely at death's door."

That first year, separated and in exile, I only had his voice, but that was enough to keep me afloat. His inner voice kept terror at arm's length, like a lullaby installed between my ears. I felt his calming presence while adrift off Trimerus' coastline, caught in an ocean current, fighting off shark fears. Then for another long stretch, I had one hour a week with him on Courting Balcony, separated by a lattice partition.

This past, poxed year was the best of the worst. We'd both been sent to the long, high-ceiled royal great room. The place the king had once sat and held court. Now it housed the dying in rows of litters, narrow corridors between each row. Doctors and nurses used to attend us, but they'd all died. Now we tended ourselves. The only people we could approach were the ones afflicted with pox who had recovered.

My infirmary cot was toward the entry door against this cool, stone wall. Jesus had dragged his cot to the row next to mine. The space between rows was so tight I could reach out in the night and touch him. We were two of those no one expected to live. Some of us had passed from plague to cholera or dysentery. Those who had all three at the same time were no longer with us.

We'd been jammed together with no regard for propriety. No separation of the sexes, no royals or commoners. Just people, wheezing on the hem of existence. Perhaps one day, we'd limp into the garment itself. The greater chance was we'd be heaved onto a burn pile with no garment at all. Regardless of my misery, I was with the man I loved, the man who loved me.

We burned together, delirious. The plague twisted our guts and chuckled. Jesus knew my pain, and I knew his. In my better moments, I bathed him with rags dipped in cool water. He returned the favor, when he was able.

In one sweet moment, middle of the night, he let his memory out for a ramble. "Abba wouldn't let me even touch the Torah 'til I was eight, but before that, he made me wash my hands to just *look* at it.

"He said, 'The meaning of each word in the Torah is a jewel. The light inside each word changes as you meditate, turning words to the Light. Such power in beauty hurts me.'

"At the time, I didn't know what he meant. All I knew was that we Jews were people of the Word. Abba kept talking, 'All words were meant to be spent joining us to God, joining us to each other. We were never to use words to separate—people from other people, people from God, or people from themselves. Gossip and slander were the worst, even worse than profanity.'"

Jesus' voice faded into a soft snuffling. I sat on the side of his cot and stroked his head. He missed his abba. He often felt like a failed messiah. Both his father and sister were killed on his watch. In the dark, his words flowed over me, around me, under me—but I had nothing much to say back. I felt stupid as a stone. He was my river, rolling me over and over, teaching this stone to speak.

During day hours, when we were less in the grip of dark and pain, his eyes on me were too much to bear, so I'd watch his eyebrows. Shaggy, chestnut, luxurious, hanging over chocolate-brown with honey flecks in them. They did a complicated dance—rising when his story climaxed, furrowing when doom played its drumbeat, arching when wonder or suspicion was afoot. Miss an eyebrow-twitch, miss his meaning.

For example, his *words* spoke about giving mercy to the hag who'd dropped a poxed head in our well water. But then he pulled a face, and I busted out laughing.

Before my laugh racked into a cough, he commented, "your laughter sounds like bells in the night."

I stopped coughing long enough to say, "I'm going to be sick. How can I rise to the status of an almost beautiful belle of the ball if I'm vomiting all the time?"

The thing was this; I'd been laughing so hard that I threw up and pooped at the same time—my body out of control. Puke and poo looked weak. Jesus cleaned up after me with a rag, a torn strip of some dead person's clothes destined for the burn pile. After, he got a clean rag and bathed my sweaty face and neck.

When he had finished, all was quiet. I spoke into the sounds of a storm that beat on the windows overhead. I shared my nightmares—being eaten by a giant grandma spider or being cooked alive on an altar. This night-time confession whispered out of me with enough emotion to knock the enamel off the back of my teeth. Outside, thunder rolled.

Jesus said, "Even Father sometimes needs a good scream." Lightning flashed. "But once his thunder's come and gone, his lightning chops the wood. He executes judgment for both the quick and the dead."

I knew I wasn't part of the quick, but not so sure if I wouldn't soon be part of the dead. I was never sure if I'd wake in the morning. Life itself was chancy. I tracked time by chalking hash marks on the wall. We were a day shy of forty days and forty nights in this Pain Palace. Jesus said, "Moses spent forty days and nights on the mountain, pleading with God before he got his smoking tablets of stone. Father rained on Noah forty days and nights before a rainbow came. Goliath terrified Israel forty days in the

Valley of Elah before David showed up with his slingshot. Another day and we'll be there. Let's see what God will do."

I thought about what he'd said, and then I asked, "why didn't you heal us? You could have, you know." He said, "Father tells me I'm not exempt from the pain that chooses me. I'm only to avoid the pain of betrayal, betrayal of Father, or betrayal of me. Windy helps me stoke my appointed fires, sort my pains, and keep only what's necessary."

During one long, thrashing night, Jesus said, "When that next bubo-volcano in my groin is about to erupt, I can't think deep thoughts like this. I can't think about Father or who I am, who I'm not, or even who I'm supposed to become. Thought gets lost inside pain."

"Claudia," he said, "We both hurt the same. Father's will. He refuses to give the world only a thin gruel of kind words. Instead, he gave me."

I fumbled for words. "I can't feel your Father's presence. I can't take comfort from words off a printed page, or even words I've memorized, words from your Torah or my wisdom books. When my body's exploding, all I want is to crawl inside *you*."

Jesus said, "All the words I memorized as a child come back in my better moments now. Torah becomes a hospital in my mind, even when I feel desolate as a lamb in a lion's den. Nothing shiny about me or you in this Pain Palace. We hurt, we doubt, we continue. We *are* our truest selves."

He fell silent. That was all the energy he had, and he gave it all away. Note to self. *Never trust love till you see what it costs your lover.*

Middle of that sleepless night, I wanted fresh air. I longed for the ramparts, but the climb would require sitting every second step. As it was, we leaned on each other for strength to make it all the way to the end of the hall. We turned to go back. Two men trotted by us in that hallway, carrying a litter between them. We pressed ourselves to the clammy walls so they could pass. A corpse lay on their litter, the detached head resting beside its body. The men headed for the kitchen. Acid burped up, searing my throat. Someone's main course?

I was glad this still sickened me. Most of my fellow survivors didn't ask where their cut of meat came from. Expectations for 'normal' had been whittled away, one bite at a time.

I said to Jesus, "Was that who I think it was? I couldn't see the face on that head."

"Gemellus was a brave man, Claudia. He listened hard last night as Tiberius longed for a non-poxed corpse. He sacrificed himself, so his uncle could eat meat with his wine."

Probably blowflies and beetle larvae were tunneling tiny labyrinths through Gemellus' guts already. What kind of communion would that provide?

Before I could speak my uplifting thoughts, another two soldiers met us. They carried another body on another litter, but this one was alive, groaning, his face twisted into a grimace. All Julius' body parts were present, with an added arrow buried in his thigh.

We stopped the threesome. Jesus stooped, his hand on Julius' shoulder. I sat cross-legged behind Jesus on the cool stone floor.

Julius said, "The enemy must have known we were coming. They were waiting. Gemellus edged his head out the sewer exit. Immediately someone struck it off. Then a volley of arrows flew down the tunnel. It all happened so fast. Their leader, a one-eyed guy, huge."

Jesus queried, "A giant? I've heard of this man, someone named after Polyphemus, the Cyclops—son of Illyrius and his goddess wife, Galatea."

Julius winced. "One-Eye shot the arrow that hit me. We pulled what was left of Gemellus inside and bolted the iron grate shut. Then, as we crossed the courtyard, his head catapulted over the wall, courtesy of their siege ballista."

The two soldiers picked up Julius' stretcher and made to leave. Jesus held onto the lead soldier's sleeve. He said, "You're a brave man, Pontii. Loyal to the emperor."

Pontii's voice guttered. "Perhaps that's true. Even so, I've had enough carved off me. Now, I live in darkness and hope for nothing beyond this moment. And that's even more true."

Jesus looked at him, beard to beard, "the best truth worth knowing is on the other side of dark."

Pontii stank with a dark kind of fear.

Jesus continued, "Father's kingdom is like that. It shines in the dark, like a city on a hill, but only those who love, see—and that's the truest thing we've said so far."

Jesus' face scrunched up, eyes to the right. He shook himself like a wet dog, like he was trying to ditch some future memory. "Pontii, remember this talk about truth, against an interview we will have one day." [3]

Pontii turned away and headed around the corner for our infirmary.

I said, "What were you thinking when you crunched up your face back there?"

Jesus replied, "You were hiding behind a drape in the shadows, daydreaming, waiting for suffering to pass you by."

I asked, "What was I hiding from?"

He said, "I'm not sure of anything but this. I felt like a worm, you were terrified, and Pontii had ironed his face flat as a sheet of iron."

3
SLOW

The Negev's noon bake clamped down on me. Our spice caravan, thirty camels and two burros, bumped southbound through Moab territory, southeast of the Dead Sea. My friend, Joanna, had overheard Chuza, her accountant husband, talking with King Herod. Seemed like the king was planning for me to service him again, and soon.

We left the next morning. I fingered the letter in my hand. I'd received it by courier as we were packing to leave Rahab's. I read it over again, rubbing the ink on her parchment, missing Leah like rain misses its cozy cloud when in freefall. "Sister, meet me in Egypt. A siege here in Scodra is imminent. Everyone is sick, but I ask you to pray we will escape. Inquire for us at the central synagogue in Alexandria."

The sun melted boulders, sand, and road into a mirage of yellow brown—another variation of the same numbing, dumbing desert day. Sulfur smells wafted off the Dead Sea. The ruins of Sodom, infested with wild jackals and creeping, creepy things, lay off on our right side.

Mules and camels clopped forward, or the sand blew backward—one or the other. I moved from stupid to stupider with sameness, but that was all right. The world was full of things I didn't want to know. For example, I didn't have to know where I was going—the ride itself was enough for today. Goodness's body beneath me soothed my jangled nerves. Destinations were over-rated. I just needed to get gone from wherever I'd been. Alexandria would wait for another day.

My chin dropped again on my chest. I felt a fly crawl the space between two toes. My almost-four-year-old squirmed against my front, reaching for his father. Hope, our six-year-old daughter, napped against my back. My bookends kept me upright.

Meanwhile, my inner me's dragged themselves into bicker-fest. Cutter brought back all the fights between ma and Achan, fights about her conscripted work as a courtesan in the royal harem. Harlot said, *mother was lucky to be a singing, dancing Jew in Eglon's court.*

Shame harrumphed and hissed about nothing in particular and everything in general.

Laz walked beside Goodness. I glanced at my quiet husband, whisper-thin, knobby at the knees and elbows. He looked up.

Fragile asked, *Why did you let that man get inside us? Men eat us out, rip us apart, and leave us dangling, exposed.*

Cutter and Bruise complained, *you didn't ask us for advice.*

Shame said to these three, *listen up, girls. Luuuv takes hostages. Loves a glass splinter working its way into our heart. Love's a get-inside-and-rip-us-apart mantrap!*

Then Shame looked at me. *And you, you let this love mistake happen, not once, but twice!*

All my me's clustered in a circle, fingers pointing at me like little spears.

I said, *do you realize what an energy suck you all are? I'm the chooser. I chose for Jesus to re-do our foundations. I chose Laz to build the shell of our house. Now, together, it's our job to furnish the interior and learn to get along.*

Another voice, so soft I could barely hear it, interrupted my-me's. *Love can mess you up, but also stitch you up. Remake your-you's into a woman you don't yet know. I'm always just a breath away, ready to help, but only when you inquire. I don't barge in.*

I heard what Laz didn't, my voices mingling with Windy's voice. He saw what I couldn't. All life's bits buried in the bake. He took Mike on his shoulders and pointed out a lizard shading himself under a rock, red ants moving on a line to some important destination, a rafter of turkey vultures tearing a coyote's carcass apart under an acacia tree.

Our lead camel driver, Emil, directed his beast off the King's Highway for no apparent reason. We proceeded to find ourselves in an especially vacant patch of nothing. The camels had circled. We ambled over to where Emil stood with Zayan, his younger brother. Both men gazed at me with something I'd grown to know as hunger. Zayan planted his feet, stuck out his chest, and licked his lips.

Emil pulled himself up to his full height, maybe five and a half feet. "You know why we're here?"

Laz twirled his sidelocks between two fingers, looked around. "You wanted an open patch for mid-day prayers?"

Emil's grin flashed teeth bright as dice. The grin bobbed his greased moustache up and down on either end. This marvelous patch of waxed hair distracted the eye from his acne-scarred face.

He said, "Look at my feet."

Emil motioned with his chin. Laz moved closer and set Michael down.

Emil said, "You two, father and son, take one side of this rock. Zayan will get the other side."

Mike toddled forward between Laz's legs and grabbed an edge. Together the three of them lifted. Water's cool, sweet fragrance rose to meet my nose. A foot or so down beneath the surface was a ledge. An old wooden bucket sat inside the loops of a coiled rope.

Emil said, "You draw up the first ten buckets. After that, others will take turns. Thirsty camels, thirsty people, hungry people."

Who would have known a well was here? I wondered how many wells had I walked over and not known?

Escape suggested, *maybe we drop into this one and disappear.*

My mother was fond of saying—*if you drown, let it be in a deep well, not with your nose in a cup of water.* She repeated herself a lot, as the dead have an annoying habit of doing. Right now, my nose had been stuck in a cup of sameness, but the journey had swapped that cup for a deep well of darkness.

I sat veiled on Goodness, still, in the shade of a grandfather cactus— the kind with white fuzz hanging down its thick shaft. I was confused by my crowd inside, unable to sort sense into myself.

Laz pulled water from the earth, thawab tucked into his loincloth. Sweat dripped off his chin as he repeatedly poured water from the dripping bucket into one water bladder after another.

Mike dart-and-shadowed between his father's legs, chasing geckos across the crushed mica and along the dry rivulets, smooth and glittery in the sun.

Hope knelt on all fours and watched a preying-mantis lay eggs under the shadow of my cactus. The mantis moved along, leaving a line of tan gook behind her. Tiny iridescent eggs, encased in goo, sparkled in the sun. Hope was perfectly still, enrapt.

I daydreamed, Escape ridding me of the present moment.

Shame said, *what an embarrassment that you've buried so many memories in the sand. Or is that your head in the sand, and your memories parading in plain sight?*

Emil slid sideways a few steps into the space between us, like he might be wondering what it held. His eyebrows were so black they had a purple sheen to them. His short sword hung on a diagonal through his sash. Its hilt, crusted with jewels, glittered in the sun.

Zayan came 'round Goodness's other side and brushed against my leg. Emil twirled his moustache and spoke with a voice thick as wet sand. "My brother and I know many things about this desert, little lady. Ways to live; ways to die. Essential knowledge. Useful knowledge."

Zayan looked pointedly at Laz. "The few shekels your husband paid, a good down payment for you and your two children. Unfortunately, not enough for him to survive this journey. Once he's gone, expect other payments during the long nights between here and Alexandria."

Zayan pulled his cloak up and over his head. He now was naked, except for his loincloth—ready for his turn at pulling up water—but more than that, ready to preen. His shoulders were wide as an ax handle. Not an ounce of fat on his body. He slipped his hand under my cloak, ran his rough fingers up past my knees; lingered, then squeezed his intention into me. In case I'd missed it.

Abruptly Zayan broke in, "We have plenty of time. Emil and I have many wives up and down The King's Highway. We share a villa in Dhiban, next door to the synagogue, a block from the king's castle. We also share women. We will expect you at our place tomorrow night, won't we, Emil?"

Moustache twirled and bowed.

My Harlot-me smiled saucily, "Whatever it takes to keep *everyone* in my family alive and well, including my brother, Laz, and his orphaned children."

The two brothers glanced at each other, sniffing the wind for truth or lie.

I said to Harlot, *what a liar you are.*

She replied, *I had a good teacher. Your mother, her husband, your father, the list goes on and on. Besides, who tells the truth anymore? It's way over-rated.*

Bruise purpled herself into the conversation. *Cutter 'n me tell the truth. We'll leave marks on those guys. Give you 'n Escape time to leave.*

I listened to my life and took a deep breath. I prayed, *God, you have more than one part. Seems to work out well for the Three of You. Maybe all my-me's can learn a trick or two from You—different from the tricks I used to do. Help me, help us, stay alive.*

4

LEAH

Middle of the night. I bolted upright and felt for Rabbus. He was gone. I was alone in bed. My sister's face flickered in my dream. Her mouth was open, calling to me from some dark place, mouthing her pleading for help.

Slow, what can I do for you when I loiter here, far away, at death's door? That letter I wrote you? I don't think I can make it.

I examined my skin—a poxed spider-web of veins gone wild, eruptions oozing. My bed stank with sweat-soak and tears. Dead son. My daughter washed early from me in a flood of blood. The old and young were always most vulnerable. I felt very old, very young.

Rabbus and I had taken untimely born Gabriela to the fires. He'd put his mask on, put her in a pink blanket, and we had taken her together. His huge hands had swallowed her like a fired offering to Moloch, the Moabite god who ate children.

I held his arm as together we walked toward the fires. We got to the maw of that furnace, where we were to leave her. I said, "let's kiss our daughter goodbye. But first, you must take off that mask you've been wearing of late. Can I help you take it off? You've said you're afraid not to wear it. That you might die of the plague. But I have a different question, husband. Can you survive your mask?"

He remained silent a good long while. We stood and held our daughter. He said, "Inside your question is a quest. You'll need a lifetime to wrench me from behind my mask, wife."

That was a few weeks ago. We'd not talked about it since. But, in a different way, I'd brought his distancing up again, just yesterday. "Husband, please. I need all of you here with me if I'm to survive this plague."

He looked at me from behind his mask. He said, "Wife, the best I can do is be a part-timer—part, here; part, with all who've died. And the truth is, I feel like a graveyard. Our children haven't gone anywhere. They're all still here, buried inside me—parents, first wife, grandparents too. None of them shut up! All cry for my attention."

I told him, "If I left now, I'd have more of you? Better that than this frail life."

He walked toward the door, cemetery quiet, and closed it behind him. After he left, I tried to sleep, but as I drifted off, I remembered Slow. She'd sometimes say when I was a little girl, "Sister, I sweep up those nasty cockroaches in my skull and sort them into boxes, nice 'n tidy. Keeps me from going bat-crap crazy." She never taught me how to do that.

I took in a long breath, as much as I could hold, and let it whistle slow out my lips into the dark. There the vision came again: sister's face. After mother was killed in the stoning pit, sister made me safe. She tried her best to be a junior mother. I remember her saying, *Leah, you're smart. Especially brilliant with music and feelings. And you're much prettier inside than me— pretty where it counts.*

Slow mothered me when no one had mothered her. I further stilled myself. A vision floated in front of my eyes—the chief rabbi in Dhiban, alone in a room with ma.

Windy said, *Yes, child, that man is Slow's abba.*

But, Windy, we're sisters, aren't we?

Windy replied, *same mother, different father. But you've known this all along, even when your heart didn't want to see. Your mother was busy serving the king, servicing the rabbi.*

And I was busy feeling ugly. Busy sitting in the dirt outside our hovel, slapping wet cow-pies on the stucco wall of our house. Busy watching them dry. Busy crying from sheer emptiness and boredom.

Yes, child, and I was busy scooping out space inside you, space to hold all your giftings.

I hate your gifts. Hate this plague and loss and loneliness. Hate my memory of the drunk father you gave me. The times he would call a cow pie by my name and drop it in on the fire. Stoke the flames and warm himself by it.

Windy said, *Ouch. That hurts. Hurts bad.*

She was silent for a long time. I felt her enfolding arms. She held me, like under Eagle's Wings when she mid-wife'd Gabe into the world.

Windy said, *memories are like the mythical Chimaera.* [4] *That walled city is only a few miles from Scodra. People vow that houses, people, and lights dance inside those walls—and the music changes unpredictably, chimerically.*

Windy, why speak this weirdness in my ears?

These are crucial life lessons, child. All you humans give meaning to your memories. The memories dance and change. Cow-poo, for example. Remember the day Jesus knelt beside you in Mary's garden? You were composting her new vines. He brushed your face with his fingers. You touched that spot once he was gone and left a streak of poo on your face.

Yeah, I remember.

Now, child, focus on father calling a cow-pie in your name. Do that, and you feel abandoned. Remember Jesus' touch, and you feel loved.

Ok, I get it now.

Good. Another thing, child. Each time you and Rabbus have sex, I sort a thousand seeds. They dance; I change them. I choose which ones live and which seeds die.

But Windy, you let two seeds sprout—my children. Then you killed them. Even Rabbus feels gone. Like you took him too. Why? When I remember the husband I used to have, my gone babies, I want to scream and cuss and beat you with my fists.

Go ahead. Grieve. And while you scream, and beat, and cuss, remember faith grows in the dark. You learn to trust Me when you step into thin air at my request. Now, child, believe and act on this. Rabbus and you will hold each other and your children alive, with great joy, on this good earth.

I looked at Windy with wonder and doubt, hate and love. I said, okay, let's go. I'm ready to take my next step. I'll leave all those mysteries for you to know. [5] *But please hold me up, Windy. Hold me while I walk. Hold me when you blow my memories, past and future, into view.*

She hugged a yes into me. *Hold on to Jesus while he's here. And then, when he's gone, I'll hold you. And we're busy right now making a future memory.*

Sound of small caligae clomping in hallway outside my door. Clatter of key in lock, creaking of opening door, opposite mine. Caligula's room. I dragged myself out of bed.

I softly opened our heavy, oaken door. Rabbus had oiled our hinges. I was silent as a chick under a mother owl's wing. I crossed the hallway, stopped and listened. Light under the door flickered, slivered, pinkie-sized.

Caligula whispered, "The sacrifice was made, the gods appeased. The remaining sacrifices are gathered in groups, in the center court, all of them, as we discussed."

Silent breeze swirled past my ankles. Darkness flowing into more darkness.

"Our guide and his boat await. Your gold ensured our safe passage to Rhodes."

Guttering chuckle from Tiberius.

Caligula's hoarse whisper once again, "Time flees, and so must we. There's room in the boat for him, you, and me. Polyphemus' hordes will be over those ramparts very soon."

5

JESUS

Anudge in the night. I rolled over, exhausted. Dry heaves crowded my throat. I swallowed hard, sat up on my pallet, disoriented. The room was half-full of poxed people. Twenty-five of us remained alive, defying the odds, refusing death. John lay on his cot at my toes, snoring. Claudia, on the pallet next to me, also swung her feet over the edge of her cot, placed them firmly on the floor next to mine.

She said, "Everyone's stink in here reminds me of me. If I wasn't such a mess, I wouldn't know who I was."

I nodded in agreement. "Was that you kicking me just then?"

"No. I'd curled up, facing the wall. A boot would have had to come out my butt to kick you."

I barked out a gob of phlegm into our shared chamber pot, "Nice visual."

She laid back down and rolled over, facing away from me once again. A slight groan whispered into the dark. Time passed. I laid back down, groggy. Moved my foot across the small space between Claudia's pallet and mine, pressed the ball of my foot against her ankle, for comfort. Drifted off.

Another kick. "Ow! You kicked me again, Claudia!"

She twisted her head over her shoulder. Felt my foot on her ankle.

She said, "Sit up. Look at me. I haven't moved. I'm pretending we're sleeping together instead of suffering apart."

Sound of John's snores mingled with others, a riffling wave through the dark.

"I'm such an idiot, Claudia. Windy's trying to get my attention."

"Ok, say something like, 'Speak, Spirit. I'm listening.'" [6]

Windy didn't wait for me to ask. He said, *day forty has arrived, Son. Your time in this Pain Palace is finished. Go to the castle's balustrades. Take John and Claudia with you. School is in session.*

"Let's go, Claudia." I shook John awake. "Up to the ramparts. Time to leave Rozafa."

Claudia's voice, weak, in the dark. "You have to help get me up and clean me up. I'm lying in a disgusting pile of me."

"Okay. Where's that bowl of water? Ok. Here. Let me swab you down."

She let me wipe her face and arms with the cool, wet rag. She moved her hands lower. "Oh, Jesus! How embarrassing. I leaked and then rolled in puke, poo, *and* I got my period. You've talked about unclean in your scriptures. I take that down to a whole new level. Gimme some wet rags and a dry one."

A few minutes passed. A sigh, babble of someone talking in their sleep, mutters, and thumps. A door down the hall slammed. Sound of rag squeezing water in a bowl. Rag plopping on the floor.

"Help me up." John and I helped her stand.

Together she and I walked down the hall to the stone stairs, a four-legged human lean-to. John followed us. Up a step, rest. Repeat. The building groaned and popped, moaned and wheezed.

Claudia listened and then, in a quiet moment, muttered, "you'd think a coven of demons was prowling about, looking for fresh meat."

I said nothing, kept pressing upwards in the dark.

Finally, a fresh breeze whiffled down the steps, trickling into my nose.

John's voice, "I'm here, two steps below."

A militant voice from above, "Stop!"

Another softer voice, "Husband, relax. It's only Jesus, Claudia, and John."

I said, "We were told to come here."

Rabbus whispered in my ear, "Leah heard the same voice. That's why she's here. And Tiberius is just outside the door with Caligula."

Claudia said, "Insider info, Rabbus. This castle jig's almost up."

He smiled grimly, let us pass. I grabbed a smudge torch off a wall sconce.

Claudia spotted her uncle, "Stay upwind of us, Uncle. We stink, but the fever's broken."

Tiberius said, "Tonight, I'm worried not about body stink, but the smell of treason. I sniff it out but can't place it."

His eyes flickered around the circle, scrutinizing each face, then moving on, "Danger surrounds me."

I ventured, "Your father, Augustus, told me the line between treason and loyalty ran through his own heart. Whichever part he fed the most, won. Why would that be different for you, Sire?"

Tiberius faltered. "All outside signs tell me this—we're close to the end. Cal suggested I organize survivors into groups of ten. One will kill the other nine and then join the remaining mercy killers. The man with the short straw will kill his fellows, then fall on his sword. Those in the infirmary can die without an assist."

Claudia said, "Thanks, Uncle. We infirmary vets might be useless as a bubo to *you*, but we're still people. And the Hope-God remains. Did you think of asking his help before you kill everyone?"

Tiberius sniffed, "Uh, right." His tone was dismissive.

I prophesied, "Sire, boys look for right and wrong done in blacks and whites. Bad guys and good guys. But men know they grow stronger in the fight between two rights. For example, it's right to want to live and leave with Caligula in your little boat down there at the dock. It's righter to remain. Sire, stay and see God at work."

Tiberius stayed on course with *his* topic. 'When the barbarians come over the wall, they'll torture us all. There's no cruelty in mercy killing first, correct?"

My Partners and I remained silent.

Claudia and I took a step to the ramparts, rested our hands on the cool stonework. The ramp was a hundred yards to our left. Slaves, guarded by soldiers, feverishly hauled fill dirt up the ramp, inching toward the top. Enemy forces, thousands upon thousands, far as the eye could see, geared up for battle.

Our few remaining legionnaires were out of weapons—arrows, spears, even rocks—gone. All the weapons they had were short swords and daggers.

A shadowed figure off to our right.

Claudia said, "Come closer, cousin Cal. Join us."

Claudia's cousin positioned himself shoulder to shoulder with Tiberius. They turned their backs to me. The two thin men turned their heads back and forth, whispering while they scanned the enemy's progress.

A booming, baritone voice, from without, "Throw your God-man over the wall, now. Obey, and I *might* give you a quick death instead of a slow one."

Tiberius turned to me. "He's challenged us every hour for the past forty hours. None here dare answer him."

Windy said, *Look up, Jesus. Look up.*

Above us, all around, thousands of flaming angels. Windy said, *Father has sent your friends to showcase his glory in you. Ask Father, in a loud voice, to open their eyes. Those who believe in you will see, according to their measure of faith. Those who refuse you will remain blinded by unbelief.*

I prayed in a loud voice, "Father, open believing eyes!"

Claudia, Rabbus, Leah, and John all looked up and immediately fell backward on their butts, pushing against the wall, fingers slatted in front of squinting eyes.

Tiberius and Caligula turned around, nonplussed.

Tiberius said, "What is there to see? Enemies, night sky, stars. That's it."

Claudia hid her face in my chest. "Those guys up there scared the pee out of me. Wet myself again. Tell them to go away, Jesus."

I sat down next to her in a small puddle of urine. I put my arms around her. She trembled uncontrollably.

Tiberius stood in the doorway, under the threshold, one foot already on the top step leading down. Cal pulled on his sleeve from below. Tiger-stripes of yellow torchlight and shadow cut the emperor in two.

He looked up again, squinted, "My eyes have taken leave of my head just now. What looks like fired embers, all around, are moving toward me."

Caligula's head popped out the door and looked around once again. He said, "I see only what's in front of me. And we need to get a move on with *my* plans; ah, *our* plans. Hurry up, lover."

Tiberius made motions to go. Claudia grabbed ahold of his ankle. "Believe in Jesus, do as he says, and all will be well. Abandon his command, and all will go badly for you."

I sat with her in a puddle of shadow and urine. I said, "Sire, those who are with us are far more than those who are against us, even if you can't see them with your physical eyes. [7] Sire, remember those past times the Spirit has spoken to you in visions, those times that Father saved you from shipwreck, fire, ice, and a pride of lions. Call to mind the time when this same Leah, in front of you, resurrected you from the dead. You've been gifted with far more experiences of the goodness of God than most people. If you don't learn from all these experiences, you're no good to yourself or the people in your empire."

A haze passed over his eyes. He shook his head. "I can't think about shades of right and wrong or learning from my past. What I do know is this. It's wrong for me, the Roman emperor, to be tortured and die at the hands of pagans. *That* would be a tragedy."

I replied, "Tragedy is the stuff of not learning or learning too late. Sometimes, decades too late; other times, a second or so. Learn loyalty to the God who created you. Believe in the Son that He sent. That, by far, is the rightest thing that you will ever do."

Tiberius fell over on his side, one eye still in deep shadow. His squinting right eye caught the flare of my torch. He banged his head with his fist, eyes wild.

Windy let me see through his eyes. The night sky had filled with tiny streaks of gold shooting all around. *Angels* on the move.

Clatter of grappling hooks. Sound of *men* on the move, men coming over the ramparts.

6

WINDY

It was night. King Eglon VII splayed across his bed alone, on the fourth floor, the top floor of his royal palace in Moab's bustling capital city. That afternoon, at sunset, he'd stood alone on the ramparts, facing west across Dhiban. A tangerine sun blazed the city's horizon, its color so breathtaking it almost moved him to tears.

Now, toward midnight, he stared at the remains of a late-night snack. The peach cobbler was his favorite. Eggie's neck had disappeared into an enormous upfold of fat, squeezed between shoulders and skull. Gold necklaces obscured his fat-wedge. He played with the single, obscenely opulent diamond earring that dangled from his right ear. He jiggled it before digging ear wax out of that ear with his polished, extra-long pinky nail.

He mused, *everything stays the same. We 'haves' eat ourselves to death; envy eats the 'have-nots.' Everybody wins.*

He'd had to drag himself up the stairs lately. Why hadn't he put his bedroom and toilet on the main floor next to the dining room? So much easier to toddle from one throne to the other—and then off for an afternoon nap.

He scratched his bald pate and bent over a leathery scroll in the guttering candlelight. He checked his right big toe to see if a spike had been driven through it. *No, only his gout flaring. A rich man's diet. So hard to say no to food, one of life's few remaining pleasures.*

His valet had delivered, as requested, the history annals of his kingdom. A careful review of his glorious works would put him to sleep, as usual. [8] Eggie's gut doubled down over his knees when he bent forward. His blurry vision inched along, hitched to his pudgy forefinger.

Wait a minute! He'd not seen this before. His singer-lover from years back, what *was* her name? She'd reported ongoing thievery, and he'd had her stoned? Vague drizzles of memory fingered through his brain but promptly disappeared. Yawning sulci gobbled memory of morning's events by afternoon. Lacunae, like a rising ocean, swallowed islands of recollection.

The king felt bumfuzzled. *Hmm. What to do? Something to be done after all this time had gone?*

He swooped a curved forefinger through the cobbler, lifting the sticky sweet peaches into his mouth. On impulse, he hauled his bones out for a midnight stroll. I swirled oxygen through the back alleys of his hippocampus, those darling twin sea horses, sparking a brief eddy of recall.[9] *What was her name? Ester?*

The king made his way to the front of his castle, slowly, painfully, leaning on gold-knobbed, cedar walking sticks. Ornate daggers engraved their shafts.

Every stone, every stair in the castle was memory's match-striker, sparks flying off in the night, disappearing just as quick as they were lit. Here, on this spot, Ahab's sons flew the box kites he had made for them. And there, a little further on, Ester's daughter, Gomaria, played on his lap while a buck-toothed performer juggled pitch-black kittens in the courtyard. Up there, on the balcony, Ester serenaded him.

And behind the stables, only a short drop down, Ahab's teenage son chased his little sister, Abby. Sound of hushed snuffles, 'no Emil, no, please....'

He'd thought at the time, *I should check on those two.* Failed to act.

The castle drowned in memories. *Who knew which were true and which were made up?* All the memories I flash-danced, ghosted. He wondered to himself, where are memories kept once they've flown the coop? Maybe they'd turned into seeds and were stored in a barn somewhere.

All this remembering and thinking left Eggie a wee bit depleted. He sat down next to Ehud, his midnight gatekeeper, the one with wild, white angel hair, like burning spiderwebs, even at midnight.

The king mused, *Ehud's about as thin as I am fat. A silo to my castle. Then a thought—he's my madeleine, my barn. He stores what's left after mischiefs of mice gnaw my noodle.*

"What was that singer's name the Jews stoned awhile back, Ehud?"

"Ah, you mean Ester, the one who you said smelled like myrtle and sang like an angel. That one, Sire?"

Eggie startled. A memory trace flared briefly once again. He'd thought of her, and forgotten her quickly. She'd sung for him. By God, how she'd sung! God's own voice soared out of her as if she had teased Music up through the earth and out her throat. Yes, he remembered his heart beating furiously as she sang. Even now, tears rolled down his cheeks as he brought to mind her gifting.

She'd sung, and they'd dined on fresh catfish, and then, perhaps she'd offered dessert. He absently licked his chops. These memories roused him briefly, then whispered away. Eglon sighed.

He said, "Ehud, why am I so glum?"

"King, perhaps you rue her demise. She became inconvenient."

Discordant music, memory and truth, played between his ears. Neither danced easily with the other.

Eggie roused himself. "Perchance, did a child come of this dalliance with the Jewess?"

"Indeed, Sire. That was a possibility but never confirmed. So many ambassadors, regals, emissaries visited your court in those days. You loaned her out to many of them. But I digress. Ester asked you to name the child. You called her Gomaria, after your mother's second cousin, twice removed."

Ehud winced, remembered. *That child looked like someone else I knew. Who was that?*

"The child was eight or nine when the turn came in the road, Sire. The chief rabbi asked your permission to stone her. I think perhaps he was envious. She'd preferred you to him. And the woman *was* very beautiful indeed."

Eglon asked, "Has memory lodged in my big toe these days?"

"Uh, Sire, I doubt if gout holds memories. But both prefer sweets. Perhaps our present gets folded into the past, deep-fried with feeling, and topped with sugary hope for a better future."

"Huh," Eggie said. "If so, I can binge all that with a side of cream, and it won't hurt a bit."

Ehud smiled and patted his friend's knee. I'd made and remade afresh all their 'bio-bits'.[10] And, after all, what remains of people, after the toll of time, are their memories.

Both Eglon and Ehud snored, one more loudly than the other. Their heads tilted sideways toward each other. One of Eggie's walking sticks had lodged in his gut, fat folding over it. Ehud moved in his sleep. The walking stick fell out of the king's gut. Ehud tucked in, holding his friend up. [11]

Eggie's laurel leaf crown slipped onto Ehud's head, seemingly by itself. The gold circlet seated itself in the old man's silvery strands, glinting in torchlight burning so bright above them. Both had swapped sleep-seats in this dance where all sleep, some wake up, and time turns treasure to trash.

A knock on the castle gates. Soft, then louder, insistent. Two of the king's men looked at the gate from the stalls where they groomed their horses.

One shouted at Ehud, "Get the door, gatekeeper!"

Ehud pushed Eglon upright and teetered to the gate, unaware he wore the king's crown. He walked to the smaller door within the door, the eye of the needle. He slipped open the peephole. No one there. He turned to go back to his sleeping bench, but on second thought, opened the smaller door—the one rich folks find impassible. He slid out, effortless. [12]

There, on the ground before him, was a young woman. Her angular, oddly beautiful face was uplifted. Tears streamed down her cheeks. She held a sun-bleached, broken skull in both hands.

Ehud examined her desert trophy. [13] The old man with the dazzling hair and golden crown knelt beside Slow. "What is the meaning of this, child?"

Escape had been weaving a net to keep her sanity but wandered away, leaving only Bruise. That child examined the stick figure before her and said, "Gabriel? Is that you, archangel?"

"I'm a nobody, lovie. A stick walking through mist. Any important men in these parts, if they ever existed, are all gone bye-bye."

"But you're golden and silvered. Here's my mother, Gabriel. You remember her, don't you? Her name was Ester. She once loved the king and sang for him. She wants to be remembered."

He studied Fragile, "You do have the look of need, if not lunacy."

"Bad men want me, Gabriel. They want to kill Laz, bruise Hope, cut Michael."

Ehud studied her words like an ancient runic stone, the Mesha Stele, encoded with cryptic meaning. [14] This child's speech was beyond his ken.

Sound of a man falling, *oomph!* Eggie had taken a tumble, gone splat. "Come in, dear Gomaria, for that is who I think you are. Help me with the king."

He motioned to the cavalry warriors leading their horses back toward the stables from a night sortie. One horse plopped a fragrant, steaming pile at Cutter's feet.

Ehud said, "You can see for yourself. All the king's horses and all the king's men can't put Eggie together again. But maybe you and I might sort two wrongs and make a sort of right. Perhaps something good might come of this."

The older man and young woman moved as one, working to waken Eglon. Ehud poured water from an urn. Slow studied the water, bathed her face in it.

Ehud shook his head, "First, use the water to get dirt off the king's face."

Slow considered his words. Wiped away her tears, seeing things half-clearly. My touch and a gentle man's warmth had half-glued her dissociations together.

She reconstituted a false memory and spoke with conviction, "Father, wake up! I'm home to remind you of my mother, your lover."

The king's glazed eyes looked at her, stupefied.

Harlot insisted, "Mother's here."

She placed the cow skull on his gut. The concussed king went from merely demented to a true *folie a` deux.*

Eggie laid down the bleached cow skull, blinked at the young woman, and touched her face wonderingly, "Ester, you'd died. The worst mistake of my life. But you're back, my angel voice, fragrant with lavender! How I wish I could still make love, as we once did so often! But alas, not possible. How *else* can I thank you for warning me of those thieves?"

Slow stifled a sigh of relief. "You remember me? What thieves, Daddy?"

Eglon's gimlet eyes glimmered with confused clarity. He stewed. Desire, vengeance, and remorse bubbled. He blubbered to his new-old, lost lover, "but of course, my Lavender. You always called me 'daddy' in our private

41

moments. Do you remember how much fun revenge once was and will be again? Memory is poor indeed if it only works backward. [15] Come to my palace tomorrow night. We'll party!"

Older man and younger woman, each broken, sat and talked into the night, swapping lies and memories. Overhead torches smoked on the edge of extinction. Ehud snoozed.

Sometimes the two were demented king and concubine, sometimes father figure and stand-in daughter, sometimes two puzzlers staring at a slew of jigsaw pieces with the box-top gone missing. Truth was, both were strangers I'd placed in a stone niche of a city wall at three in the morning. These two shuttled spools of memory and imagination, weaving a new story on this loom of Our choosing. Each passed the peace to the other in this desert cathedral, replete with smells and bells. I officiated. Time flew beneath the shadow of my wings.

7

CLAUDIA

We all heard the grappling hooks, saw the enemies' helmets coming up over the ancient, crumbly wall. The sky above was pink, the color of salmon eggs blitzed through with yellow streaks. The air below was a thick, low-lying black cloud. [16]

Uncle turned, ready to bolt down the steps. Jesus took his arm. Caligula's dark eyes flashed. He grabbed his uncle's other arm and pulled hard in the other direction toward the interior stairs.

Uncle looked back and forth from Jesus to Cal. "The last time you pulled or pushed, Jesus, we crashed out of hell into a pride of lions. Cal, the last time you pulled, I landed in bed."

He swung his head to Jesus. "In this situation, I'll follow you."

Caligula took off in a frump, spitting on Leah as he passed. His sword's scabbard rattled the railings. *Sound of hob-nailed boots banging through the door and down the dark stone steps, falling and fading.*

Jesus took a few steps toward the ramp. He said, "Do you see more clearly now, Emperor?"

"I wonder if I have what it takes to see at all, either the light or what I see by it."

Jesus said, "Walk with me and you'll learn to live lightly and freely, learn to believe your beliefs and doubt your doubts."

At that moment, we came face-to-face with a one-eyed giant. This man, maybe three times my size, had leapt up and onto the outer wall. We could see him within the orbit of Jesus' torch. His armored shoulders rose in the dim light, like the wings of a wraith. He wore a patch over one eye, and the remaining eye glared at us. He let loose a cry of bloodlust, sword high overhead.

Grappling hooks clattered beneath his feet. He stomped their sharp edges into the loose mortar beneath his feet. Weight of unseen warriors, pulling upwards, tightened the hooks.

Suddenly, the castle's wall was pulled from under Polyphemus. Morning mist alone held the hooks, and then they dropped from view. The giant was left suspended in mid-air.

Jesus held out his arm, palm out, and simply said, "Stop!"

Polyphemus stood immobile in mid-air, on Jesus' word alone. His eyeball glazed over like an interior hailstorm had hit the back of his eyeball. His down-slashing sword bit hard into something like invisible rock.

The blinded giant held his sword in mid-air—or did his sword hold him?

The soldiers under his command, beneath him on the ramp, were also struck blind and immobilized in mid-scream.

A voice in my head. *Claudia, see what happens when rage weds unbelief? Their children are all blind and impotent.*

I said, *Windy, this is the first time you've spoken directly to me.*

A distinct wind-cuddle wrapped 'round me. Strangest, softest, strongest cuddle I've ever known. She said, *look up.* I did.

Can you see the angels throwing a party, furiously dancing the Hora in circles, arms flying high above them?

I did, by God, I did! They were foreground in my field of sight. And, truth be told, my eye only caught a glimmer from behind my hand. A Presence radiated from them like maybe a million zillion suns. I couldn't begin to look directly at this Light without my head exploding into sheer Light.

Windy said, *Father is laughing with pleasure in his Son, and in you too, Claudia.*

I was so stunned I fell on my face, irradiated by belief, flattened by Love. Long moments passed in the radiance of that certain sort of knowing. The Voice said, *show them how to cooperate, Claudia, not fight and compete. Don't tell, show. Show them, and you will know your place in My family and be blessed.* [17]

I took Windy's words under advisement, not knowing what or how or who to show anything—other than Jesus. I squinted into the courtyard's interior. All survivors in Rozafa's courtyard had been lashed together with ropes in groups of ten, one mercy killer in each group awaiting a signal from the emperor. Each mercy killer was stilled when Jesus said, "Stop!"

I shook my head. *Was everyone frozen in place, or had my eyes stopped working?*

Jesus interrupted my doubt. He lifted me to my feet. His somber smile bathed me with light that seemed to know both light and dark from the inside out. We faced the courtyard.

He called in a loud voice that carried through the castle's interior—a voice heard by anyone with even half-a-heart for interior things, "Turn your heads toward my voice. If you believe and hope in me, my Father will set you free. It is for freedom that you are freed." [18] No one moved. Possibly because they couldn't.

Jesus turned from the courtyard, giving them time to consider their fate. He said, "Tiberius, please help me with Polyphemus. He needs a gentle let-down."

Uncle leaned toward Jesus and muttered, "Why waste our chance? Kill him and the rest of these traitors."

"My Father could stop your breath at any moment, Emperor. He already has, once, and then given it back again, only so you would believe in me. Show the same mercy you've been shown, and it will go well with you. And one more thing. Send for Caligula, who now crouches by the sewer grate, waiting for you to escape with him. Bring him to me."

Uncle motioned to Rabbus. "You heard the man. Send for Cal. And you, Rabbus, come here. Help me get this giant out of the sky."

Jesus seemed strengthened, exuberant, as his Spirit blew these happenings about like fall leaves in a swirly wind. Uncle and his bodyguard positioned themselves as close beneath the giant as the crumbled rampart would allow. The giant was still about ten feet out, over where the wall had crumbled, beyond their reach.

Uncle said to Rabbus, "If he lets go now, he'll fall about 150 feet to the base of the wall. What to do?"

Rabbus said to John and Pontii, both standing by, "Get over here. It'll take a small group to lower this giant."

Rabbus spoke to the giant, "Swing your feet toward my voice. Get a rhythm going, more sideways movement with each swing. On the third in-swing toward me, let go of your sword. We'll catch you."

The giant swung back and forth in the sky like an overgrown child playing on a sky-swing. He used his sword hasp as an axle. On the third swing, he let go.

Giant faith worked. At this moment, letting go was more important than holding on.

He fell sideways, his momentum throwing him wall-ward. The four men each caught an arm, leg, or hank of hair as he hurtled toward the wall, collapsing on top of Caligula, who had just arrived from below. Polyphemus pulled himself away from my cousin and sorted himself out. I went over to the giant and led him to Jesus. There at Jesus' feet, he sat on solid rock.

Jesus asked, for the first time, "Do you believe in the Hope God, the one you cursed a few minutes ago?"

The blind, bemused giant, head down, mumbled, "Who is he, Lord, that I might worship him?"

Jesus said to him, "You're looking at him right now, but only if you use an eye of faith. No need to see more or hear more. That will come later."

Caligula sat against the wall, in earshot of these proceedings. He could hear, but he'd been blinded. Someone had put a rag round his head, shielding his eyes.

Jesus' glance passed over my cousin and rested on me. He said, "Claudia, could you climb on my shoulders? We're going to pick up my new disciple's sword. Leah, would you and John join me on either side? We'll all going to need each other."

Leah helped steady me because I was tippy with weakness and fear. Jesus got down on all fours. I hiked my short smock high on my thighs and clasped my legs around his neck. I was still wet with my pee—gutter perfume. Jesus stood. Leah and John linked arms with his arms on either side.

Jesus held my bare, grimy feet and said, "Claudia, be free of your stink."

I took a deep breath and felt fear drop away. Whatever it was I smelled now wasn't bad, just human—like someone I hadn't known. I looked up, outside of my *me-focus*. A hard thing for a self-absorbed person to do.

Words came out of my mouth, surprising me. "The sword is out there." I pointed up at a diagonal to where Polyphemus had been hanging. The sword had not moved an inch. It remained still, stuck in place, out there in space.

Jesus looked up at me and then left and right at his friends. We were on the very edge, fifteen stories above the rocks below.

He said the same to us as he had to Polyphemus, no difference in his tone or words, "Do you believe in me?"

I said, "Yes, but I hope this doesn't mean what I think it means."

John said, "I'm willing to die with you."

Leah said, "Windy already told me earlier today that my next faith step would be into thin air, at your request. What are we waiting for?"

A strong wind began to blow. [19]

8

SLOW

Our caravan made camp outside the walls of Dhiban. Laz and I bedded the children down inside our tent. He told them their favorite bedtime story, David and Goliath, and they all drifted off to sleep.

My mind drifted too. Shame said, *well, you dragged us all back to your old hometown. Satisfied?* She tilted her head, parsed me into pieces, and promptly forgot to put me back together, as usual. I wandered away from our tent into deep shadows, away from the caravan, eyes all affright. This was last night when I happened on silver-hair and the fat man.

Today our family went shopping in the capital city. Goodness carried our children. Laz led me, and I led Goodness through Dhiban's walled warren of shops and alleys. We came to the town square and tied our burro to a hitching post. I wanted to keep an eye on him.

Inside, Laz splurged on a teensy bottle of absurdly expensive perfume for me, the kind for enticing the living or anointing the dead. I wasn't sure what tonight's party might require.

While he perfume-shopped with Mike and Hope, I dodged across the crowded street to a hardware store. Cutter made one thin purchase, about six inches long. We returned to the dress shop. A lavender dress caught Harlot's eye, ma's exact favorite color. While in the dressing room, Cutter bound the six-inch, straight-edge razor to our right thigh with two strips of twine. I put my clothes back on.

All the while, my-me's were annoyed with the smell of pee. Had Fragile squirted on Escape? Or was this another?

Laz stopped at the city well. We filled our water bladders and slung them over Goodness. I whirled us around a time or two, eyes squinting, nose wrinkling. No one there other than a crowd of town people doing life.

We walked past shantytown outside the walls. My childhood home had once been here. Nothing remained but caved-in mud walls and a fallen roof. Everything there, like me, flattened under the weight of all we'd seen. Wild weeds and hot winds swirled trash across the knee-high remnants.

Laz watched at a distance, his keffiyeh wrapped tight to keep the grit out of his eyes. I laid on my back where my bed had been and gathered my-me's inside folded arms. I breathed deep, blowing dust swooshing through us, expanding my hollow spaces wide enough to hold an orphanage.

A stray thought wiggled through my ears. *Welcome home, daughter. Time to reclaim your-you's from the lost and found.*

We returned to campsite. I said, "Laz, I smell pee everywhere I go. I feel like a jug stuffed with peeing monkeys. Is this my stink, and I'm finally able to smell it now that I'm home?"

Laz hugged me inside his strong arms and didn't try and smudge fake cheer all over me. *Good husband, well done.*

Hope and I basin-bathed, shampooed. Each dabbed perfume back of the other's ears. We looked and smelled gorgeous. One of us was possessed of an almost adult mind—her mother, less so.

Laz cleaned up pretty well, dressed in his sabbath keffiyeh, tan cloak, and new sandals. He watched the children as they threw rocks into a culvert and played tag.

He leaned over and blew on the campfire coals, ticking items off on his fingers, "So, let me get this right—you think your real father *might* be Moab's king. He's lost his mind, got fat, gone impotent, and discovered your mother told him something about thieving. He thinks you're his ex-lover or daughter, and I'm your brother. Have I missed something here?"

"You missed how grateful I am that he's impotent. He remembers how much fun it was, but little porkie's lost his prong. Also, he forgot what and who thieved from him, but accepts his own written histories."

Laz said, "And what's this about me being your brother?"

"If it takes lying to keep you alive, so be it."

"You do know God hates lying." [20]

"Truth's a luxury I can't afford, Husband. If money's left in my purse at the end of the day, I'll spend it on truth."

Laz sat with his mouth open, thinking of a come-back when Hope dragged Michael up to the campfire. She shook her little brother off her ankle. His nose was bleeding, and he wailed, "Ma, she pushed my face in the sand."

Hope said, "He's lying, and that's the truth! We got tired of tag and stoning, so we played Whack-a-Mole and Find-a-Well. I picked up the edge of a flat rock like nice Uncle Emil did yesterday. Mikey stuck his face under it to see the wigglies down there, and the rock slipped out of my hand."

I comforted my growing boy, and Laz picked up Hope. He offered them a date from his pouch of dried fruit. After the children went back to play, I asked, "You have a better plan to keep your throat from getting slit and your wife from getting raped?"

Laz effortlessly switched conversation partners. "God, please provide a sacrifice Yourself."

About then, Ehud hobbled around the side of our tent. Harlot greeted him. "Ehud, meet my brother, Laz. His wife, Gomaria, split. His children call me ma; they're over there playing."

He scratched his head and gave me a knowing sort of nod. "King asked me to escort Queen Ester to his banquet room. Also, Ahab the rabbi is there with his family."

Laz whispered, "The plot thickens. This is the rabbi fond of stoning women? Hey, want to get gone now, skip town and the caravan?"

"I wouldn't miss a reunion, though neither candidate for abba, king or rabbi, knows the real me."

Laz said, "What's real is kissed mist, vapor on the move."

"Isn't this how most daughters and fathers really are, just a little more in your face?"

"Ah, I don't know. Mary and Martha can tell you next time we're in Bethany."

Escape answered hopefully, with our usual optimism, "Only if we make it out of Moab."

We left with Ehud for the palace. My stiletto chafed on my leg, but I walked with my shoulders back, and head held high, just like Queen Ester of long ago. At this party coming up, if I perished, I perished. [21]

Ehud led us through a maze of narrow streets, stopping outside a humble adobe home in a long row of identical other adobe homes. Not too different from the house where I'd grown up. His silver hair glistened like fine mesh wool in the sun. An old woman, going bald, sat in a linden wood rocking chair. She creaked as she rocked, or was that the chair?

Elsa eyed us somberly, quietly. Peaceful looked good on her. This, in spite of the off-white booties she was knitting for grandchildren she didn't yet have. But there still was hope. After all, she and Ehud were only in their 80's.

Ehud said, "Elsa would be happy to provide childcare for your little ones while we attend the banquet. We'll be out late. Elsa's stories will get them to sleep."

The palace guards thoroughly frisked Laz but gave me only a cursory once-over. Ehud brushed off their questions with a brusque flick of his finger.

After we passed through the gates, two servants washed our feet, a man and woman. A valet led us into the grand palace's receiving room. Eglon reclined on a dais, propped up by pillows all around. He sucked an olive off a toothpick. The green, stuffed olive made a popping sound as it disappeared in his face. Three other men leaned toward him, facing away from us, everyone in animated conversation.

Eglon's shoulders' rose when he saw me. He held the air and then released the heaving intake. His exhaust caused his shoulders to fall. Probably a good example of what happens to all kings and kingdoms.

His guests lounged just a few inches below where Eglon's sigh stopped. The king motioned to Ehud. "Who's that man with my queen, or is that my daughter or my lover?"

Ehud advised, "King, that man is her brother and watch-guards her honor. She's daughter of your ex-lover, Ester, the one who warned you of thieves."

Recognition briefly flared on the king's face. His body, encased in plentitude, relaxed. He glowed with adoration when he stared at me, his resurrected lover-queenie-daughter—along with a few me's he couldn't see.

He couldn't keep my identity straight to save his soul, so we were on even footing. I let my patchy memories dance lightly. Some of them even might have been real.

Eggie sucked in another breath and shouted, in a voice too garish for anyone but the guy in charge, "Here comes the Lavender Singer, boys! Va-va-voom!"

The men stood to greet the new guests. The two younger men, resplendent in gold-trimmed, silken garments, fragrant colognes, and red-checked keffiyeh, trailed behind their father. The spice brothers turned away from the king to greet us. The elder son, Emil, was a parody of himself, gold necklace twinning his sly smile. He kissed my hand and whispered hoarsely, "Queenie for a day, is it? Zayan and I are *so* looking forward to a royal dessert once we're done with the Demented Dumpling."

Zayan nodded agreement. He put me in mind of a carnival freak who eats glass for a living.

Their father, Rabbi Ahab, had decked himself out with golden phylacteries on forehead, right bicep, and right wrist. His bright, blue-green eyes, identical to mine, flashed in the candlelight. Eyebrow ridges formed lines below his widow's peak.

The rabbi stooped, weighted by what he carried—Torah, phylacteries, and black woolen robes. Windy whispered, *behold your father. He's heavy, like you, with all that cannot be seen—the weight of past sins, sons' misadventures, wife's recent passing, and his shamed, septic daughter, your half-sister.*

I turned from the wealthy Jewish brothers, my half-brothers, who'd risen to the rank of princelings by the oily ease of their slippery judgments. I pulled back my veil and bowed low before the king, "Oh King, my voice is not as beautiful as was my mother's voice. However, I would still like to sing, sing a humble song just for you."

9
CLAUDIA

My knees hammer locked around Jesus' neck, joining together at the ankles. He took a step of faith into thin air, off the ramparts, fifteen stories up. The air held us. He took another few steps further from the balustrades, positioning us under the sword. We were far enough below the sword that I had to stretch for it.

I said, "Jesus, aren't you being unreasonable? Couldn't you step up to the sword?"

Leah, on Jesus' left side, commented, "Windy usually requires a stretch. That way, you get to grow."

John added, "Jesus does his part. Windy does hers. Now, stop complaining and reach for that stupid sword."

I reached inside for some higher power that might stretch me toward heaven. I felt those little bones in my back go pop-pop-pop, widening with effort. I barely got my fingers around the sword's handle.

Then I looked down, got dizzy, and forgot I was seated with Jesus. Totally lost it and fell off his shoulders. John happened to catch me by my ankle on my way down. I dangled there upside down, screaming my fool head off, smock over my face. I was blind to anything, but this morning's puke stains on the cotton smock, half-inch from my eyes. I flopped in mid-air, free leg kicking, arms flailing, naked to the world above and below.

A smooth updraft gradually lifted me back on Jesus' shoulders. *Thanks for righting me, just as I am, Windy.*

Had Jesus had put his heart in mine? It was the only way to account for all those extra heartbeats. I looked around at our cluster of air travelers. Leah steadied John. Jesus held Leah. Windy held us. No one lectured me about unbelief or public nakedness.

Jesus said, "Claudia, can you feel our support? We're solid, beneath you. Now, back to work. Reach up."

I shut my eyes to impossibility and opened my ears to Jesus' voice. I gripped the bronze sword handle and yanked with all my strength. My military father and Rome would have been proud of me. My face felt hot, probably bright pink or purple. Sword was not impressed with my efforts. It stayed stuck, solid in its mid-air vise.

Crap! I wasn't cut out for mid-air sword grabs. Give it up, Claudia.

One baby cherub out of that cloud of witnesses must have read my thoughts. She tried to reach down and help me, but a bigger seraph held her back. I heard the big one whisper, "She can do this hard thing. How else will she ever get strong?"

Jesus' voice buoyed me, "No strain is needed. Act from your seat of power. *Let Windy breathe you.* A gentle pull—all that's needed."

I pretended I knew what he was talking about. *Who was I kidding?*

I tried again. I grasped the hasp of this giant sword with both hands. Ok, here comes my best "gentle" pull. Pulled hard, straining. Nada.

I got distracted by the dancing cherub. Clear, crisp vision of Windy flowing through my blood and breath. [22] *Ahh, a sigh of wonder.* As the air went out of me, my arms relaxed. Sword accompanied hands' instroke toward my heart. [23]

What fell in my hands was a plowshare with a sharp point to it. I tried not to cut myself from what I'd sky-harvested.

I said, "Hey, Jesus, think we all can scoot back to the castle wall? This thing's heavy."

Jesus turned to Leah and said, half-joking, "What do you think? A little sky-stroll, or back to business?"

John, from fifteen feet away, said, "I went for a wander while that whole sword thing was happening. I had to turn away from that Roman wench's brazen nakedness. I left. But now, I'm stuck like she was."

His wide eyes lost their focus on Jesus and rolled around in his tipped-back head. His arms cartwheeled, and he looked ready to fall off some invisible faith-ledge.

Jesus walked over to him. "Cousin, could you reach over to Claudia and grab ahold?" John's reach was fueled by desperation, not desire.

Jesus looked up to me and smiled. "Do for him what he did for you."

I grabbed John's flailing right arm and pulled him to me, transferring his dead weight to Jesus' side. John grabbed ahold of his cousin.

Jesus didn't have to use me, but he did. Why?

Leah turned aside and waved to Rabbus, back on the ramparts. I caught her tipped-up chin and slight smile. *Hey, look at me!*

Rabbus, inspired, called out, "Keep your eyes and ears on Jesus, wife. Best way to keep grounded." Leah took a sneak peek at Jesus' face.

He said, "Let's go back."

We returned to the castle and walked past slack-jawed Uncle Tiberius, who had been giving a blow-by-blow commentary to blind Caligula. Polyphemus also had listened to Tiberius' description of our whole skywalk.

Jesus stooped at a distance from the stupefied giant. He said, "Rise, Chieftain."

Polyphemus got on his feet, groping for who he could not yet see.

Jesus asked him for the second time, "Do you believe?"

"Yes, Lord. I want to see."

Jesus said, "Leah, could you take this splendid man and lead him to me?"

Pleasure washed over her face. She took Poly by the hand, as she might have done for her son, had he been still alive, and led him to Jesus.

Jesus said, "Polyphemus, I'm here, even if you can't see me. Remember that—I'm always right here, available. My Spirit's as close as knowing the right thing to do when the rules don't apply."

The giant allowed himself to be led by one who was a third his size, led onto uncertain ground. Blind Poly, the giant, was listening to Jesus. My friend had been belting out a praise song, dancing in place, and raising a hallelujah.

Tiberius told Cal what Jesus was doing. Cal said to Pontii, standing beside him, "It's clear, at last. He's taken leave of his senses." Pontii nodded.

What was clear to me was something else—neither of them could hear the music.

The one-eyed guy, still led by Leah, approached Jesus. God-Man stopped his song and hugged Leah. He rested his right hand over the giant's remaining one eye.

Uncle hovered behind him. If he'd had a tablet, he'd have been taking notes.

Jesus asked for the third time, "Do you believe in me?" [24]

Polyphemus said, "Yes, Lord. Save my people and me from ourselves and the devils that surround us."

Jesus said to all who were present, "According to your faith, be your sight."

A few things happened just then.

Many within the sound of Jesus' voice started yelling, "I can see!"

My eyes came into crystal clear focus.

Uncle said, "I see, but in halves."

Caligula screamed, "I'm blind!" He howled, turning in circles, hand over his eyes.

Leah, Rabbus, and John all said more or less the same thing, "What are you talking about? Nothing changed."

The giant's one eye gazed clearly at Jesus' smiling face. Jesus seemed lit from within by a Light far greater than any one human was meant to hold. I stepped up next to Jesus, held Poly's hand, and smiled at the new disciple. A few minutes earlier, he'd have been delighted to hand me my severed head. Now he smiled back at me, a quirky grin under his one seeing eye. He almost looked handsome.

Jesus said, "Polyphemus, in the land of the blind, you, the one-eyed, are chief. Take your new plowshare and cultivate the souls of your people. You alone among your warriors see clearly enough to lead them to me. Go back down the ramp to your soldiers.

"Touch each man's eyes, and say, 'You are healed and given hope, in Jesus' name.'" Jesus handed the giant what his sword had become.

Just then, I remembered Windy's words to me. I said, "Jesus, Windy spoke to me! She asked me to *show* people how to cooperate. Poly could give us a hand here before he leaves. Maybe he could release stuck enemies in the way he was freed?"

The giant overheard my request and nodded. This guy was a doer.

Jesus smiled gently at me just before he sat down. More accurately, he collapsed. He'd used up his constitution and run through his by-laws. My body must have gone on a sympathy strike of sorts because exhaustion crumpled me too. I felt rock beneath me and Jesus beside me—and I was glad.

Before either Jesus or I could move, Poly picked us up gently, one in either arm, like we were small children meant to be cradled. He set off down the steps into enemy territory, conquering his enemies in fresh ways unimagined an hour earlier. I held onto his neck ten feet above the ground with both arms.

Jesus looked across the giant's broad chest at me and shrugged. "Enjoy the ride."

Having no choice wonderfully clarified my course. We went to each death squad in the courtyard. Rabbus and Uncle followed behind closely. Poly leaned over from the waist, got on eye level with each Roman.

He practiced saying to his enemies what he would soon say to his followers, "You are healed and given hope in Jesus' name."

Everyone in that group was restored their sight and freedom of movement as the words came from the Poly's lips. Each mercy-killer, to the man, slumped to the ground. Their daggers remained planted in mid-air. Damnedest thing I ever saw, next to that sword trick.

Jesus and I took turns. We kept one arm around Poly's neck and with the other hand, plucked each dagger out of the air, turned it around, and handed back a trowel or pruning hook to the intended killer, handle first. Each released mercy-killer received his alchemist's gift from an expectant Jesus and one plague-poxed survivor.

My part in this whole shebang, besides dagger plucking and trowel shucking, was to say two words, "Follow him." I pointed to Jesus in the giant's other arm.

In this way, all nine hundred sixty victims of siege and plague and soul darkness, except cousin Caligula, were set free by a believing giant, an exhausted Messiah, a poxed waif, and a wee helping from the Almighty.

10

WINDY

The king sat up straighter when Slow offered to sing for him. A memory spike fastened a flap of tangle into plaque, right there in his mid-brain. The curvy waitress, Propinquity, offered a serving of Desire—also known as Crumble Cake.

Slow picked up an old harp that sat in a corner of the room. She dusted her mother's harp off, tightened the strings, and sang tenderly in a throaty alto. Her vibrato on the sustains lifted her voice to the ceiling. The syncopated rhythm, with slinky shoulder lifts, perfectly stitched the notes together. Her smile danced slightly, lightly shifting between the king and rabbi.

Slow sang an ancient version of Israel's national anthem-to-be, *Hatikvah*:

> *"As long as Jewish souls still yearn toward Zion,*
> *Our hope is not yet lost.*
> *As long as dewdrops fall on mothers' graves,*
> *Come home, my people, home come, in peace, to your homeland."* [25]

Slow's harp and voice ransacked sorrow, drenching her father. Ahab, a full-on synesthete, soaked in the sensations that rode off his daughter's fingers and out her throat. He experienced her song like crème brulee, savored in tiny bites during a massage. Fireworks shot stars of blue onto a white field between his temples. Ultramarine blues blended toward magenta, drifting around his toes when she lingered on the low notes.

Eglon also dusted off Ester's memory and did a turn with her on memory's dance floor, right before her memory was put to death. The silver-haired wise man sat cross-legged behind the reclining king. He whispered,

"She did well. Meanwhile, the thieves who stole from your treasury enjoy the bounty of your table."

The smoking flax in Eglon's eyes kindled into a crackling flame of jovial inquiry, "Tell me, Emil and Zayan, how many years has it been since you so loved flying the kites we made together?"

Zayan answered, with the merest crust of an edge, "We're no longer children, highness."

Eglon tossed off the inflected disrespect. "So, is the spice business treating *us* all well?"

Emil answered, "Ah, my sovereign, it is indeed hard work, backbreaking work, day and night, north and south, back and forth. Zayan and I stopped here only to deposit our tax tributes, great king. Tomorrow we travel further down the Kings' Highway toward Egypt—where we will earn more for our king and his kingdom."

Ehud turned to the rabbi, "Your sons' names have become famous throughout the realm, Ahab, for all they've done and left undone."

Ahab shook himself back into the conversation. He'd been busy remembering—*so this was Ester's lost daughter! She looked just like her mother, but more so.* He worked hard to shake off a looming sense of threat, murkier than hell. One eye turned in, searching for the source of his pain; the other eye turned out, scanning for danger. He rubbed his temple, the right one that pulsed pleasure and spiked pain, a gathering crescendo of transient ischemic attacks.

Ahab's body, this fragile container and mingler of senses, harbored an excellent memory.[26] He remembered what the king could not—both men had fallen head over heels in love with Gomaria's married mother on the same day, at the same party, when she sang and played the same harp Slow had played moments earlier. Ester had also worn a lavender dress and used the same perfume. *What devious gremlins were at play here?*

Memories of love lost leapt from Ester's grave and wrapped both legs around him. Purple ecstasy spasmed. Joy jumped him with pink oranges and white lily's fragrance. Harlot showered him with luscious love's memories, stolen from time at the temple, time with his boys, and time with Me. She almost blew his top, but not quite.

The darker depths of memory took Ahab down. When Ester jilted him for Eggie, Envy's waves swamped his boat. Unwanted memories, like a great fish, gnawed his body. Near the end of one impassioned love-making session, Ester had said, "Ahab, we can't keep this up. We're married to others. And my other lover in the castle demands more and more."

He'd argued back. "I'll divorce my wife once she recovers from being poorly. Give me time. We were meant for each other."

She'd replied, "The minyan looks the other way when the king takes a Jewess lover. But if *our* affair becomes public? *They* will stone me." She and he knew who "*they*" would be. His sandals would slip through her ruby issue as he walked away, unnamed, unharmed.

When Ester dumped Ahab a few days later, Envy sliced and plated him at this very table where he now sat. On the spot, Ahab hatched a plot thick as a nest of viper eggs. He announced before all the honored guests, "Our synagogue wants to use this time to announce a gift to our beloved king. Ahab mentioned a large sum. Everyone sucked in their breath, *such enormous generosity!*

Ahab's gift was not a gift. It was an obligation. No sooner had Ahab been seated than Eglon stood. He promised to give his good buddy whatever the good rabbi might ask, up to half his kingdom.

Ahab joined him. He put his arm around tipsy Eglon's shoulders. "I know *exactly* what I want, dear friend. And not something for *me*, but for my God. *Righteousness*. I want that harlot, Ester, executed for adultery." He didn't mention adultery with whom and for how long. Such indelicacies were tucked under the low table, with the dinner napkins.

Eglon could not recant on his public promise. He'd overlooked this inconvenient mistress stoning and busied himself with other affairs of state the day of the stoning.

The waiter tapped Ahab on the shoulder again. "Sir, honey with your coffee?" Ahab took his sticky baklava and watched the date honey being stirred into his coffee. Eglon's voice re-directed his attention. The king had heaved himself off the couch and now joked, "My body's a full-on organ recital—gout, constipation, skippy heartbeat, and more. Illness harps at me like a two-string lyre with one working string. But, never fear, Your Grace has special after-dinner entertainment in store."

Eglon absented himself. Zayan and Emil scooted closer to Slow, one on either side, while Laz discussed Torah with Ahab. Zayan leaned over and peered down her cleavage. His fingers slipped under her dress and up her thigh, lightly dancing their way toward Cutter's straight edge.

Harlot playfully slapped his fingers and whispered in his ear, "You're very naughty!"

Emil eye-waved his brother off with a head shake, *later is better!*

Zayan relented, "Quite the poser, aren't you, *my precious?*"

The king toddled back from his bathroom pee-break and spoke to his longtime friend and sons, plus those two strangers sitting next to Ehud. "Ta-daaa! Here I am! Now that dessert's done let's take a short drop. We wouldn't want to leave reward left hanging, now, would we?"

The platoon of guards tromped before and after the dinner guests, bronzed helmets all a-gleam in the smudge torches that hung on the walls, every ten paces. One locked door after another fell behind the royal key-keeper as they journeyed deep into the castle keep.

Once the final door was breached, the guests were escorted to the front row of four chairs. Each was seated in a high back chair of pure gold, covered with llama pelts. Neatly stacked gold bars shimmered behind votive candles in this church where wealth was worshipped.

This was Emil and Zayan's first visit to the royal treasury. Their eyes were wide with wonder and wantonness. Emil fingered one of the llama pelts, remembering exactly where he'd found this one in Ethiopi and how much he'd inflated its value when paying his taxes. He'd forgotten what of his soul he'd traded for such inflation.

Ahab noted the thick velvet curtain before them. He whispered to Zayan, "Son, that's an exact replica of the veil in Jerusalem, the one that separates the profane from the Holy of Holies."

Eglon said, "Emil and Zayan, my honored guests, please approach the curtain for your prizes. Our treasurer will reveal how your rewards have stolen their way into my vault."

Zayan demurred, palms down, as though refusing the last piece of cake on a royal platter. "Oh no, great king. We need no reward for our efforts on your behalf."

Eglon would not be put off. "Ah, my princelings, don't deny me! In fact, I'll add to the suspense. We'll blindfold you to heighten the mystery of this after-dinner theatre. Yes, indeedy, that's exactly what we'll do! I've always loved game shows!"

The brothers rolled their eyes, smirked, and let themselves be gently blindfolded by the laughing guards.

Eggie tittered, "Oh, guaaa-rds! Please. Add to my suspense. This is delightfully unbearable! Tickle their wrists with cords of silk." Guards bound their hands behind them.

Eggie crowed, "Oh yes, let the show begin!"

A snare drum rolled. Eggie cried out, "And now, behind Curtain Number One!" A pause. "Oops, silly me! Curtain Number One is the *only* curtain."

The royal snare drum rolled for the second time. The velvet curtain swished back. Two slender, narrow stacks of gold-colored curcumin were positioned side by side, a few feet apart, in front of stacked bars of gold, floor to ceiling.

Laz whispered to Slow, "those curcumin spice stacks are far more expensive, ounce for ounce, than the pure gold behind them. End users cut the spice into dilute mixtures of turmeric or curry, but this pure stuff is devilishly expensive."

The curcumin had been pressed into heavy cubes—sheets of spice between panes of glass. Each of the two platforms was a six-inch cube of golden spice bound on the corners with sharp, metal edging. The spice brothers were led, side by side, to their separate blocks. Standing room only.

King Eglon nodded, and a noose dropped, as if by magic, over each of the spice brothers' necks. Zayan queried, "What's this?" His voice was surprised, not far from panic. Emil's feet jittered a bit, then stilled. Guards cinched tighter the cords that bound them and removed their blindfolds.

At this point, Ahab panicked. Years of laughter in both men's houses, dinners of state, negotiations between the Jew and Moabite—all these memories splashed across Ahab's inner sight-scape, colors done in shades of purple. Ahab released a breath and rubbed his throbbing temples. The pleasant memories leeched away into the room's dim recesses. Sound of tambourines in his inner ears, sensations of prickly cacti in his fingertips, and the creeping smell of rich food gone rancid. The thought crystallized. *Eggie's going to kill my sons.*

11

SLOW

Laz and I sat in the only two chairs on the back row. No one could be seen sitting in the three-seated middle row, but a cool breeze swirled around the third chair and nowhere else.

King Eglon sat on the remaining Chair of Gold in the front row. Ehud approached him. He held a black robe in his outstretched hands. The king stood and shrugged on the robe. Ehud wandered back beside our chairs. He whispered to Laz, "the king no longer serves as a king, for the moment. He is now High Judge of all Moab."

Eglon the Judge said, "Emil and Zayan, you stand on your just rewards. My treasurer, quite fastidious, has weighed your tax theft to the exact ounce. My guards recouped what was mine from your caravan. My chef hammered and layered the spice. My engineers polished the glass, my ironsmiths bound the edges. My Chief Rabbi will now recover what is mine from beneath you."

Guards escorted Ahab to his eldest son. Emil looked past his father to Eglon. He pleaded, "High Judge, I'll restore to you fivefold, no, no, tenfold, what I mistakenly have taken. An honest mistake. Forgive me, kind and generous ruler of all Moab, Maker-of-Kites for us as boys, Lord Potentate Most High, Compassionate Sovereign...."

Eglon addressed Ahab. "My hearing isn't working too well tonight. Did you hear someone passing wind? And, come to think, my noodles don't work so well either—the one on top, and that one down there." He winked twice, theatrically.

Eggie eyed Ahab askance. "I'm not quite sure who you are. I think you might be an old friend, but you put me in mind of someone who stands on his scriptures to gain an elevated view of others' sins. But, seeing how my memory's gone all pudgy on me, I never can trust who's a friend, who's not. Ehud recalled for me just yesterday how you, or someone just like you, threw the first stone at someone quite dear to me.

"'Fulfilling all righteousness,' you said."

Ahab stood, silent as a thrown stone.

The king continued, "I wonder. Do all Jews *think and speak* righteous but forget to *do* righteous? Or is that just you and your offspring? Ah, no worries. We'll even the scales tonight. "

Ahab made a face. "High Judge, the stoned singer, Ester, abandoned me. I couldn't stand it. I had her executed in haste and now entreat your forgiveness."

"Kneel, Jew. Kneel before your own law. Execute righteousness. Does not Moses demand it? Your law resides in your phylacteries—the boxes on head, heart, and arm. Perhaps you might slip a little law from head to hand? Now, do the deed."

Ahab's face flared, bright red. A bulging blue vein in his right temple throbbed.

Eglon's voice, harsh, "You lied and murdered to salve your pride. Your sons have stolen. And, alas, I also remember a rape, Emil, from behind the stables off the main plaza. Your little sister, as I recall."

Eggie didn't appear to remember any of their forty years of good times in this town—watching the same vistas, discussing the same wars, arguing politics and truces, celebrating birthdays and death days, christenings, and weddings.

He said, "Here, read the law to your sons. Someone dog-eared the correct passage for you—even underlined it using curcumin ink." He lifted his copy of the Torah and ripped out the page he wanted, handing it to Ahab. The rabbi gasped at such sacrilege but said nothing.

The judge said, "You may now read your law and let it read you. Read past the words, rabbi, into the red meat of it."

The kneeling rabbi closed his eyes and recited the judgment, his head shuckling up and down. After, he half-turned his torso, kissed the holy page, and set it on the golden chair. He looked down at the oriental carpet, elaborately patterned in oxblood reds.

Eglon said, "Rabbi, no more delays. Recover my stolen taxes."

Ahab crawled toward Emil, his most loved son. He bent, head to ground, at Emil's feet, "Forgive me, my son."

Emil lifted on one toe, tenuous. Ahab removed the stolen spices from beneath him. The drop was short. Only six inches.

Emil kicked furiously, stretching rope and neck as a unit. But, alas, his longest toe barely touched ground, giving him hope. He pushed up with that toe, restoring a bit of wind in his pipe.

Eglon's mask of joviality tore loose. "Stealing and lying are bedmates, my kite flyer. But here's the thing. Neither elevates your standing before judge or king, not even an inch."

Emil balanced on his big toe, face twinging toward cherry red.

Eggie sat comfortably on his golden throne, a few feet away. His face twisted as I watched. He grabbed his right big toe and massaged it furiously.

He said, "Emil, wouldn't you know it! Both our big toes are merciless tonight, which leads me to a question. I wonder. Would you trade strict law for a mercy that's not strained?"

Emil was a merchant who'd traded in many places. He furiously nodded his strained chin. [27]

Eggie said, "Tell you what. I'll give you the same mercy that your father gave Ester. But I can't remember how that went. My memory's not so good." He winked. "But hang on. I'll send the scribe for my journals. History tells all."

The obsequious scribe hurried out the door. Eglon continued, like a professor of physics, "The long drop, or even the standard drop, will break your neck nine of ten times. The short drop preserves your life longer. And that's the good and bad, in a nutshell."

Eggie waggled his finger, "Half hour at the end of a rope makes for a very long life."

Emil's eyes bugged out. He could no longer speak. The scribe returned at a trot, bowed apologetically to this empurpled merchant, who lived presently at the end of his rope. He delicately placed the journals on the king's lap, bowed deeply, head scraping kneecaps.

Eggie was gleeful, "Ah, here we are! Let me see. What did Ester point out? Justice does require a thorough discovery."

Eggie wagged his finger. "So *terribly* sorry, merchant. Your Grace takes a long time. We dumplings dement by degrees, or is it decrees? I never can remember. But we wouldn't want to cheat due process, would we? I *am* the High Judge, you know."

He sniffed, looked down at Ahab. "Yes, you're in luck, Emil. I found the offense. Hmm." He tsked. "I read that truth is found in the tension between opposites. Like gravity and grace. One pulls down on you, the other lifts you up." He sighed. "Unfortunately, Your Grace is indisposed. I need a brief potty break."

Eggie toddled off to the vault's vanity. Sound of urine splashing, stopping, starting again. Repeated. The High Judge returned, after his not-so-wee-pee, and went on about various theological tensions for some time, all the while keeping Emil on toe.

The elder son took a fiendishly long time to finish living. His face turned deeper shades of magenta. A rich sapphire soon became him, before his kicking became spastic. About half an hour dripped by on the water clock. Each drip sounded like a gong. The only other sounds were the turning pages of history.

The perfumed elder spice merchant became quite still. The smell of his final poop tangled in Ahab's nose with his son's cologne.

Zayan had quietly watched his brother's horror show with huge, round eyes. He had tried to slump and quietly hang himself without much ado, but the soldiers held him up.

Now his hour had come. Time for his dance with death. Time to know Terror. Time for Terror to know him. The younger prodigal didn't plead or flatter. Instead, he cursed his father, the king, and this pissant, forgettable kingdom of Moab. He spit at Eglon and declared he'd enjoyed every coin he'd grafted. He'd do it all again, given the chance.

Eglon said not a word. Escape and Fragile hid my face in Laz's shoulder. Laz shielded us. We held on.

The king prodded the rabbi. "One down, one to go." Ahab continued rocking on the floor, shards of sound jagged in his mouth. He crawled over to his only living son. He begged forgiveness from his wife's favorite boy and placed his head, nose down on the carpet, pulsing temple a few inches from Zayan's spice block, becoming in that moment as still as the hung brother.

Zayan took charge of his ending, pushed off and back from his spice block, body supported by nothing but his own neck. In one move, he kicked his platform out from under him with all his might. The metal corner caught the bulging vein in his father's head and severed it—a skull-crack, kill shot.

In one fell swoop, patricide and suicide. No big toe, balancing nonsense for him. He hung limp, twisting towards lower regions. A very few minutes passed. Zayan's earth time, done. A voice whispered in my ear, *he will provide a perpetual feast. Those inside the Shade know how to gnaw long and well.*

Guards cut both bodies down, arranging them on top of their father. One brother's head rested on each of his shoulders, feet flopping out to each side—a three-self cross on a bloody Oriental carpet.

Eggie wafted his righteous right hand in their general direction. "Hmph. Unsavory odors emanate. *Definitely a stinky-poo*, Ehud. But two short drops with a rabbi sweetener, not bad work for one hour."

He played with his diamond earring, the size and color of a robin's egg. He turned to Ehud. "Glad *that* party's over."

He moved to leave and cast a cursory look behind him. He asked Ehud, "Who are those two people, and how did they get tickets to the show?"

Ehud smiled, "No matter, my lord. They came for dinner but instead went to school. Tomorrow they're on their way to distant lands."

The king scratched his bald head and departed with his retinue of guards. Ehud walked over. He pulled a straight edge razor from his side pocket and laid it on my left thigh. "A matched set. Let tonight be a lesson in speaking and spending truth. Any other coin in your purse is counterfeit. Understand?"

Harlot and Cutter nodded slowly. Fragile looked for Escape. Ahab's daughter slowly nodded, shivering in my shoes.

Ehud said, "Take both weapons when you leave town tomorrow. You'll need them elsewhere. But here? It's folly to hide chicanery from this king, long as *I* live."

Shame cast my eyes on the three corpses that held each other in death. She spoke, "We're ashamed, Lord of the Night Watch. But you must understand we're terrified, not terrorists."

Ehud waggled his eyebrows. "All the same for 'true believers.' What a shame! Ah well, one day shame will grow into humility."

We left Eglon's palace, found our sleeping children in Elsa's care, and we passed through the city's gates on our way to the caravan. Laz looked toward the vermillion sky, now pinking.

He said, "And our next homecoming? Bethany, with Jesus walking beside us."

12

JESUS

Polyphemus pleaded, "Jesus, I don't know how to lead these people. I'm a warrior, not a regent. Your wizard stuff is *way* better than Bato's puff or Drusilla's magic. Take me on your ship. I'll fight for you."

Claudia flicked a glance at Poly's empty scabbard and then examined the giant plowshare in his hand. We stood on the pier, ready to board Tiberius' new warship. Augusta had sent *Tiberon*, a flagship, with four other, identical quinqueremes, docked on different piers.

I said, "Poly, you delight me. I hear your prayer, and Father *always* answers prayer. He's told me that this time the answer is 'no.' He's sending you to your people. He also told me something for my journey that I'll pass along to you too. 'Go where you're sent. Stay where you're put. Give what you've got.'" [28]

Poly nodded. He slowly turned around in a circle, kicking the ground.

Claudia approached him and took his hand. "Poly, answered prayer can suck. I've gotten a lot of 'no's' from Jesus' Father."

I added, "How else will the kingdom spread far and wide unless we each work in our backyard, led by Windy? Don't fear, servant-leader. Windy will lift you in the future, even as He lifted us all yesterday."

Poly objected. "I don't get this Spirit Kingdom thing. I deal in real— bodies, time, space."

Windy exhaled from my mouth, "You're being schooled. Your body is big, but your clear-seeing spirit, small. We are all who we protect and what we stand for. This sort of sight requires depth vision. Your one-eyed vision is monocular. You have no depth perception."

Poly's face fluttered through five shades of not-understanding.

I continued, "you and I are more alike than different in this way. We need one inner eye that sees beneath the surface of things and one outer eye on Father's destiny and destination for our lives." [29]

Poly gazed at me intently. He heard what he could, let the rest drop, and for such a giant as he, that was a long drop. "You're saying, Master, that we're more alike than different, you and me?"

I replied, "My father put me on earth to grow up, just like you. We're all being schooled from one threshold to another, faith to faith. Windy will guide you and me with His eye and Her voice—but only if we are vigilant."

"I've got wax in my ears and sleep in my one eye, Master. I don't know how to lead."

"Poly, here's the fascinating thing. You don't *have to know* what you need, where to go, or what to do. My Spirit intimately knows your not-knowing and rushes to fill the gap you mind." [30]

Windy whispered, *you yammered too long, Son. But he took all he needed—that you and he are alike. The rest is already un-remembered.*

Windy schooled me with more on the pier that day, but I, like Poly, couldn't hold onto it. All I could take in was that He liked that I'd loved Poly the best I could. The other parts of Her lesson plan would come 'round again when I had space for another info dump.

I pulled myself back to the present moment, in time to see Poly turn and march, militant, off the pier. Claudia and I climbed up to the captain's deck. This Roman quinquereme had docked outside Rozafa Castle on the River Drin with Lake Scodra glistening in the distance.

Captain Sejanus called out, "Away! Next stop, Rhodes!" All five decks of rowers started stroking our 140-foot-long vessel toward the Adriatic.

Claudia stood next to me, leaned on the railing, and faced into the freshening wind. She said, "Jesus, I'm still recovering from pox, siege, and airwalk. All that buried me."

I said, "What do you mean?"

"If I had any lingering doubt about the god part of you, it got buried in thin air."

I said, "I'm a believer in resurrection. Hard to keep a good doubter down."

Claudia smiled. "Last night, in Poly's fancy house off the main square in Scodra, he provided so much stuff—food, bath, bed. The thing that killed me was the hot bath. With soap. I didn't know whether to eat it or scrub with it."

I smiled. "This morning, I broke down and cried over a piece of buttered toast and a sunny-side-up egg that Poly brought me. The yolk in the egg was the color of ma's giant sunflowers, the ones that face the rising sun outside her kitchen. I so want to see them all again."

Claudia said, "We counted the seconds together for more than three years in that scummy, pox-struck, scabietic castle. Every comfort I'd ever known vomited out into a phlegmy hairball."

I said, "Windy tells me that we grow bigger inside with that kind of wanting—like a pregnant woman. [31] I don't have to like her words, just trust them. Abba mixes simple things to grow belief—like a fried egg over-easy, air-walks, unstuck swords. Together they break the back of my doubt."

"I keep forgetting you have doubt too. You seem so sure ...."

"I'm sure of Father's care. But I never know how it all will work out. We live under Father's maximum-love-minimum-protection plan."

We fell silent and settled for a hug. We looked behind us at shrinking Rozafa—the siege castle with a ramp sloping up one side and catapults still in place—this land of the cannibalized, the castle of the disappeared, betrayed, beheaded.

Claudia gazed at this many-layered castle. "Simple mystery doesn't begin to describe the luck of the draw—who dies, who lives, who barely squeaks by, and who gets raised on your shoulders."

I said, "I've lived only a twinkle of earth time—short twenty-eight earth years. But what's bred in my bone is this: Father is good and his will, inscrutable. For instance, why did he 'bless' me with this gift of pumped-up empathy? Do you know where that store is located? I want to take it back." Claudia laughed, pointing east toward Bethlehem.

We lapsed into quiet before she whispered something the wind took and lost. I queried with my eyes.

She repeated, "I wouldn't mind carrying your child. I rest my case like I want to rest in your bed, not the one next to it."

I answered, "I longed for you in those bone-crunching infirmary nights, lying side by side on our cots. I wanted that more than I can say. But that is not the one precious life I was given to live."

Claudia cried, head in her hands, "I want married life with you more than breath itself."

I knew enough to stay quiet. My eyes alone invited her to keep speaking.

She asked, "Can you suck the hurt out of all the pain?"

I was tempted to speak, but Windy put a bit in my mouth.

Claudia kept crying, full of what was not to be. She turned her face to me, eyes awash. She said, "It's not too late for us. The book of memories is still open, and together, we hold the pen in *our* hands."

I got lost in her longing and mine—felt them mingle together. To save ourselves from crumbling, we turned away from each other's eyes and looked at Scodra, now a pinprick on the horizon. I said, "Those winding streets back there in Scodra, the ones now disappearing in the distance? They sparked flashbacks of my younger self in Alexandria, Egypt—and even briefer flash-forwards of my older self, to be sacrificed in Jerusalem."

Claudia shivered uncontrollably. We both fell into memory mill's grist wheel, the one that turned backward and forward. Waves at the prow slid past the gunnels. Oars slapped, sails snapped.

Tiberius approached. He had his arm around Caligula, who wore a sky-blue silk bandana over his blind eyes. Caligula, unaware of our presence, slid up beside us at the bannister, holding tight to Tiberius.

He growled, "Uncle, when do we get to kill that Jew for blinding me?"

I roused from my reverie. Claudia delicately coughed. Tiberius looked me in the eyes as he whispered into the wind, "How d-d-do you kill a god, Caligula? It is the gods who kill us." His old stuttering habit had mysteriously returned.

I remained silent.

Claudia spoke to her cousin, "Jesus didn't blind you, Cal. You blinded yourself with unbelief. It's not so much that you *can't* see. You *will* not see."

Cal said, "Love's made you blind to this Jew, cousin, not me. I see well enough to keep love in the family and not mix our blood with mudders. They're wet dust, blowing off the road."

Tiberius intervened, "Enough. There's p-plenty of unbelief and b-b-blindness to go around. We Claudians are all part of one grand destiny. We barely managed to keep our heads on our shoulders before mother rescued us with these ships."

Claudia said, "Uncle, I'm confused. I thought *Jesus* stopped your head from rolling off your shoulders. Now you're saying *grandmother* rescued us from that fire?"

"Well, families do com-b-bust in all sorts of ways. And she *did* send these warships, niece. F-f-finally. After three years."

"Uncle, did you see burning embers become angels, a giant sword become a plowshare, and Poly get a new heart? Did Jesus not save you from getting frozen in hell's entryway? Didn't he redirect lions toward feral goats?"

"All that is true, but memory feels like vapor when *now* I want what I want."

"Uncle, God's Word has lived among us. Even as we ate each other. But even now, your unbelief makes him weightless as a dust mote."

Uncle squeezed Cal. He looked at me and said, "You feel wafty when you're not amazing. Could you jen up a batch of amazing and r-r-reverse Cal's blindness? He's a wee bit put-out with you. We need a fresh miracle if you don't mind. Don't want to appear p-p-presumptuous, but it's been a day or so since the last one."

Claudia said, "Uncle, Cal's a sympathy suck, but he's the sort to rake a dustbin of broken glass in your head when you're not looking."

Cal summoned up a gob of mucus and blew it her way. She dodged, and it landed beside her on the deck.

I said, "Sire, only those who truly love truly see. Why hope for clear seeing when love is absent?" [32]

The emperor said, "that must be one of those Jew sayings. Haven't heard it."

Caligula sniffed, "Tibbie, you're getting all tangled up in this clinging vine of a wandering Jew. I wouldn't take two seeing eyeballs from him even if he served them up on a platinum platter. We have our magicians in Rhodes. Let's decamp this dreadful conversation for our stateroom. My mouth and tongue see very well indeed."

The two lovers made a beeline for the captain's quarters. Rabbus and Leah also went to their sleeping quarters, eyes bright for each other. John meandered to and fro—listless and shrouded in silence.

I stayed with Claudia on deck, listing with the waves, holding lust at bay. Claudia didn't help. She took my right hand and adored me with her eyes. I nestled her into the crook of my left arm. I rested one eye on her and the stronger one on Father. He'd given her to me—to love and lead into wide, open spaces, not a cloistered marital bed.

Sea mist poured over us. Illyria slid by the gunnels, and Windy ghosted us out of sight, further into the morning's light.

13

SLOW

News spread quickly of the spice brothers' execution as well as their father's death. They were all spiced, wrapped, and racked into their cave graves before the next sunset. We attended the late afternoon funeral. Paid wailers pandered on as the dark began to deepen, rolling up light like a scroll, and hiding it beneath the western dust. A rabbi-in-training stumbled out *correct* words that didn't feel *right*.

A veiled woman in black sat alone on the pew reserved for family. She arrived late and left early. She carried a peculiar odor of heavy perfume hiding something beneath it. Knowing glances rippled among the other Jewish women.

We didn't stick around to sit Shiva. Unloyal, inappropriate, and unloving. But there you have it—none of my-me's gave a crap. Instant family, instant departure. Cutter sliced attachment loose as an eyelash.

The new caravan commander, a Moabite named Hooka, was Zayan and Emil's first cousin. He'd made the trip to Egypt only once, a few years back.

Laz asked him, "You sure you remember the way? Alexandria and Moab are not so close."

Hooka puffed his pipe and said, "How hard can it be? Follow the King's Highway all the way down. If I don't remember a turn in the road, I'll get my concubine to ask for directions." He rode up and down the line that first morning with his chest stuck out, whip-nipping camels to get a move on. One sitting camel squirted a stream of spit on Hooka's cloak before he could get out of range.

Traders slotted themselves into place within the caravan. Everyone sought safety in the middle. The front and back positions rotated. The last camel drivers rode backward, scanning for danger from raiders and robbers, particularly the Amalekites. [33]

Goodness juddered along, bouncing my two children and me in the saddle. Kindness followed, loaded with luggage. We had segued between two larger dromedaries. The camel in front carried a veiled howdah—a one-room castle with a pointy, painted roof that glittered in the sun. The strapped-down sedan chair rocked back and forth on the camel's hump as he padded along the sandy track.

This massive camel, Whiskey, had belonged to Emil. But who now rode in his shady carriage? A nosey hit-and-run wafted my way from Whiskey's direction, smelling more of pee than camel fart. I said to Laz, walking beside me, "Know who's up high on the mighty?"

"Dunno. But whoever's there is giving spice a bad name."

Hope's back plastered to my front, and Mike's back to hers, the three of us sitting in a row. Hope said, "It's Turquoise Eyes, ma. Grandma Elsa went to her house the night you were with Uncle Ehud."

I said, "Darling, did she smell bad?"

Mike said, "yep, she was a stinky-poo."

Hope put a hand over his mouth. "I ran over to her when I first saw her and asked who she was. She lifted her veil and smiled at me. She's beautiful, ma, looks just like you, except one eye's bright turquoise and the other one's white!" Laz and I looked at each other. Unanswered questions passed between us.

Late that afternoon, we made camp around an oasis located on a crooked line between desolation and emptiness. The oasis consisted of fourteen date palms fringing a no-name pond with a gurgling spring at one end. I followed the veiled howdah woman in the black burka to the spring, trailing at a distance.

She sat alone. Her sheer, black veil topped her equally expensive, black silk dress. She'd found a few bulrushes to hide behind, on the far side of where others filled their jugs. She had submerged her feet and bottom in the cool waters.

I sat down in the mud next to her, stretched my legs out into the water—a respectful distance apart. I tipped my water bladder at the surface, letting clean water trickle over the lip. Cool bottom water soothed my butt and feet. We remained silent, us two, not burdening the air with words too heavy to hold. No thread tied us together, and there was plenty of legroom for lies.

The water took its long, sweet time to fill the skin. I lifted the bladder high against the blue of the sky, watching for leaks. A small dribble from one corner. Nothing much, but by mid-day, it would empty the pouch. Happened a lot. I brought out a needle and thread from my pocket. Repaired the leak with a few tight stitches.

I plugged the top of my bladder and leaned back on my hands, squishing mud beneath my fingers.

Sounds of children playing at a distance. She said, "You have beautiful children."

I interrupted, "Inshallah. As God wills."

Silence. Then, "Yahweh wills I get shit, piss, and a wandering eye that hides out of sight. My bowels and bladder leak like sieves, and no one can stitch them shut. Call me One-Eye, Stinky, or the Witch. Take your pick." Her voice had legs strong enough to kick down the walls of a synagogue.

Escape wanted to run. Shame turned up her nose.

I said, "What's your story?"

She started to weep. I guess that was her story because there weren't any other words to go with the tears. Her shaking shoulders were plain, as was the sharp intake of air and its ragged exhale.

I then realized in a flash, this is the woman I saw at the funeral yesterday, the one who zipped in and out. I'd caught wind of her then, and come to think of it, back in the marketplace.

I scooted my bottom through the mud to sit closer. All my me's had edged past where we knew to go. I prayed, *help me see her as you do, Windy.*

I said to her, "My stink's same as yours. Just takes people longer to recognize it."

She pulled back her veil. Her one bright turquoise eye, the right eye, stared directly at me under a raised eyebrow. A glimpse of blue-green iris hid in the top right corner of her left eye, but the rest of her eye was white.

She said, "If you get past my stink, then you have to deal with my eye. I can't hold my poop or pee, and I can't keep my 'Evil Eye' from running away. I think she's hiding from what I don't want to see."

Then, after a patch of quiet, "Even in death, our brother's stink is shrouded in spice. Abba's stink is different, colored in tones of grey and sounding like a dirge."

Oh yes, this woman and me, we shared the same father. Ahab's eyes, her eyes, my eyes—all the same color.

She looked me in the eye. "You just figured it out, didn't you, sister?"

I nodded and said, "my child, Hope, didn't call you Stinky. She said you were Turquoise Eyes, the beautiful."

A dark bark of grief exploded from her mouth. She laughed like someone who would collapse a cave on her head just to see it fall. After, she recovered her quiet—face cryptic as a moonscape.

She said, "ah, so that was my niece. She flitted in and out. Must have been the same hour Eggie and Ehud were busy killing abba and our brothers."

I answered at an angle. "What stops you from sitting Shiva? I would think everyone would want to sit with you. Ahab, ah Abba—anyway, that man's loss must have crushed the few Jews left in Dhiban."

She said, "I couldn't stay. Instead, I sit Shiva with Whiskey—and add a little of my own. But in the morning, I'll be sober and men in the minyan, still mean. If I stayed in town, those men would see to it that I'd be stoned. Both me and my child."

My gut twisted, "You're with child?"

She nodded. "Too dangerous to speak truth in Dhiban. You know, of course, the town's name means 'wasting away.' I'm done with wasting. Done, I tell you. Just like Noah, Abram, Sarah, and Jacob were done with toxic people in their day. Noah built an ark, Abram left Ur of Chaldees. Later, he left Lot to Sodom and Gomorrah. Sarah banished Hagar. Jacob left Laban. And you? You left Jericho. Everyone's got to leave someone, somewhere, sometime.

"Bottom line? Draw a line between good and evil if you want to stay alive—particularly the good and evil inside you. But outside evil's a good place to start. Easier."

A wave of sadness surprised me. Real tears, not make-believe ones, coursed down Fragile's cheeks. "I'm so sorry for how lonely your life must be. And then, those executions …."

Turquoise said, "Tell me what happened, please. I have to know."

I told her, in detail. "It was horrible. Emil lingering and twisting on that one toe of his, and then Zayan killing Abba as he fell."

My grown-up me said, "At the end, Ehud schooled me in truth. Put my native liar to death."

I was silent for a few seconds before Harlot admitted, "Her resurrection is imminent."

Turquoise's kind, green-blue eye flashed a smile, "There's a time and place for loving lies to substitute for cruel truth. Abba was a pro at the oblique lie, tucking absolute truth down deep. One of the last things he said to me was an encouragement to go ahead and lie. He said, 'Abigail, it will be easier for you to visit my brother in Egypt. They'll believe stories of how your husband died along the way, for example. As it is, I can't be responsible for what happens once your pregnancy is discovered.'"

I laid my hand on her shoulder, and she didn't shrug it away. I said, "So, Abigail, you were named after King David's second wife and first true love?"

"Yes. But unlike her, I have no one to husband me. I'm over seven months gone with child, and the father was one of our brothers. I'm not sure which one—could be either."

"Ack. Mother's husband, Ach, taught me sex and hired me out as a whore."

Abigail shook her head, ruing our fate. "Abba and brothers would have thrown the first stones at me."

I said, "Beauty is a curse we both share."

Abby reminded me, "Ugly and plain people, men and women, get raped too. Rape is about power. Sex is the tool to hammer it in place."

My hand slipped off her shoulder and took her right hand. Together we rose. Her wet dress revealed her belly bump. She shook her dress out, adjusted her veil, and we walked back to the circle of campers. All around us, evening cooking fires crackled, fueled by a load of camel crap. Spiced meat hissed and snapped in frying pans, one end of life supplying the other.

The sounds and smells helped me locate me. I'd checked into some weird wrinkle in time where I met a new sister and old grief. Now we all returned to this caravan circle with its chatter, dust, sizzle of meat, and the earthy smell of Laz's armpits when he hugged me.

I motioned Abigail to sit by the fire. Laz took in my new friend with a glance, "Once I saw you together, I talked with Hooka. We decided that I'd become your appointed guardian-protector and deliver you to your family in Egypt."

Abigail nodded once. Her shoulders relaxed.

I said, "Thanks, husband. There's enough care here for *all* of us." I caught Abigail's eye, nodded to baby bump, and handed her some carrots to chop on a cutting stone. I peeled a few beets. Laz wandered off, smoking a shared pipe with other men, arguing, laughing, resurrecting problems from their graves, and unbinding them—as he was wont to do.

High overhead, chevrons of long-necked pink birds unfurled, silhouetted in sun's afterglow, southbound. More migrants looking for home.

Hope came up with her little brother in tow. She said to me, "Hey, ma and Auntie Turquoise, look what we found!"

She sat between us by the fire and showed us something that looked like small, sharp-edged bones, caked in sand gone solid.

Abigail said, "Hope, these are once-upon-a-time living creatures. We call them fossils."

Hope asked, "How did you learn that, Auntie?"

"My father, Hope. Abba was very smart. He taught me what I know, ear to ear. My eyes don't work so good. One's lazy, and both get letters and numbers backward. I can't read or do math, so I learn by listening. And my name is Auntie Abby."

Hope smiled at her, the same as if she'd understood the quick lesson in geology. She said, hopefully, "I'm learning my letters and numbers. We can learn together! That will be fun, Auntie Turquoise-Abby."

Michael toddled over and held onto Abigail's ankle. He offered her a smile guaranteed to ignite love in a new mother's heart. Abigail rubbed his back, even as she gazed somberly at the cooking fire. She looked like someone carrying her memories in a bundle, someone content to feed the fire, one stick at a time, from that store of remembrances.

The eastern canyon went to scarlets in the day's dying light. Desert bats swooped over us and back to their caves—eerie, jawbone faces darting in the firelight, then disappearing just as quick.

We welcomed our new auntie. A slippy, pee smell wafted into our circle, one drop at a time, mixing with all life's other odors. And for all the world, it smelled like family.

14

GOODNESS

We'd been back on trail for a week. Our group had cut down a road off the main highway into a cool, narrow wadi. Slow rode me, as usual, and my angel led me. Only a small angel, hardly more than a cherub, but he said, "don't forget your ancestor was owned by a man named Balaam. I did cool stuff with that ass, and I will again, with you. Stay alert." [34]

Kindness, my foal, plodded along, loaded with stuff. Smoke, the big she-camel ahead of me, had a cute kid, Wisp, who trotted beside me, bareback. We used our tails to switch flies off each other's withers.

Laz carried Michael. Hope slept in Slow's lap.

I glanced behind us. A black cloud, the size of Slow's hand. All else, bright blue.

I stopped under a shady ledge with Wisp, and we licked a rock wet with slime. Yum. This stuff lived in the wadi's dark narrows, near ground weep, and loved cracks in canyon bottoms.

We rested. Both children explored up a side rabbit trail with their father. Lots of laughter above me, but I didn't look. I was busy slime-licking.

A new smell. Water. But not slime water. I reared back, sniffed the air. The hair on my nose stood up. I bolted up the side rabbit trail toward father and children.

Slow said, "Goodness, whoa! Stay!"

I kept scrambling up the rabbit trail. Gotta join Laz and the kids. Got to get to higher ground. He was up there, straight ahead, on a ledge thirty feet above us.

Slow jerked my head straight back and lashed me with her long rope, "Goodness, no! Turn around!"

I turned my head around and stared back and forth between her eyes and the white streak in her hair, hoping she'd trust me. Maybe she'd remember Rastus. Remember the kind of bone snapping that happened when I obeyed the angel and kicked Rastus' legs, breaking both of them.[35]

Slow said, "Okay. I give in. You're a smart ass."

I obeyed my angel. Climbed to higher ground with Slow still on my back. Laz and the children were wrestling with each other, down on the ground.

New sound, roaring sound. A wall of water, maybe twenty feet high in the narrows, flashed around the bend, pushing boulders in front of it.

Slow screamed down in the wadi to her sister, "Abby, Flash flood! Quick, climb!" Flood boomed loud. Crashed through canyon. Rainstorm followed flood.

Slow flopped off me and scrambled to lower ledge. Reached for sister. They grabbed each other's hands. The river ran through them.

Slow screamed, "Help, God! Hold me and my sister!"

I lost my footing. Angel slid me down toward the flood below. Then, angel on my shoulders slid me on my back into a rock hole. I got stuck.

Angel poured me full of warm light and spoke again to me in Mule. Angel said, *have a seat, Goodness. I made it for you in honor of your pal, Mercy, who gave her life for Leah. This is the Mercy Seat.*

Then angel spoke Human from *my* mouth to the two sisters, "Reach up! I'm here for you." My angel, Bright, stood behind me. So much Bright closed my eyes tight, and my jaws went loose.

A rope dropped in my mouth. I bit down. Other end fell between sisters' hands. Behind me, Bright pulled. I rested. Sisters rose. Sisters got to ledge—bloody, bruised. Bright spoke again in Mule. *Chomp,* Bright said. I chomped. Rope held sisters beside me. They hugged my neck, one on each side. I looked back at them side to side. I like hugs.

All of us looked out over the ledge, looked at flood's leavings. Rocks and water, running wild. Kindness gone missing. I felt sad. I saw a sagebrush beside cave. I ate.

Sister said, "Goodness is eating bush and opening a space. Looks like a cave behind the bush. The more he eats, the wider the cave's mouth. Looks like home, for now."

Laz said, "Does it always take an ass in Moab to speak God's voice?"

My mouth was covered with sage. Smiled to myself. Hidden, all safe.

15

WINDY

The capital city of Rhodes hosted the Roman emperor and the ruins of Colossus. One was a fallen Wonder of the World. [36] The other, a fallen man. Tiberius had built two villas on the island. One was a country estate on a bluff overlooking the sea. The other was an ornate palace downtown, near Colossus' ruins.

On this day, in dim light, Tiberius and Caligula lounged in a private spa, rotating between steam baths, polar plunge, and sauna. The younger man's smooth, unlined, teenage body lounged next to the emperor's wrinkled, sixty-seven-year-old frame. Tiberius was bald, save for a sliver of hair that rimmed the back of his head, looping a silver smile from ear to ear.

Steam coiled around them. They reclined, passing a sweet-smelling pipe back and forth, pupils dilated. The smell of this smoke, in and out of their lungs, was an iron fist in the air, clamping down their abilities to think clearly.

Cal took his time scrubbing Tibbie's body with a loofah, soothing and massaging his body. "Uncle, these local magicians are second-rate seers and third-rate healers. They've done their best dog and pony show, but to no avail."

Tiberius smiled dreamily, not hearing Cal's implied request. He inhaled, held, and exhaled the opium, a fast-coming devotee of the long pipe. He reached up with his right hand, reaching high to the heavens above. He lost sight of his fingers in the sky-steam. He raised his other hand, breast-stroking into the heavens, clouds above meeting cloud from within. Both clouds took only a brief note he had passed this way, but this heaven-swimming was as close to true love as he'd ever known.

Besides, his Cal-craving had become quite irrational—a craving a bit like short men have for platform shoes. This physical craving was brilliant due only to dullness of spirit in the rest of their relationship. But for the moment, chemistry chugged along, taking them with it.

Cal repeated his complaint. Tiberius heard a voice coming from somewhere outside himself. He replied, "Leave it to me, darling. Another healer is almost here."

The door swooshed open.

Rabbus appeared, "Did you call for me, sire?"

"Indeed, bodyguard. Present your wife to our persons."

Rabbus left and returned shortly with his wife. Leah stood by a steamed-up window, back-lit with a sideways streak of bright sun, hair haloing her face. She felt the cool, wet mist crawling up her ankles.

Cal inhaled deeply on his pipe. He was unable to see further than the end of his arm. Tiberius gazed through the mist at this wisp of a woman before him. She'd been hollowed down to shadow and bone by plague, starvation, and loss.

Tiberius' voice pierced the fog, "So, my resurrection princess, Jesus has refused to play nicely with short-sighted Cal. And this lover-boy needs new eyes. Not new life, mind you, just a working pair of orbs. Child's play for such as you."

Leah fidgeted, slid her toes around the slick floor, averting her eyes from the naked men.

She called on me, *Windy, what to do? Please speak, Spirit!*

I answered, *Take a conscious breath. Inhale, hold, exhale. On the exhale, the words will be given from your mouth.*

Leah exhaled into the smoky mist, "I am God's instrument, under Her authority, His power. Father and Spirit mingle inside Jesus, inside me. They would delight to honor Consul Caligula's hope in God."

Caligula piped up, "Must be crowded inside with the Mingles, Jew-girl."

Leah replied, "This mingling confuses the humble into greater faith. Even the best minds, at some point, have to shrug and step into thin air."

Cal missed the point. He quipped, "His this, Her that. You Jew Mingles must be switch-hitters, like me. My three sisters certainly kept me up many a night." [37]

I kept speaking through Leah. "Consul Caligula, Yahweh is neither male nor female, but both and more. All people are made in the image of this God who is far above your wildest visions."

Caligula grinned, "He's not been inside my head lately. But vision is the point of this short-sighted interview, *little* Leah. Vision. Say the word to heal my eyes. Refuse, and we can't be responsible if you get a sudden *attack* of—well, who knows? So many things snuff life out these days."

When Rabbus heard the not-so-subtle threat, his bones tightened up, and his body shook with rage. The smell of smoke made him check his chest. Perhaps he'd caught fire.

He said, "Consul, you speak to my wife, and therefore to me, like we were animals."

Cal grinned again, "We're all animals, bodyguard. A few of us, though, have bigger teeth than the rest of you."

Leah put her calming hand on husband's shoulder. "Consul, do not confuse me with either animals or God. I can say the words, 'be healed,' all day long. Nothing will happen other than words bouncing off eyes blinded by unbelief. If you recall, you chose blindness. Jesus said, 'according to your faith be it to you,' and blindness struck you at that exact moment.

Caligula and Tiberius squirmed. The exposed emperor became aware he had no clothes. He dropped in the polar pool.

Leah's sharp-sight probed future mist. "God's power must mate with your belief, Consul. If you refuse to do your part, you cut yourself off from God's part." [38]

Tiberius, from the polar regions, flicked his finger; terminated the interview. Rabbus and Leah left. Once the door had closed, Tiberius climbed back on the dripping marble table, face-up, and took a long hit on the pipe. Cal's hands soothed and stroked him. Tiberius' eyes filled with longing for such skin as Cal's.

16

CLAUDIA

Some weeks later, Jesus and I walked together in the late afternoon. The forest fringed a shimmering pasture, emerald-colored, water-drenched. Cattle grazed peacefully in this enclosed paddock, alongside sheep in the next field over, back of a stone hedge, and through a kissing gate. The exposed ground was bright, striped with red and green veins of minerals.

John trailed at a distance, behind and to our left in the far field, mingling with the sheep. Breezes whiffled through the elder trees, dropping snow-white florets, like confetti, in our hair. This path ended at a jagged cliff's edge where a narrow Z-path led down to the slate-green sea. Rocks and sea swell boomed, an ongoing conversation. The stark, streaky face of the cliff looked like a lightning bolt had cracked off most of it. Jesus and I sat on a bench at the top of this Z-path, facing into the wind and toward Palestine.

Jesus called, "John, come join us!" John angled toward us and sat at Jesus' feet.

I said, "Let's face it. My Uncle Tibbie enjoys exile on Rhodes like a rabbit exiling himself to a briar patch."

Jesus said, "A very comfortable briar patch, distant from his mother." He looked left to the villa. "Your uncle and Caligula are frothing the piranha pond with fresh meat. Once they're done there, they'll come here as usual, to catch the sunset in their silk pajamas."

We vacated our bench. The royal couple sat. Uncle looked a little floaty. He held out a box of candy and said, "Niece, have some fresh-made Turkish delight. Firm outside, but the filling collapses in your mouth—rosewater and sugar, like a candy garden, explodes into bloom between your teeth!"

I bit into half of one, closed my eyes in ecstasy, and braked myself from gobbling the rest of the box. Daintily, I handed the other half of my Delight to Jesus.

He rubbed his lips together and waited a long time to swallow. He said, "Incredible!"

Uncle replied, "Indeed, but not as delightful as other pleasures." He poked Cal with his elbow and winked. "By the by, Jesus, in the months we've been here, the whole of Rhodes wonders about you two. You're our mystery couple. I tell you what. We'll go public and arrange your wedding next week at the temple downtown across from Colossus!"

Jesus said, "Thank you, Emperor, for your kindness—but marriage is *not* in Father's plans for me."

I steeled my soul all over again to wanting what I'd gotten, not getting what I wanted. Cal distracted me from my pity party. He said, "Didn't you hear the emperor order you to marry? Respect your lord, ruler of the real world, not your make-believe, pie in the sky kingdom candy."

Jesus said, "Father's kingdom is not a cafeteria cult. He sent me here, not as a side dish, but the main course. In fact, I'm the only course that helps your palate discern what nourishes, and what is illusion."

Caligula said, "Seer, you're disobeying a direct order from Rome's divine ruler."

John jumped in with a conversation re-direct. He pointed at the royal couple. "You, sirs, are guilty of disobeying God's divine order. Pederasty and adultery! Father will execute judgment on you!"

I thought, *this kind of talk gets people killed. Shut up, John.*

John didn't shut his yap. His bony finger got in their faces, close enough so even Cal could see its shadow. "And you, Consul, seducing an old man on your way to the top! Both of you will burn in hellfire!"

Uncle giggled. "Your cousin missed his calling, Jesus. I'm of the mind to hire him as a consultant in our personnel department."

Consul Caligula didn't take John's accusation as lightly as his older lover. He slashed out with words sheared from cut-glass. "Guard, escort this filth to the snake path. See that he takes the express route to the rocks below."

Uncle looked at Rabbus and jerked his head toward town. My almost blind cousin didn't see Rabbus escorting John toward the stables. They both mounted a horse-drawn wagon and headed toward town.

Uncle looked at Cal. "I'll deal with John later. But for now, let's not get hasty. Perhaps, as Jesus says, his Father has celibacy in mind for him."

Cal grumped. He repositioned his bodacious blond toupee. Uncle had made this hairpiece whole from the scalp of a Balkan chieftain's son. The Balkan had caught Cal's eye in the public baths. After a few intimate encounters, the new lover took an unfortunate tumble—a bit icky. No matter, that man's crop of thick, blond hair now rested on Cal's head. He adjusted his silk ascot and primly crossed his legs.

Jesus said, "Claudia and I *have* talked of marriage. But Father's priority for me is not so much my happiness as building his Kingdom. Of this, I have no illusions. Kingdom is Father's priority, and Father is mine." [39]

Uncle commented, "You sound very sure of yourself, Seer."

Jesus replied, "Father sures me. Emperor, you were once resurrected by Father's Spirit because of Leah's obedience. I will be resurrected by Father's Spirit because of my obedience."[40]

Cal swiped his left hand through his platinum hairpiece. Knocked it clean off. He groped the ground, found it, and plopped it back on his head, askew. He flicked out a waspish jab. "Well, aren't you so *very* special?"

I laid my hand on Cal's shoulder. "And you are one of the world's most magnificent haters. I don't know anyone else who can consume truth and crap out slime at the same time." I slipped to Jesus' other side.

Cal's sightless eyes burned hate-holes into the space I had just vacated. His hackles rose on the back of his neck like the hood on a cobra ready to strike.

He said, "Some of us are genuine descendants of royalty, not bastard children from backdoor affairs."

I stared wide-eyed, my tongue paralyzed for the moment. *Did he just say aloud what everyone thought, but no one dared to speak?*

I said, "I'm amazed maggots don't crawl out of that hole where you store your fangs."

I gestured to Cal and said to Uncle, "On second thought, maggots would suffocate inside your little Vacuum-in-Pajamas."

Cal produced his jeweled dagger. "Darling, please lead her to me. I'll relieve the wench of her tongue. We can take side-bets on which of your piranha will die first from eating it."

Uncle did nothing. His eyes squinted with alarm and glittered with glee, each in turn. His pleasure fueled my anger.

I ranted, "My tongue speaks truth. You think our uncle is blind to your plots of vengeance? Ah! You don't think he knows you hate him for banishing your mother and brother?"

Tiberius squinted at Caligula. It was now Cal's turn to be speechless.

Uncle calmly observed attack and counterattack. He looked like he might be at the Coliseum, spectating while gladiators disemboweled each other.

Jesus said, "Unlike me, Sire, you will die again and *not* be resurrected. You'll be smothered by deceit from a lover close at hand." [41] Jesus looked at the emperor and then briefly redirected his gaze to Cal, who at that very moment was snaking his hand around Uncle's waist.

Cal jerked his hand down and said to Jesus, "if you have such clear vision without illusion, why not share it? We could have an amazing love-fest, little lean man."

He approached within a foot of Jesus and lifted his sightless eyes. "If you choose to defy me, those consequences will also be amazing." He prophesied, "You will die on a stake, and your followers will become flaming torches for Nero and my garden parties."

Jesus trembled, grabbed my hand. I soothed his twitchy fingers. He took a deep breath, like he always does when Windy-filling.

He set his eye like a flint on Uncle. "Here's a story for you, Sire. Once upon a time, an aging ruler secretly wondered about the nature of illusion. He privately consulted a wise man. 'Seer, I feel myself getting older and younger at the same time. Which is more real?'

"The seer gave him a mirror. He looked at himself. The aging ruler said, 'I don't know what to trust, my feelings or that face in the mirror.'"

Jesus said, "The seer took an empty glass from within his sleeve. He said, 'fill it with red wine and return it to me, Ruler.'

"The ruler set out to his vintner but ran into a much younger man on his way. This young man was afflicted with charisma and dubious character."

"Immediately, he fell under the younger man's influence—an iron shaving to the younger magnet. He took the young man to healers and magicians. The young man improved not a whit, but the ruler couldn't have felt much better—indeed, he felt like a bull in heat. He wondered, *have I fallen in love or lust?* He didn't know which was more real. But since he was the ruler, he shouted, to no one in particular, 'This is love!'"

"The older and younger lovers swapped places back and forth seamlessly for some time. After a short or long time, hard to tell—or even remember— the young man ran off to spar with new warriors his own age. From then on, the ruler wandered, wearing amber colors and lenses that were spider-webbed with stress fractures."

Uncle's right foot frantically tapped, like a cricket doing push-ups.

Jesus wound down his parable. "One day, in his wandering, the ruler finally found his *true* love. Unfortunately, he had arrived too late. Love had been crucified but was not yet dead. He was so disfigured the ruler couldn't tell who he was. His built-in seer wasn't working. This lover had been side-stabbed. Ruler filled his cup with blood from the crucified's side."

Cal's neck turned fiery red. "This guy creeps me out. Let's go, lover."

Uncle sat still, his face a bright coil of regret. I released Jesus' hands for a moment. They still trembled. The space in that wide-open field was cramped for words. There wasn't enough room for even a syllable.

All I didn't know bunched beneath my skin. I whispered to Jesus, "Is this where the story stops? Corner of Truth and Illusion, with red and amber warning lights?"

Jesus finished his story, "The ruler awoke, as from a trance, back in front of the Seer. He stood before him, holding out a cup of blood."

Uncle looked down, only to find himself holding Cal's amber pillow in one hand and his ruby goblet in the other. His empty cup had been filled.

Jesus watched, hand pressed tight to his right side.

17

SLOW

Abby sat on her knees next to Laz and me, looking down on clutches of vultures feasting on the carcasses below in Death Wadi. Men had conceived a hazy plan in the dark of night and morning delivered a monster baby. Hooka and most of his camel, Smoke, had disappeared under the long drop of a crumbled canyon wall. Whiskey lay crumpled between two boulders, all four legs sticking out at weird angles.

Abby, without any warning, doubled over in pain. A small flash flood gushed from between her legs and drenched her feet. Water was brown and stinky. Sister didn't understand what was happening.

I said, "Abby, bump's graduating to baby. We can do this."

Abby said, "This is too early, *way* too soon. I'm not ready to mother brother's son."

Laz said, "I'm taking Mike. Hunters, going scavenging."

Voice said, *my labor and delivery cave awaits. Boy will birth from sister. Pay forward those gifts you got from Rahab's sisterhood.*

I took charge. "Auntie Abby is going to give you a new baby to play with. Help us."

Hope used her one pot to catch a stream of water cascading off the cave's face. She also gathered scraps of firewood. The wet wood steamed in the desert sun.

Laz eventually re-appeared with Mike, carrying Whiskey's leather saddle, sodden blankets, and a satin pillow from inside Abby's howdah. Father took son down with him a second time, along with Goodness. They returned an hour later with more treasure—spices, grain, clothes, sandals, and jugs of wine.

Finally—on one last trip down to Death Wadi—father, son, and Goodness brought back chunks of camel's liver and a skinned leg. They stuck the meat on a spit over the smoking fire.

Abby walked in circles on the ledge, knelt, squatted on all fours, rocking her rear back and forth, humping her back like a cat, then sloughing it like a cow, each movement flowing with a humming-groaning. I got on hands and knees next to her on one side, doing cat and cow with her. Hope and Mike thought this looked like fun, so they joined.

Sister said, "I don't want to feel what's coming. And the past should stay behind me where it belongs." She twisted her head and looked back. "But when I look at my behind, it's enormous."

I laughed. "That's where we're headed, the panting and pain of it all. Sorry to tell you, but this will hurt like hell."

Abby writhed. She yelled past knuckles she'd jammed in her mouth, "Oww! God, seal my poop and pee, where brothers tore me—all my hollow places. God, don't let me leak on my kid." Sweat rolled off her forehead and dripped off her nose.

Voice said to me, *Sister's boy is stuck. He corkscrewed inside—butt's down, not his head.*

Windy, what to do?

No answer, for now. It wasn't time. Dusk pulled in its shutters; night fell. We moved inside cave's mouth, nestling against a pinkish-white cheek of stone.

Abby moaned and mooed in turn, on hands and knees, shoving her torso a foot or so forward, then backward, like her arms and hands were scrubbing a washboard. Her head poked out of the smiling cave's mouth, then retreated, back and forth, a preview of the coming birth.

Spirit took my hands and massaged Abby's sloping back. I hovered beside her, brought her to her feet, and we danced together along the ledge—dancing down the baby.

Sometime in the night watch, the world moved backward. Mother earth's plates, directly beneath the cave, moved on their own accord, trembling. Goodness, in his sleep, pushed backward against the cave's vault. I backed between Goodness's front and back legs and spread my knees open. Sister spooned backward between my spread knees, leaned against my chest, moaning and taking shreds of comfort. Voice said, *baby's backing out. Still stuck.*

Hope and Mike sat cross-legged outside the cave, backs to us mothers, facing the fire with their father, sucking marrow from Whiskey's cracked bones.

Mike whispered to his father, "Is Auntie Abby dying?"

Laz said in Abby's hearing, "This is normal, old as time itself. Your ma went through this when you were born. Hope's birth ma, the same."

Abby asked me, "What should we do now?"

Voice said, *tell her she's doing fine, obey her body.*

I repeated, "Respect your body. She knows what she's doing in this waiting game."

Abby said, "How can I respect a body that has betrayed me? I squirt stink like a skunk working overtime."

"Well, now's the night to change that story, sister. Leah told me something. In her birthing cave, she heard a voice. Maybe not too different from what I'm hearing. *"Trust what's heavy. Exhale. Let heaviness pull you to earth. Baby wants down, wants to go down. Open. Hug the pain."*

Voice said to me, *Open to all your you's, Slow. Let them mend. She's ripped apart from abuse. So were you. Mind and mend. That's how rips knit together.*

Abby screamed, "Hate feelings! Hate pain! Hate open! Hate vulnerable!"

Abby paced, twisting her back like she was trying to throw off a monkey. Hope and I stayed with her, on either side, not more than a foot away. We kept her between ledge's edge and the fire.

Moonlight washed over us. I said, "Pain doesn't come to stay, sister. It comes to pass."

I needed Windy's words. Abby needed my words. She had told me, "Words never came easy. Letters on a scroll turned inside out, upside down. I became muscle and wire, beating brothers in their outdoor games. Then life changed one day behind the stables. Emil tackled me in a game of kickball, and tackling turned to tickling and then into something different."

Just then, she let out a shriek. She pushed away from me and rose on all fours. Her moans rose to a crescendo—growling like a bear, panting, beet-faced. She looked like someone pushing 500 pounds straight through her.

Voice coached me. *Boy's butt cheek's pushing on her plumbing. My light is sewing her tears tight. She pushes. You encourage while I sew her fistula together. Father guards. We're all needed.*

Hours passed, slow. Contractions came more quickly. Fragile held Escape when the littler one wanted to run. Together they, we, rocked Abby and milked the rest periods. We felt her body relax, now and again. Children slept. Laz snoozed. The moon inched across the skies, a slow march. Orion kept watch 'til he dropped below the horizon. I guess even constellations need naps.

In the barely lightening skies, Voice finally spoke once again, clear in my ear. *Get everyone up, now! Sing and dance this baby into the world. It's time.*

I told Laz what I'd heard. Hope heard what I said to Laz. She squatted in the middle of fire's remains, grabbed two handfuls of warm ash, and rose from the ashes, twirling and singing, throwing ash to the winds and turning all the flakes into a floaty covering—ashes to beauty.

Laz, Mike, and I joined Hope in an ancient hora from time-out-of-mind, slowly at first, and then faster, faster. All my me's joined in, except Shame, who sat in the shade, watching. We dancers surrounded Abby. She squatted, knees apart, in the middle of our circle.

We stopped when I could dance no longer. I moved Abby back into the cave's mouth, resting her back against Goodness's tummy.

I took a peek under Abby's singlet. Her buttocks had parted. As I peeked, she launched. In one fluid move, she lurched backward onto Goodness's back, howling raw-throated. In the same backward move of his mother, baby's butt crowned. Purple grapes popped out and met night air. First sign of *boy's* arrival, entering the world balls first.

I said, *what to do, Windy?*

Voice said, *relax, Slow. I birthed the universe—talk about a long labor! Since then, I've birthed every child ever born on this speck of dust. Breech births happen every day, all day, around the cosmos.*

I muttered aloud, "Uh, ok. But this is *my* first time as a midwife. What's next?"

Let her twist and turn, Voice said. *The child will un-screw himself out of her.*

Abby dropped back onto all fours—screaming, pushing, twisting. Her child rotated down and around, clockwise. Out popped his tiny legs and feet—plop, plop.

Voice said, *Slow, give a gentle pull. Pull right and down. Yes, good. Long, slow pull. Okay. Let go, now*!

I listened, obeyed.

One arm slipped out, then the other, followed by a face full of cheesecake. Folded-over boy aimed toward mother's silk howdah pillow, missed, and landed butt-down on the good earth. Abby settled on him, momentary, and the top of his head wore his mother like a skullcap.

Two feet of cord hung from boy's belly. Cord and child trembled in dawn's light. I tied off the cord. Laz took my new straight edge, the one Ehud had given me, and cut the cord in one short swipe. I held the new baby in one hand, de-cheesing nose and mouth with a clean, wet cloth. I jiggled the still, silent boy up and down.

Voice said, *twirl him around by his feet. Swing him around. Your whirling will push poo out of his nose and mouth. Swing him now and ask Father for him to live!*

I prayed, "God, get this kid breathing, please. Live, baby boy, live!"

Abby watched me twirl her tot. Another contraction. Slush plopped out of her, afterbirth, tinged brown with poo.

Silent, still baby.

I panicked.

Voice said, *Swing him around again, faster. Give his bottom a wake-up paddle with the flat of your hand when you're done.*

I listened, obeyed.

Baby wailed, first breath.

Abby cuddled her little one. "Hello, beautiful boy. Your name is Ahud—Abba's brilliance, Ehud's loyalty."

I floated my eyes from the new mother to the old earth. Desert stretched bleak and endless beyond canyon's walls. I sensed all the lives that had been birthed and killed on this very ground. All were here, ghost worlds beneath my feet, the thin air quivering with what once was.

God interrupted my meditation for a public service announcement. An earthquake. I held on to *all* my children and Laz. The earth began to shake, gently at first and then violently. Wadi walls all around collapsed in a rolling wave, giving corpses below a divine burial beneath tons of rock. Our ledge cracked off and tumbled to the wadi's bottom, along with all the other outcroppings left and right of us.

Columns of dust bloomed high over the new plain, blowing back and back again toward Dhiban and Moab, a town and country where we would never again live. Sun peeked over the earth's curve, clear, bright. High places had been made low; valleys, exalted. My-me's and outside family huddled in the hollow of God's hand, rolling with Her aftershocks. The hills that remained clapped their hands, booming applause across the desert.

A reddish scree ramp stretched before cave and entry ledge, angling down, pointing south toward Egypt.

Abby leaked clean tears. Michael ran over to her, sliding to a stop. "Why you crying, Auntie? Did I do something bad?"

"Oh no, child. These are happy tears. You're an excellent uncle for Ahud."

"Can I hold him, Auntie?"

Abby put Mike in her lap and Ahud in his lap. Mike looked over his shoulder at her, "Wow, Auntie Abby, that was so much fun! I've never made the earth dance. Could we do it all over again?"

18

WINDY

Caligula, in the darkening night, felt his lover's alarm. He said, "Tibbie, what did he do to you?"

Tibbie faintly pushed him away, but Cal held on. He groped his lover's goblet, sniffed at it, and like Tiberius, tasted. His eyebrows also raised in alarm. He grabbed the cup out of Tibbie's hand, walked a short distance, and swirled in a circle, arms extended, spraying Jesus' blood all over the ground. A field of blood-red Jerusalem Cross flowers sprang up wherever the blood hit the ground. Cal found himself surrounded by red crosses. A sea of red spray surrounded him. He felt flooded, like he might drown. He clutched his throat and screamed, "Help me, Tibbie! I can't swim!"

Pontii, standing behind him, said, "Consul, those are just flowers. They can't drown you."

Tiberius, for his part, mumbled, "Decide what to do with this storyteller, Cal. I can't think straight right now."

Cal calmed down and fired up his straight-scheming thoughts. New gravitas met old ambition. His near-blind eyes brightened like two silver coins. All the silvery education inside his tongue sparkled with authority. "Jew, you're done. Tomorrow, Pontii's guards will stick you on a stake." He pursed his lips, fingered them. "Along with anyone who takes after you."

Claudia was undaunted. She shook Tiberius' shoulders with both hands. "Wake up, Uncle Tibbie! Look at the basic difference between these two men. Jesus hasn't figured out a way to light up others' lives without setting himself on fire. Cal lights his ambitions by setting others on fire."

Caligula ignored her. He said, "Pontii, shackle these two. We'll light 'em up tomorrow at my garden party."

Pontii looked at the emperor. Tiberius' eyes had cleared for the moment. He said, "That's a bonfire too far, Cal. Pontii, get the Seer and his cousin on the first ship out of here tomorrow. I don't care where they go; just get them gone from Rhodes. Claudia, you can stay or go. If you leave, I'll send Pontii and a platoon as bodyguards."

The emperor next turned to the young man behind him, "This was a test, Cal, to see if your judgment had improved. It hasn't. Go back to your quarters. I'll come to you in due time."

Caligula's shame was obvious to everyone. He stormed back to the villa along the gravel path, head held high to the stars, and ran into a tree. A nearby servant handed him a lantern, "My lord, please, take this torch. I'll help you get home."

What had been a steady fire in the servant's hand became uneven in Caligula's trembling hand. The servant held his other arm and guided him. They passed Leah at a darkened spot on the path.

She hailed him, "Consul, where's Jesus?"

Caligula spat, "He's on the next ship out of here, and good riddance!"

Leah went one way, Caligula the other, led by his manservant. Along the path, sole detached. He threw the sandal away in a fit of temper and limped home.

Once the servant had departed from his apartment, Caligula fumbled through his chest of drawers. His fingers found a gift from his grandmother, Augusta. He held the carefully stoppered vial of amber liquid and scribbled a note by the candle's light. He bent so close to the fire and paper that his eyebrows almost caught fire.

He called for Cassius, his personal slave. The slave's hair was the exact color and length of Cal's hairpiece.

Caligula said, "Young Leah, Captain Rabbus' wife, is feeling poorly. I know how important she is to Jesus. Make a pot of freshly brewed tea. Place it with some cookies on their dining room table. Add this potion to the tea. It'll help her sleep. Poor girl's distraught. One spoonful is enough. Stopper the vial and return the rest to me. Also, give her this note." Cassius bustled about, doing his lord's commands.

Meanwhile, Jesus sat in a carriage with Claudia, waiting to depart. Leah walked toward him, sparking his memories—as if a chisel were striking iron. Little Leah, Rabbus, and Slow fleeing Nazareth at three in the morning. Rabbus and Leah's garbage dump funeral-wedding. Leah gathering herbs along the path up to Dragon Hill. Leah leading Polyphemus by the hand to himself. Leah grieving for her two dead children.

"Jesus," Leah said, "you're leaving on the next ship? Leaving me all alone with a mute husband and a crowd of unbelievers?"

"Leah, Windy is always present."

"Do you remember, Jesus, another time when you were leaving, I said you reminded me of a diamond peace ship, spraying rainbows of color from a sun within you?"

"Yes, and you also said those colors were the sufferings of shattered Light."

"Exactly. I feel the same way now, but this time, I'm shattered."

Jesus put his arms around her and then released her to me. She walked away as I blew through her. She felt disoriented, floaty. At the end of her hallway, separated only by a stone wall, were niches filled with old bones. She peeked through the door. A few niches were still empty, awaiting new arrivals.

Leah turned from the catacombs and opened her apartment door. A steaming pot of tea, cookies, and a note all sat in a cluster on her dining table. She sat down at this table and rested chin on hands, elbows propped in front of the teapot. She fumbled with the ivory-colored parchment. Luxury slipped between the pads of her forefinger and thumb. The writing was in an unremembered hand, a slanted grid of loopy troughs and ridges.

Brewed with you in mind. This tea will help you sleep. The initials at the bottom were smudged.

Leah's hand trembled. Bony fingers held sugar cookie up to candle. Her fingers were so thin that light shattered around them, silhouetting bone and translucent, pink flesh in front of the flame. Tendrils of bitter almond steamed 'round her fingers and sugar cookies. She poured herself a long draught of the amber tea, stared into the steam wisps. She imagined eyebrows arching in the steam. *Ready yet?*

Her children's faces played peek-a-boo in her mind's eye, looking at her through a field of red flowers shaped like crosses. Her mama stood behind them. Gabe mouthed the words, *Mama, come to us. Sister and I miss you. Come home, Mama. Come to us.*

Her door opened. Caligula said, "Hello, little Leah."

19

LEAH

There was absolutely nothing imposing about Caligula. Indeed, he was quite a small man. But he was one of the scariest people I had ever met. Candlelight fell into his eyes like a body into a grave.

I said, "Consul, Rabbus is not here."

He smiled, kindly. "Jesus sent me. He wanted to make sure you had received his gifts. I can smell his tea, so I'm happy the servant delivered it to you. Did he also bring the cookies? Jesus made this tea, you know, with his very own hands, just for you."

I wasn't used to the consul being so personable, but something didn't feel quite right, even though I felt floaty. Was it my imagination, or were his lips twisted up at the ends? He'd forgotten his wig and his head seemed extra lop-sided, bald patches shining beneath his combover. He'd changed clothes to a green silk tunic with matching leggings.

He made a show of taking off his shoes, fingered an enormous emerald stone on the middle finger of his left hand.

I said, "Consul, I'm not used to visitations from royalty, particularly without my husband present."

Caligula showed his teeth. "Ah, but of course, my dear. Both of us being young, sexually active people. Not seemly. No, not at all. And I do so like thin, petite women such as you. My appetites are, shall we say, omnivorous. You remind me of a favorite partner—my little sister, Agrippina."

I examined my fingers, folded together in my lap. "I'm inhospitable. Please share a cup of tea with me, in Jesus' name."

Caligula felt his way across the room, hands out to either side. He stumbled on Rabbus' chair beside me and sat down. His knees touched mine, and his fingers groped across the tabletop. "I'll have a cookie. My appetites swamp me."

I stood and moved to the kitchen sink, carrying the teapot with me. Over my shoulder, I offered, "Please wait a moment. I'll get a cup for your tea."

At the sink, my hand loosened its grip on the teapot, all of its own accord. The teapot shattered on the stone floor.

"Ah. I'm so sorry, consul. I'll make a fresh pot for you."

He said, "Oh no, a glass of wine would be fine."

I filled a glass with white wine. The candlelight danced on the wine's surface.

My cat, Squiggles, slinked around the corner, stepping delicately between the broken shards. She licked some spilt tea.

I walked around Squiggles and cautioned her, "be careful, Squig. The floor is full of sharp edges." I sat back down at the table with the consul and pushed the glass of wine across to him.

Squiggles mewled loudly, raced in circles, and fell over on her back, stopped breathing. Her legs twitched.

My hands flew to my mouth. I stood abruptly, knocking my chair over. I took a step toward Squiggles, totally focused on her. I didn't hear the consul approach from behind me, and his voice seemed to float through some kind of air syrup.

"Let me comfort you."

Consul pulled me to him, buried my face in his chest, ground his lower body into mine. Trapped my arms beside me. Backed me up against the stone wall that separated our apartment from the catacombs. Felt like he was pushing me straight through the wall.

I got frantic. He didn't let up his pressure. Instead, he pushed my face into his chest, smothering my screams.

He whispered in my ear, "I'm not a monster, you know. Am I not merciful to follow Jesus' command? Why, just yesterday he was nattering on about the excellence of the narrow way. Just for us righteous ones, you know."

He kept up the pressure. His voice took on a sing-song impersonation of Jesus, "Yes, indeed, the path to life is exceeding narrow. [42] But no worries, Leah. I'll draw many people to my bosom. You are among the first. I am meek and mild like Jesus—and treacherous as hell."

My last prayer was, *into your hands, Father, I give my spirit. Find a substitute for Rabbus. Free him, Jesus.*

Gabriel came—bright, clear, shimmering.

He said, "It's time for *your* homecoming."

20

WINDY

When Leah died, Caligula seized and fell frothing on her husk. He jerked and quivered for a few minutes on top of her, a leaf in the storm. Chewed his tongue to ribbons. Grand mal seizures do that to a person, even one with a silver tongue.

He awoke after some time, dazed. Stood shakily and stepped on Squiggles' head as he passed by, carrying Leah's corpse on his shoulder. He dumped her body on the unmade side of the couple's bed, the side that sagged lower than the other. Her little body got lost in that husband-sized depression.

Cal felt her face with his fingertips. Her features left him open-mouthed—cheekbones like porcelain china. So thin, so delicate, for a mudder of mixed race. A torrent of spit and blood flowed from his mouth, drenching her face.

A sliver of the broken cup stuck in the pink ball of his right foot on the way out—a brief sting, nothing more. He walked across the hall and slipped into his apartment.

His door had no sooner closed than Rabbus arrived from his trip downtown with John. He clunked down the steps, armor rattling with each step. He opened the door, calling, "Sweetheart, I'm home!" Her cheerful reply was missing.

He turned, saw Squiggles, the shattered cup, a half-eaten sugar cookie, and a note on the table. His boots crunched shards of teacup on his way to the bedroom.

Leah lay crumpled like a rag doll on his side of the bed. He shook her. "Wake up, Leah! I'm home. Wake up, my darling!"

He thought, *her body's not stiff, not cold. She sleeps.*

Even as a river swamps a teacup, denial ran through him. He picked her up, effortless, and moved to the kitchen. They sat together at the table, warm wife in his arms. He kissed her bloody face, saying, "Wake up. Naptime's over, dear. I'm home. I've come home."

Her head hung limp, eyes closed.

He glanced at the table where they took their meals together, so silently of late. He picked up the note on the table. Her head flopped sideways, thumping softly on the hilt of his sword. The door opened, and Cassius popped his head in.

He said, "Shall I take away the leftovers I brought from Consul Caligula, my lord?"

Late the next morning, Emperor and Consul cantered on their horses near the Port of Rhodes. They'd made up from their tiff the night before. Caligula's stallion, Incitatus, pranced, muscles rippling in the morning sun. Caligula would one day nominate this horse, his favorite, as a high priest of Rome's Equestrian Temple. [43]

The two royals stopped for coffee and croissants at a local patisserie. Adjutants rushed to hold their horses. Once inside, Cal settled for warm chamomile tea and no food. This soothed his ravaged tongue. Imperial Guards hung around the bakery, front and back, in a loose perimeter.

After, they wandered through Colossus' ruins. They held hands, stopping to smell the primroses scattered among the hemlock. Caligula limped, favoring his right foot.

Tiberius inquired, "Hurt your foot, lover? Your ankle streaks red."

"Oh, that. A passing sore. Here today, gone tomorrow."

He spoke of himself but without insight.

The crumpled Colossus was frozen into a fruitless conversation with himself. One part wondered to another how they might, once again, gain glory.

Three outriggers, rowed by twelve men each, pulled a merchant ship, *Alexandria,* from the docks toward the open water. Small figures at the masthead waved to them.

Caligula eyed the emperor. His torn tongue, flapping blindly over eye teeth, spewed the ragged words, "those Chews thail on that thip."

Tiberius shrugged dispassionately, "Not for me to say if the Jews sail. Shake the ground around you. Find out stuff. It's your job as consul."

Cal plopped his pillow on fallen Colossus' nose. As was his habit, he arranged himself rather than just sitting. He lifted his right foot, delicately, and placed it over his left knee, "No need to th-ake the ground, wuver. This is Whodes. Ground thakes all by itself." He chortled.

Tiberius suddenly felt stifled. *I can't take a deep breath.*

Caligula continued, "last night Wabbus went on a tear."

Enough air squeaked through Tibbie's throat for Cal to hear the hoarse whisper, "A tear?"

Tiberius frantically whirled around, desperate. Where was his protector? *I'm suffocating. Panic trilled in his chest.*

Petite mal seizure zipped through Cal right then, stayed and left in two seconds. Eyes rolled briefly up in his head and he smelled bitter almonds. Cal shook his head, stood up, and his head cleared.

He thought, *close call. Can't fall and froth. Lover's watching me.*

The emperor, implausibly, drew breath once Cal stood up. "Ah, the sea breeze is so salty and sweet, all at once."

Caligula put his foot on Colossus' face and queried, "How do I look?"

He struck a pose, right hand back of his blond pompadour, chin raised imperiously, chest sticking out, gut sucked in, right knee bent.

Tiberius was annoyed with such posturing. "You're favoring that right foot and talking like a dweeb with rocks in his mouth. Damaged goods, lover."

Caligula reeled inside. *Was he being dismissed?*

The emperor continued, "Mind you don't wander into the sea—you know, in your diminished state."

Caligula's feelings sunk. *Tiberius' subtle style of execution had always been suggestion. If I don't fall on my sword, footsteps will come by day or night. He's done this so many times. Onto another boy toy.*

Tiberius nailed shut Cal's coffin shut. "Let's find Rabbus."

No need to find Rabbus. He'd found them. He ran through the streets toward them, banging Cassius' severed head along the cobblestones behind him, dragging the head by its long, blond locks—*bap, bap, bobble-de-*

bap. His dominant left hand held his sword. He ran up to Caligula, "Ah, murderous royal!"

Caligula scampered behind his uncle, screeching, "Away, fell execu-thuner!"

Imperial bodyguards closed the distance, curious to check out the loosed head their boss shook in the consul's face. *Might be a story here.*

Caligula screamed through his bloody spit, "Guards, Awwest this… murderer!"

Tiberius held his hand up, palm out to the guards, "Hold."

He turned to Rabbus and gestured to Cassius' head, "What is this execution, dear man?"

Rabbus pointed to Caligula, who stood cowering behind his protector, sword in one hand and jeweled dagger in the other.

Rabbus flicked his gaze down, "This man murdered my wife—at that man's order!" He pointed at Caligula.

Rabbus wound Cassius' head around by his hair in a spiral, a stone in a slingshot, and let loose at Caligula. It was a good shot, zinging past the emperor's tipped head and bouncing off Cal's face. A gout of blood hung from the consul's wispy beard.

Tiberius went into Imperial mode, "What say you to this charge of murder, Consul?"

Caligula swiped at his bloody face with his silk hanky. He shouted, "Wabbus' wife cwoaked. *Tho what?*"

Rabbus' hand trembled with the effort to not run both men through with one thrust. Eyes wildened, neck cords bulged, face purpled.

Rabbus pulled a flask from his belt, "Cassius confessed before he died. He said that *you*, Caligula, made this viper's brew. She must have fought you. A teapot was shattered, our cat poisoned, and Leah's body dumped on our bed. This note, done in *your* handwriting, was on our table. What more evidence do you need of guilt, Excellency?"

Tiberius waffled between truth and illusion. *What to do?*

Caligula crossed his arms. "You know me, wuv, I burn grathe toward vulgars like Vestal V-v-virginth burn midnight oil."

Tiberius queried, "So how do you explain the tea, the note, the timeline?"

"Obviouth. Th-he choked on her own thpit. Dea-ff by phlegm. Happen-th all the time among commoners."

Rabbus' held up a leather flask, "This flask was in your apartment. If you're innocent, drink. If not, fight."

Tiberius intervened, "Both of you, scabbard your weapons. The matter is inflamed, as is Cal's foot and tongue. I'll decide the outcome within the week. Perhaps a duel when Cal's healed up."

Caligula felt chills down his spine. *No need to walk into the sea with rocks in my pockets. If I have to fight Rabbus, I'm doomed.*

Tiberius kept talking, "For now, Rabbus, give me your word that you'll stay clear of the Consul—and that you, Caligula, will scheme no harm to my bodyguard."

Cal held on harder. Rabbus' head slumped. Sound of sword rattling into his scabbard.

Sallow-faced Grief, smeared with white make-up, put her hook through Rabbus' nose and pulled him into her slipstream. White water of madness washed him homeward.

Tiberius' voice followed him as he walked away, "My condolences on your wife's passing. She was a real saint—and the only one who's brought me back from the dead."

Rabbus didn't acknowledge the comment. He kept walking further and farther than where either he or the emperor knew he would ever go.

Tiberius motioned to Cassius' head at Caligula's feet, a platinum blond mop at either end of his body, and neither belonged to him.

He snarked, "Pick him up, Cal. This is what comes when vengeance schemes with ambition. All that's left is a bloody flood."

He brightened, "Fortunately, once in Capri, we will write the histories. I'll dictate, you scribe."

Cal calmed. *Okay. Tibbie's mood had shifted again. His plans could still work.*

The older lover kept speaking. "This situation can be fixed. History is past. Fiction is future. We'll cover the former with the latter, shaping what's past on the wheel of fantasy. No one need read 'Disaster.' 'Dynasty' sounds so much more noble. Give me pliable facts, and I'll spin 'em into fiction. Disguised history—yes, that's the ticket."

21

CLAUDIA

Pontii so annoyed me. He hovered. I just wanted Jesus to myself, and he would inch up and play the Roman card. "We Romans gotta stick together." He eyed Jesus at the starboard side of *Alexandria*'s bridge, "provincials ricochet from dangerous to magical—they're not ordered, like us."

"Ah, Pontii. We've crossed so many borders—and not just borders of countries. We started with my being a royal and you, across a fence, a no-name military grunt. And then I walked through the nice-girl-to-murderess border with Postie. After, the border between you as guard and me, your prisoner, on Trimerus. Then, we crossed from marriage proposal to some sort of fatal attraction on the skiff sail from Trimerus to Aternum."

Pontii smiled, briefly.

I continued, "I saved you from being killed by my uncle on Dragon Hill after Bato had skinned and castrated you. He wanted to kill you and bury you deep so the lions wouldn't eat you. Jesus moved you back across the eunuch-to-man border and back from being skinless to being covered by skin again. Now we're crossing from Rhodes to Egypt."

Ponti smiled at me, hopeful, but I was without mercy. My lethal mouth kept flapping. "Through it all, Ponti, I've rejected you, loved Jesus. You've rejected Jesus and loved me. As it was, so it is, and will be."

Pontii, a man dedicated to silence, lapsed into a lengthy oration. "What happened to you? You used to be hotter than sex on a stick. Now you favor saints?"

"Burned through my lifetime supply of sex, I guess. Maybe someone whacked off my gonads when I wasn't looking. Maybe too many border crossings. Some part of me dried up while another lit up. Maybe spirit for sex. Weird how I do that either-or thing. One day, maybe Windy'll witch me into a happy medium."

Ponti grinned, "We're alike. I've not found the middle ground either."

I said, "Some borders have gone missing. The plashings between me and not-me have come undone. You and me, more human than otherwise, you once ball-less and now me desire-less."

Jesus walked up behind us with another man who stood next to the kedging anchor's housing. He stepped into the light.

Jesus said, "Surprise! Julius is traveling to Egypt with us."

Julius said, "I got wind of your leaving and paid my passage at the last minute. Alexandria feels like a homecoming of sorts for us—the place we first met as boys, Jesus. I know the guy in charge there. Prefect Cornelius took over after my pop left. He doesn't let a fart loose without written permission from Rome."

Julius turned to Pontii, "We two got the worst of it there in Illyria, soldier. Skinned alive, both of us, before our flayer turned into a hog and ran into the sea, courtesy of Blue."

John also joined our group. He said, "Blue was amazing. I still don't miss her as much as Millie, the woman locked inside the mastodon. She froze to death, poor gal. That was awful, seeing her chill into a block of ice."

Julius looked confused, "I don't remember any of that. You sure your imagination hasn't gone missing with this Millie?"

I shook my head, "You and Pontii were dying fast. Leah 'n me smeared stuff from her paste-pots onto your raw guts. Whatever *that* was brought you back. And, by the by, she gave me full paste pots, with instructions, before we left. In case you get skinned again. Might be a fresh loss around the next corner. Never can tell."

Pontii looked away, caught sight of huge Colossus shrinking to less than life-size—as time and space do to all giants. He said, "Wave to your boss, Julius. He's standing there with Cal, who seems to have grown another blond head on his feet."

John looked over Jesus' shoulder. He tipped his head to one side. His eyes glazed over as though he were staring into a mystic ball of molten glass.

He said, "Rabbus just bounced Cassius' head off Caligula. It's in the dirt at Caligula's feet. And one of Cal's feet is poisoned, by his own doing— but unfortunately, he'll recover.'"

We were all stunned with this offering. Even Jesus seemed caught unawares.

John continued to stun us all in his dead-pan, emotionless monotone. "Cal smothered Leah last night in a fit of shame-rage, using Cassius as a ploy. Rabbus mistook her death as poisoning. Now his soul and body burn, two sides of one leaf. He'll come home to forget his heartache and get into lots of trouble."

Jesus stared at a patch of ravaged hillside on the Rhodes coast, a slope of sticks burned black from a recent forest fire. He said, "In a year or so, a new forest will replace those charred skeletons. Dormant seeds needed that fire, like a slap in the face, to wake up. A new forest will rise from that ash."

I said, "Loss keeps us living, is that what you're saying? Even though it's not one-off. Loss burns through new stuff all the time and hands us ruins day by day."

Jesus nodded. "Windy blows where He will, crackling spark into flame. I follow, picking through the ashes. Father's Fire-follower. And that journey will cost me everything I've got."

He said these words and then slid to the deck, trembling, back against the bulkhead. The wind blew through his beard, and a tear lay on his lower eyelash. I slid down next to him, side to side, knee to knee, rested my cheek on his. I wiped his eye with the flat of my forefinger. Got a taste for his tears—salty, mixed with heavy. An image came to me when I next looked at him, like a spiked strip of sadness had wrapped his head roundabout like a crown, pressing in, puncturing.

Roman sails bellied overhead, puffed full of Windy. Weathered deck thrummed a quiet vibrato. Sails' shadows flickered over us and then away, back and forth in the ship's rocking. We plunged down waves' trough, heading for the sea's barren, black floor. Then the hull caught, rose again, sailing soft into sea's chop and swell.

After some minutes of being rocked by the wind and waves, Jesus nodded, "I didn't want to believe you, John. But Windy whispered her 'yes.' Leah is home now. And hear me well, all of you. I'll make a way for

Rabbus. Don't know where, when, or how. But that knowing's been bred in my bones."

John said, "We've been taught to believe saving one life is equal in merit to saving the world, is it not?"

I looked up at Jesus to see what he would say. Pinpricks of blood had popped a crown around Jesus' brow, and he bled. My jaw dropped. Did I cause this, or was it fated? I'd always thought Fate was the lazy person's religion, so I threaded some dark needle of not-knowing and settled on Mystery.

I took a small pot of Leah's salve. Anointed his head. Rubbed the paste on each small stab wound. I soothed his chestnut hair, stroking it away from his squeezed-shut eyes. He leaked grief all over me. Drenched me with himself.

Mourning wound through my lips, impetuous, and danced a slow hora in my heart. I no longer questioned these paradoxes. They flowed from God-man, preparing me for what barreled down spirit canyons our way, like a flash fire or flashflood of twisted grief. He turned his face to me and said, "She knew. She knew she was being shattered. If only I'd heard her, listened deeper, differently…." He began to sob, and I held him.

I murmured into the wind, *God, your most awesome work was done in the kindness of your Son.* I rocked Jesus. The wind and waves rocked us. Together we sailed on our pinpricks of time. *Ah, Beloved—time's scant, time's scant.*

22

SLOW

Abby rode Goodness and cuddled Ahud in her arms. The rest of us walked down the ramp that God had quaked into place. We all headed south, away from our fancy hotel room over Death Wadi.

Laz said, "We'll take the patriarch, Jacob, as our mentor. He moved at the speed of slow. Children and new mothers had no trouble keeping up."
44

Our feet made a new trail over old debris. Beaten trails, at least for today, were for beaten people. We made our own trail, taking each twist of the canyon in turn. One rocky overhang looked like a chipped angel, barely hanging on.

I said to Abby, "We walk among the fallen. Long canyons' fall and brothers' short drops. Both put ground under feet. While we're walking and talking, give me Ahud—he's had enough to drink and will sleep now."

She handed Ahud off to me. She said, "Every step's a calculated fall, isn't it? Throw a leg out. Lean into thin air. Hope your toe strikes something solid before your face smacks rock. Repeat."

Hope said, "I'm in each step you take, Auntie?" She began to dance down the ramp, eyes closed and arms floating out to either side, sleeves from her robe like the wings of a bird. Each knee held high, one foot teetering in front of the other before it touched ground.

Hope conjured up a story on the spot, "Once upon a time a cloud child air-walked over canyons. She lost her balance up there when the wind stopped blowing. Just as she was about to fall, an eagle swooped beneath her, lifting her up and up to waterfalls where angels waited to play with her."

Hope paused and then said, "Maybe I should leave my heart with the fairy angels, Auntie? Sometimes, just sometimes, I think it's too heavy to dance or fly away."

Abby said, "Hope, faith is like the wind." She pointed to an acacia tree in the shadow of a cliff. "Love is heavy with earth. Keep both in your heart—wings *and* roots." Abby's words blew over or through the child. Either way, Hope kept dancing and twirling, leading us all toward Egypt.

About mid-morning, Abby said, "I need to get down. Stop for a pee and poo break over there in that crevice. I hear sounds of a tiny streamlet, a good hand washer. And, Slow, either my nose is tricking me or gone missing. Is there still something on my face between my eyes, with two holes in the bottom? I can't smell my stink."

I said, "Maybe God healed you, Abby."

Abby cocked her head at me. "Huh! Didn't even think of that." She put her head back and laughed with sheer abandon. Never before or after have I seen that kind of glee caused by pee and poop getting a fresh stopper.

I was unspeakably grateful for what smelled like a newly contained body, too long torn. And, come to think of it, my pieces were hanging together better than in days gone by. Maybe both comings-together were best seen walking forward while looking back.

I kept Ahud while Abby went off to do her business. Laz sat in the shadow of the wadi's eastern wall, smoking. Our children organized a rock-throwing contest and appointed me judge of their stoning spree. I officiated my first-ever joyful stoning. Hope won.

Abby returned a few minutes later—relieved, clean. She said, "I love, love, love leaving my toilet behind me. Do you have any idea how it feels to be a continual walking, talking toilet?"

I had some idea and told her so. "I know how it feels to be a flat-backing, whoring semen storehouse, always leaking what wasn't mine. I was delivered from *that*. Does that count?"

Her eyes flooded with a shared sense of too much sadness, grief stored in tricked bodies.

She said, "Between the two of us, sister, we've been given plugs for all three holes down there. Guess it's our choice how we use our plugs."

As I considered the wisdom of her comment, I heard a branch crack above us. A wake of buzzards looked down, cawing and hopping away, leading us away from their nesting places. We obliged them, kept heading southbound, moving like slugs. Relief leached into my bones—no one hunting me, no flashflood threatening me. Smells of the desert filled my nose and crowded out bad body memories.

I said to Laz, "Maybe we could build three homes on top of that wadi top over there, one for us, Abby, and a guest house. We could rest up there, out of harm's way, the rest of our lives. What do you think?" [45]

Laz said, "Sure. We could set up an outpost for passing oryx." He paused, "Some of the best victories I've ever experienced came from walking away from battles. My enemies exhausted themselves waiting."

I sighed out a song of deliverance with each step further from Herod's purple room of shadows, a barely bearable lightness of being. I found it hard staying tethered to the planet.

We went 'round the next wrinkle in the wadi and the next. Chalk-bright earthen crust baked in the sun-shot afternoon. Sweat evaporated into salt scrim left on skin.

Toward dusk, our narrow canyon gave out onto a jagged, arid desert-scape. No people, no water. Plenty of sapping heat, broiling sun. Plenty of craggy chaparral dotted with sabra cactus and wormwood. A cloud of dust swirled off to our left, twisting like a dust devil of discouragement. I told God, *I can't handle a mouthful of grit. Please, no.*

The cloud obliged me and collapsed under its weight. Left us alone to bake in the desert's oven. Even our empty flasks were parched. Ahud sucked Abby dry.

Hope and Michael came clinging, "Thirsty, Ma, thirsty!" Desperation-inducers they were, no experience required. Such a human quality, thirst. Born from bodies that are vulnerable, craving, aching.

I said to Abby, "I feel like Hagar when she dumped Ishmael under the wormwood bush—lost, dying of thirst in the middle of nowhere. Being hated is a distant second to being dead."

Laz, irrepressible, offered, "Wasn't her Ishmael dump right before an angel led her to a well?" [46]

The one of little faith, me, said, "Husband, why don't you open a vein and give your kids a drink?"

Instead, Laz pointed to a tendril of smoke fingering its way up the edge of a rose-colored ridge. He held my sweaty hand and murmured, "Let's have a look. Can't be more than a mile straight ahead. Where there's smoke, there's water. Right?"

The sun galloped west in its downward arc—going, going, gone. Green flash hovered for a moment, then it too vanished, eager to be done with the day. In the Negev, sunset and dark court briefly before they jump into bed and clench the deal. We barely arrived at the source of smoke before night fell, like an ax chopping light from the sky.

23

WINDY

A few date palms stood swaybacked and tall in a cluster close to the eastern cliff ridge. An old, black couple sat cross-legged on bedrolls between an empty saddle and a campfire. The fire crackled beneath a few sticks they'd tepee'd together. The old man played a daf. This circular frame was ringed with tin spirals that tinkled like rain and rolled like distant thunder when he hit the stretched skin with the heel of his palm. The woman mournfully played her stringed tembur, a traveler's lute, in time with his daf. The ancient couple fit their ancient instruments.

Both man and woman stopped playing when my band of travelers approached. The woman's black eyes were milky, her white hair threaded with black. The man's coal-black face was leathery and bland till he smiled—then it lit up like a split-open geode.

Laz greeted them, "Mind some company for the night?"

The man said, "Plenty of space around here, but no food. You see this saddle? While back, we ate the burro it belonged to. Now we just finished our last pancake. Used our last drop of oil. Caravan moved on last week. Where we come from, when old folks use up their usefulness, folks say good-bye and move on."

"Old man, we have food and fuel but no water. Got water?"

Old man raised a finger, pointed over his shoulder back into the cliff crevices, "trickle from a crack in the back, about 100 yards into that ravine. The trick is to hold your bladder still and be patient. Wait, catch the drip."

Laz eyed the moon's rise over the cliff. He said, "Look at that moon, resting up there on top the canyon wall. Might be too heavy to rise any higher in this thin air."

Old man said, "Here's what's left of our water—about half a bladder. Maybe enough till morning?"

We all took a sip. Mike guzzled the last of it. He said, "Is that all? I'm still *very* thirsty."

A creaky, high soprano warbled into the night air, "Samuel's lame, but I can lead you to the water now if need be."

Samuel said, "We're a fine pair. Sheba's blind; I'm lame. Between the two of us, we can see exactly where we can't go. Not bad, considering I've done eighty-five trips around the sun, one more than her. Neither of us ain't young. In fact, we're older than eighty." He cackled, and everyone laughed with him. The old guy was funny.

Hope piped up, "Ma, maybe grandma Sheba can lead us. I can take your bladder, Auntie Abby. I'll fill it full for you."

Sheba got up and moved toward Hope. Her voice twanged into a bright cackle, "Take my hand, child. I might be withered, wrinkled, and crinkled—but my night vision's good. For example, I can tell you that dark's way different than the Prince of Darkness."

I ran a shiver down Slow's spine. She said, "Perhaps Auntie Abby and I could go with you two. We have several containers that need healing, ah, filling."

Laz busied himself getting bedrolls laid down in a circle before the campfire died out. He tore off a chunk of dried camel meat, handed it to Samuel.

The old man said, "I'll have to gum this thing to death. Teeth fell out a few years ago. But thank you. Most kind."

Sound of Laz chopping meat. "Here, Mike, I have a hard job for you. Take my hammer and these bits of meat to the slab of rock beside Goodness, the one with a hollow in the middle. Beat this meat. Then chew, and here's the hard part—don't swallow. Give the chewed meat to Samuel."

Boy hammered, and Sheba dark-walked the women, plus Hope. They daisy-chained their way over jagged rocks and brittle tumbleweed.

Sheba muttered, just loud enough for Slow to make it out, "Survival in deserts requires inside light more than outside fight, children. Don't carry your own night light? Fear leaks in and out. Demons smell that stink a long way off."

Hope did a skippy-hop behind Sheba. She lost touch with Slow. In those moments, Slow stumbled more than once and scraped the palm of her hand. Hope slowed down and helped. Slow kept one hand on Hope and the other on the wall, the tall granite spire that held the day's heat. Several bats swooped by, each reflecting the other's clicking sounds to guide their mates in the dark. Soon Slow could touch both of the narrowing walls on either side of her.

Hope said, "Auntie Abby, here's the wet." Abby reached her bladder up where life flowed down. The flow rate off the mountain's crack was between a drip and a drizzle, water tricking itself around, under, and through the rock. About the volume of an old man's pee stream. The old mountain's leak slowly filled Abby's bladder.

While we waited, Abby said, "Sheba, what's this night-light stuff?"

Sheba said, "Draw into a circle, children." We pulled closer, knees kissing, except Abby, who stood and kept her bladder raised up for the mountain's drippings.

Sheba said, "Courage is the striker for night-lights. Without night-sight, you'll not make it through the deserts. Lots of ways to let life out, wandering in the burn."

I said, "Speak plainly."

She said, "You couldn't make even this short journey alone, from campfire to the back of this ravine. The same with inner journeys. Any wounded woman is riddled with blind spots."

Abby said, "Like what you have, Sheba?"

"Not exactly. In Africa, they call me a *griot*, a mirror. Hold myself up so people can see who they are."

A crackling over dry brush. Cool scales, oily, slithery—a snake coiled around Slow's ankle. She froze, waiting to die some hideous death in the middle of nowhere.

Sheba said, "Here's a case for you." She pulled the snake off Slow's leg. "Young whipsnake here needed some guidance. Lost his way and fell off that overhang. He needs fresh direction, that's all."

Sound of arm whipping through the air.

Sheba's voice. "On your way, fella—yummy lizard's in the bush over there."

Plopping crunch, crackling brush, soft gulping sounds.

Hope's voice lilted, "How'd you do that, Grandma Sheba?"

"Night-seeing improves with use. Live long enough, you learn what snakes are dangerous or only endangered. Two-legged varieties cause most of life's troubles.

"For example, shame shakes folks down faster than snakes. Drama's not required. Even a trip to the market can flatten a person with the smell of fish, or figs, or whatever—shame-attack memories have hair triggers.

"I reckon that's why the Great Spirit gave me blindness. Same one you call Windy, or Great Mother, or Great Father—all the same. She said my blindness was for those who I'd meet on the edge of night."

Slow said, "Huh. That might be us. Is this Jesus' same Spirit?"

Sheba replied, "I don't think I've heard that name. Mother slips into my dreams. Father stands beside her. They said we'd meet you in the middle of nowhere. You'd feed us. I was to take you to the water. That's all I know."

Hope said, "Ma, I believe Grandma Sheba. Windy moves in strange ways. For example, I was sitting in her lap when you were giving birth to Ahud, Auntie Abby."

Abby said, "You didn't say anything."

Hope replied, "I forgot. When the baby came out, Windy shot a beam of light right up your crack. I forgot to tell you. Bright sat behind Goodness and whispered in my ear, 'Tonight Windy's swapping openings with closings. Baby will open her. Then she'll close what's torn. Windy will deliver mother and baby.'"

Sheba said, "Brilliant, Hope. You "do" wonder *real* good. Adults get busy spending and getting. Elders return to wonder. We start laughing and ask lots of questions all over again—a sign of a second childhood."

She placed her arm around Abby and laid her other hand on me. "Don't be fooled, young mothers. Sun doesn't give reliable light. Unless you become as a little child, you'll never see what the Parents have for you."

Slow reached for Abby's water skin and let Abby rest while she kept the bladder's opening under mountain's drizzle.

Sheba said, "Inside journeys work better when you go together. Solo travelers don't do so well on wet winter nights when cold wind's whipping. Struck sparks on such nights give no continuing fire, only death by snuffed sparks."

I said, "I'm confused. Single-sparks in nights of the soul? You're a worse riddler than Jesus, and I thought he was the champ."

"If your Jesus is a true prophet, he'll know what I mean. I'm talking courage that sparks heart-to-hearts. Join sparks with fuel and air? *Fire.* Fire that moves you to speak your flaws and fears."

Slow said, "So let me see if I get this. Blab my guts out with a bunch of people on a street corner, and I'm good to go?"

Sheba's voice smiled in the dark. "No, not at all. Add one stick at a time. No more than half-dozen small sticks at a time. That gives the best light and warmth."

Abby and Slow took what she said. Hope cuddled Slow.

"Take a short rise toward courage, and you live. Shut up or shut down, you fall. Even a short drop can mean death."

Abby cried, "I'm not strong enough. I can't do this." Her shoulders trembled as she cried—quiet, unobtrusive, already a professional at hiding her grief.

Sheba replied, not unkindly, "How do you think you'll ever get strong? Fired wood stays lit only if it sticks together. Take a stick out of the fire and leave it alone? Ha! It don't do good."

Water was trickling stronger now, more than a drip. The second bladder, filling.

Slow said, "My arm's getting tired holding up this bladder."

Sheba said, "Let us join you. We'll hold your arms from the side so you can relax in the middle. And remember, children, no stink sticks when sisters face shame together. If you try this alone, you'll become a person who's made mistakes but thinks she is a mistake."

After a black, quiet moment, Abby started to shake worse. Began to wail. Slow felt her, even smelt her sadness. Hope rested her head on Abby's ankles, weighting her feet to the ground.

I circled over and around her head, just off her skin, massaging scar tissue toward her heart. Sheba wrapped arms 'round her sides. We all let Abby shake and howl, and shame slithered away, a whipped snake in the shared night.

Sheba took the flask from me, swapping places. Now we supported her arms. She said, "Samuel was a carpenter most of his life. Put up houses.

When trusses couldn't bear the weight of a roof, he added supporting timbers along the sides, angling them into the heart of the triangle. Carpentry technique, sistering. Helps bear weight that would break a truss left too long alone."

Slow said, "This makes me think of my friend, Jesus. He touched lepers, partied with me and other prostitutes, married a low-life Samaritan to my sister, a Moabite-Jewess, like me; loved a tax-collector, Zacchaeus, and his murdering brother, Rastus, ah, the list goes on. We're headed south to meet him. He sistered us."

We took our fill of this new style of sistering, walked back to the campfire with full bladders, stoppered by choice. Emptied other bladders along the way, also by choice. Sheba led us in our dark-walk daisy chain, and none of us stumbled.

24

JESUS

We'd settled into life in Alexandria for a year or so. The desert air was arid; farmhouses and fields, bone dry. Every year in this season, people waited on tenterhooks, fearful of one passing spark, one flash of orange exploding into disaster.

Julius had found lodging inside the walled city for John and me—we lived together in a two-bedroom rental not far from where I lived as a boy on the Street of Carpenters. Claudia studied theatre arts, and the Prefect had given her more upscale lodgings reserved for Roman royalty.

I'd found work as a carpenter. John trudged from dockside to the Pharos Lighthouse's furnace. He and other dockworkers kept the 300-foot-tall-nightlight burning.[47]

After work, most afternoons John and I met at the main synagogue in the Jewish quarter—two more voices arguing Torah. Lately, the conversations had taken on worried notes about an upsurge of anti-Semitic violence. Talk flickered around our circle, talk of ethnic cleansing.

Not far outside the city's walls, someone had lit a rush match, lighting a cluster of Jewish farms in a moshav. The whole Jewish settlement had burned—and their adjoining cemetery, uprooted. The graves had been dug up, and a new village constructed over them. This was so like Satan to try and erase the memory of our people—using the mouths of local gods through local priests to purge the land of a particularly troublesome Jewish crop, both living and dead.

Some Jews made backup plans but stayed put. Others left for safer cities or villages further away from the power centers. All these murmurings pressed me to Father and Windy.

After arguing Torah at the synagogue, John and I stopped at the open-air market every day, bought fruit and vegetables, and sometimes a chicken or fresh-caught fish. I cooked, and John cleaned. One day as I was serving him dinner, I dropped his wine glass on the tile floor. It shattered. I apologized and turned to get a broom and rag to clean up my mess.

Windy took us down another path. She preached a wordless sermon to me through my cousin, stirring him to stomp the glass shards in a kind of swirling dance step, stirring the glass with his foot and kicking bits of it away from him. He motioned to me where I stood with broom in hand, wide-eyed, ready to give him a stern talking-to. He used my confusion to link arms with me—and then, inexplicably, my mood shifted. I stirred and stomped with him. Stirred the broken bits on the floor, kicked them out to the furthest corners of where we could see. As I moved, Father's words came to me through Windy's voice, words I won't forget.

This is how my kingdom spreads. Welcome persecution. Be stirred, not shaken.

I didn't have long to wait. Practice in being persecuted was just around the corner.

The next week, Julius invited my friends and me to the palace, where he worked as an administrator. He wanted us to meet the Prefect, his father's old buddy. "Gotta meet this guy. He takes brown-nosing into a whole new art form."

We arrived at the Prefect's palace complex. Ionian columns, every ten yards or so, lined the outdoor corridor, strafing us with light and shadow.

A familiar figure exited the Prefect's central gardens—Caligula. He squinted at me and said, "Well, jumpin' Jupiter! I get off the ship from Capri, and va-va-voomm, who do I meet outside the gate! Looks like the family's Jules be cozying up to the Black Magic Jew!"

Claudia stepped out from behind a marble ashlar. Cal took a few steps closer to her in order to see better, squinted her up and down, and shifted his gaze to John and me. "Ah, nothing's changed. Messiah Sycophant and the Camel Boy!"

The old Claudia would have fired off an impulsive retort, skewering Caligula to the wall. This new version of the woman remained silent, eyeing him from behind watery, blue eyes and a set chin. Caligula waited for some verbal meat to get his hooks into. Hearing nothing, he re-arranged his platinum mop over his swollen forehead.

He said, "Cornelius needs to know exactly who he's dealing with—a Claudian who's forgotten family loyalty, a cunning functionary, and two slippery Jews. Pardon me, lovers." He turned on his heel and went back the way he'd come, slamming the wrought-iron gate behind him.

After a few minutes, Cal exited the Prefect's arbor once again. He looked me up and down. "Jews. History's favorite punching bag. An extinction parade, a line-up of loss. Children of ten thousand lost battles, from Pharaoh to our latest, beloved, divine Caesar." He stared hard at Claudia and added, "Plus some backdoor spawn from a forgettable affair."

Claudia grabbed his shoulder. "Don't deceive yourself, Caligula. I will always be Augustus' granddaughter. Cheap talk won't change that." She looked at me standing beside her. "And remember this—*thousands* of years from now, we will all be forgotten dust—except for him. People will remember him, not you, not me."

Caligula left without another word. Julius shook his head, "So predictable. He has a worm's eye view of the world, gets bored with any conversation where he's not the center of adulation. Otherwise, envy's his moral compass and points due south."

We entered the Prefect's cherished gardens in the center of his palace. Wet heat hit us like a sap. Claudia said, "Now I have a good idea of how it feels to be cooked alive inside wet cabbage leaves."

We three began to explore, eyes ranging left and right, searching for the Prefect. Our path, made of crushed oyster shells, crunched underfoot, releasing their chalky odor. The acre-sized greenhouse was an ordered mirror of the city itself, laid out in a rectangle with wide, tiered rows under green-tinted glass. Exotica blossomed under trellises. Brimming aisles bloomed with passion-fruit flowers, bromeliads, magnolia blossoms big as clenched fists.

We moved through mist and running Nile river water, water pumped down artificial waterfalls, water that trickled into manicured streams. Servants in purple loin cloths moved the air with long-handled woven fans, moving clouds of vapor. Plants and water colluded to foster the illusion that we were in a rainforest.

Cornelius puttered in the middle of the garden's center square, in the center of the city's central palace, in the center of the city itself. This well-positioned man stood like stacked paste, jiggling. He stood almost six feet tall, probably tipping the scales at over 350 pounds, with wispy hair strands that were more of an idea than a reality.

The Prefect dressed only in a brief white toga wrapped around his loins beneath a stomach shaped like a championship honeydew melon. His hands, covered by white linen gloves, held platinum snippers and trowel. His eyes bugged out over a veined nose and massive goiter. He stood to approach us, slathering an avuncular smile over his lower face.

Julius bowed low. He said, "Sire, behold the God-man, Jesus. He's come to bless you, as he blessed my father when we played here together as boys. Whoever blesses him will be blessed."

Cornelius's eye twitched as he stared at me. "Ah, I *so* love someone given to self-adulation—like the youth I once was. Rome has a very special project for you, young man."

He drew near and wrapped a meaty arm around my shoulder, crowding my nose to his armpit. His voice dropped into that of a conspirator, "There are far too many Greek idols around, wouldn't you agree? One on every street corner. Rome should not take a back seat to the conquered."

The Gardener-Judge said, "Thus, your humble benefactor, Prefect of all Egypt, *moi, gives you this commission:* a twice life-size, carved *Roman* idol of acacia wood twining with cedar. The *visage´* would be mine, of course. This idol would greet all those thinkers who enter our city's premier library. Yes, indeed, I'd quite love that."

He examined my face for signs of agreement, found none, and continued, "You know, dear boy, I do not enjoy honorifics of any sort or style. Honor and love are mutually exclusive, don't you think, but Honor and Betrayal are twin sisters. One twin praises you while the other finds purchase for her knife in your back. No, no, no—I much prefer to be loved. Ah, but I circumlocute. Back to *your* task, so recently devised, my little God-Man. This idol's base would be scripted with the name, 'Cupid.' A reminder to Alexandria's polyglot to love their Roman roots and royalty!" Cornelius tittered and twirled, palms up, arms and eyes extended to the sun above.

Our group remained silent. He recovered from himself, briefly. He clipped a scarlet Moth Orchid from his arbor, wound it together with a

Passion Fruit flower and a thistle of Monkey Brush vine. Thrust his offering my way with a flourish. I took the gift, inhaled the fragrance, and almost swooned with its aroma.

John worked his face. "Your Prefectness, we Jews, as you know, worship the one true God. Idol carving, Greek or Roman, is blatant blasphemy."

I shot him a glance, loosely interpreted, *why pee into a headwind?*

John stoppered his speech.

Good, John. All things in their time.

Cornelius appeared unperturbed, "Ah yes, you Jews! Freedom of speech, freedom of worship, freedom to work undisturbed. I've gone to great pains to ensure your blessed freedoms, Jews. You have so many freedoms here— freedom, for example, to obey *all* government officials placed by Yahweh over you."

I started to reply, but the Prefect's clip voice now cut me off, like an ornamental. "Freedom also to shorten the number of one's breaths if he should choose the path of civil disobedience."

One froggy eye shot a plume of stink that caught me in its spray. Cornelius gave his goiter a push, tucking it back under his chin. The goiter, festooned with warts, popped back out with a vengeance.

Cornelius used his clippers to fissure a cyclamen's fiber bowl, spilling the ground from under it. He smiled sweetly as the dirt came out. "Consul Caligula advised me to balance my boundless generosity for free speech with a renewed respect for Roman authority."

John replied, "Free speech is particularly fetching when you're alive to speak. Jesus saved Emperor Tiberius from death twice—once from lions and once from freezing in the Gates of Hell. Emperor Tiberius, unlike his rash under-emissary, might love to counsel religious tolerance on this matter, Provincial Prefect. Past prefects lived longer when they obeyed the emperor, not his minor magistrates."

Cornelius's mouth puckered like a poked oyster. He arched an eyebrow Julius' way.

Julius nodded gravely. "Indeed, Sire. The emperor sees the Seer's value more clearly than his Consul."

Cornelius' face quivered as he took in Julius' double-edged sword. He appeared lost in an inner quandary. His hands unmade a large bed of Jerusalem Crosses. He pitched their husks, like an afterthought, into a tarred Moses' basket. He fingered a bougainvillea branch with thorns spiking and blossoms going pink to scarlet, like a mounting fever.

He looked at me sternly, "I expect that statue to be an exact likeness of me, Jew."

A wave of his hand signaled that our audience was terminated.

25

WINDY

A week later, Claudia and Jesus met downtown at Alexandria's library, home to over five hundred thousand scrolls and bound volumes. The massive marble structure took up a full city block.

Claudia was in the women's section of the library. She studied Antigone's lines, the heroine of Sophocles' tragedy. [48] In the men's study section of the library, Jesus poured over a copy of the Septuagint. Dust particles hung in a gash of light, too lazy to fall.

Jesus glanced at a dripping water clock beside the high window. It was time. He slipped away from his study carousel, moved across the aisle, and entered Claudia's carousel. He placed his hands on her shoulders. She raised her hands to cover his, crossing her heart left to right, the air between them charged with compressed heat. She unhooked from the heat, exhaled. She murmured her lines from the tragedy, like Jesus spoke Torah aloud while he was studying.

Jesus whispered in her ear, "I'm so proud of you. You waltz into town, look around, and find a venue for your calling as an actress. You bone up on the part, audition on stage for the lead role, and *ba-bing*! You get the role of understudy for Antigone!"

He pulled her to himself. "Leave this work for now. Time enough, later, for tragedies. Let's go on our picnic by the seaside."

They passed under a marble arch capped with two gilded cherubs, heads touching. The cherubs watched an endless stream of people coming and going, always amused at an in-joke they wouldn't share. The two friends exited through the high-ceilinged atrium.

Alexandria's wildness closed in on them. They waded into a throbbing mass of people, packed tight. The 200-foot-wide boulevard thrummed with the clatter and chatter of passers-by. Azure blue skies and my ocean breezes washed Jesus clean from worry. He stomped a shard of glass and kicked it to the gutter, remembering dinnertime with John and sharing that experience with Claudia—enriching her life with his story, as friends do for each other.

A cadre of soldiers stamped by in formation, headed toward their barracks. A block further, on the corner of the Jewish Quarter, working women, clothed from the waist down, beguiled Gentiles from one road and Jews from the other, from a second-story window—smiling, swaying, and saleable as boxed lust.

An elegant woman, adorned in black satin, stood in another window on the third floor. She had a leather-bound book in her hands. She nodded to Jesus, pointing with her left index finger to the roof above. She turned and left the window. *Odd,* Jesus thought, *but Father would make meaning of it later.*

The younger harlots' oiled, black hair whirled down, rippling 'round their necks, half hiding and then revealing their breasts. Claudia took one look their way and yanked Jesus' chin her way. She hugged him with the passion of a woman wilted enough, scarred enough, to be more than spun sugar.

She whispered in his ear, "I choose to love you, knowing I'll lose you one day soon. But for now, *everything* is the beginning."

A tanner with sidelocks and a smudged leather apron ducked out of his shop to take in the air. Inside the open window, a child recited Torah in a sweet, melodious voice. Jesus stopped in his tracks and caught snatches of a familiar psalm. The father, stirred by my Presence, called to his son, "Apollo, come quick. Messiah passes by!"

A perky child, four years old, ran through the open door, neck twisting left and right. He was so near-sighted, he tripped over an old entry rug to his home. The Persian rug, burnt sienna, and hydrangea blue smacked him in the forehead. Jesus knelt in the entryway and hugged the child.

He said, "Let me hear you recite scripture, child."

Apollo's bright, wet eyes blinked at Jesus and then at Claudia. He reached up to touch Jesus' face. He recited, letter-perfect, the whole of Psalm 22. When he finished, tears flashed from his eyes. "Why, Messiah, do they see you as a worm, not a man?"

The force of his simple question, one that previewed his upcoming execution, nearly collapsed Jesus. He struggled to take a deep breath, his own tears wetting *his* face and then dribbling onto Apollo's face. The child's vision cleared the moment Jesus' tears hit his eyes. I had taken Apollo's unspoken prayer and interpreted it to Father, who chose that moment to heal the child's near-sightedness and stigmatism.

Jesus tied Apollo's *vulnus* to his own tears. "Your son's vulnerability is precious, sir. He will understand, in time, why others treat me in this fashion." [49]

Jesus and Claudia hadn't walked more than a few yards, around a corner, into another crowded street, when they heard Apollo yelling, "Abba, I can see clearly now! I can see!"

The couple disappeared into the flood of people. A hundred yards on, they passed a quiet alley. Claudia pulled Jesus into the quiet of that small street. She hugged him close and said, "Your gentleness dizzies and then heals me too. I trip and fall, only to rise and see more clearly. I think thoughts with new clarity. Weird, or what?"

Jesus looked into her eyes, pools of deep blue. He lightly ran his fingers across her pox scars. Her face, sun and shadow, was a study in symmetry, complementary angles.

He said, "I love the gauntness of you, woman. Every experience you've stashed into your body, every age you've ever been during your twenty-eight years—all that still lives in you. I love your lack of embellishment, the natural arc of your eyebrows, the way your eyes peer into what I say and leave unsaid, what I do and leave undone."

She said, "Does this mean you've changed your mind, and we can finally marry?"

"Claudia, I wasn't done singing your praises. Plague, starvation, and exile lie in your eyes and the shade they gather. You no longer played the 'royalty' card. You've tempered your anger. You don't look down on others over that long, patrician nose."

Claudia said, "You're impossible, Jesus. How can I get mad at you for dodging my question when all you do is love me?" She looked at a tired food vendor who'd moved his lunch cart into the mouth of the alley. "Another thing I love about you. You don't lecture in fancy words; instead, you park your cart close enough, so ordinary people like Apollo and me can get food."

He pulled her head back to him with both hands, laying it sideways on his chest, twirling a few strands of her hair between his fingers. He remembered how Augustus's physician, Hippo, had used a few of these good, strong strands as sewing thread to stitch up slashes on his arm and leg.

The weight of years wrapped his heart to hers. "You wear your scars like badges of courage. They don't diminish you. They define you. They fill you with light and a fresh wind."

He looked at Me and breathed on her. He prayed, *fill her, Windy, fill her.* [50]

Claudia's face pinked. Her body, held tight against his, felt like she was purring. He pulled back a bit and looked. Her lips trembled. Her arm, stomach, and leg muscles hummed, vibrant. She moved the fingers on her right hand and tapped on Jesus' breastbone—tap-tap, tap-tap. He queried with a look.

"Getting my heart in sync with yours." She paused. Again, tap-tap, tap-tap.

She said, "Do you think we're looking more like each other the older we get? Thirteen, the age we met, seems far away and long ago, now that we're pushing thirty."

He nodded. "Hardly can tell us apart anymore. Our pox marks even look alike, particularly this one." He lifted her hair and tickled her neck. Their laughter had time and room enough in it for them to recognize the sort of people they wanted to be—people of body and spirit, intertwined— Light mingled with flesh.

He said, "We don't need to marry, Claudia, even if I was free to marry. You are closer than that. You carry my Spirit within you. I just asked Windy to fill you with her sweet presence, and she did. She'll take you by the hand and guide you through whatever is yet to come. He'll teach you the unforced rhythms of grace—walking and working with him." [51]

I whispered, *what you asked, you got. Claudia sees you as you truly are— light in spirit, meek in heart.* [52] *Your kindness is the centerpiece of what you will teach people about the art of living.*

They swayed in each other's arms to the sound of the traffic—ordinary twenty-somethings ducking into an alley for a cuddle and Spirit-filling. Jesus stooped to pick up his backpack. They slowed their stride to an amble along the Heptastadion causeway that connected the mainland to Pharos. Sailors up to thirty miles away could catch a wink from Pharos, this causeway lighthouse, and be guided home to safety.

The couple looked to see if they could pick out John from the line of workers carrying coal in bags on their back from a bulker moored in the southern harbor. John was proud of fueling light into height, 100 yards straight up, where fires burned at the top.

Jesus told Claudia, "You know what John told me the other night when we were cleaning our teeth, getting ready for sleep?"

Her eyebrows raised, quizzical.

"He said, 'I'm not a common grunt. My job is to fuel the only real Wonder of this World, You. I carry Light to the world.'"

Claudia laughed and said, "Most people with his job would say they broke their backs every day carrying heavy bags of lumpy coal up 300 steps. John makes Light of his work."

They idled to a saunter, slipping the knot of commerce. Raw coastline stretched its arms open before them on their left. Breakers clapped joyful hands against solemn rocks. A flight of swifts tipped crescent wings across the surface, skimming for supper. I stirred drifts of cloud into the shape of two hands clapping.

The couple passed a pasture full of sheep. The sweet fragrance of alfalfa mixed with manure and corn silk trodden underfoot. The musk filled their nostrils with alive sweetness in that slender, quickly passing blip of time, a day Father and I had given to them so they could collect quiet.

They passed a gate along the road that had a sign tacked to the crossbars, *Keep Clear.*

Claudia said, "leaving space for the gate to open and close is one thing. Getting my mind clear, another. I don't even know what that means a lot of the time."

Jesus made things clear. "One meaning of that word is 'a perfect transmitter of light.' But even tougher than *getting* clear is *keeping* clear. That requires sustained focus."

Empty marshlands on their right led along a downward track toward briny Lake Mareotis. They walked past womb-like mossy caves. Silvered mudflats shone in the ebbtide, water rushing backward in rivulets, fleeing estuary for the sea. Tangled thorn bushes and yellow furze thinned into the saltings.

The couple walked, holding hands, savoring the silence. The lack of press to talk tendered their spirits. Half an hour passed in this way, companionably, each savoring the other, both quieted by nature.

Noise of a loud crowd chittering. Jesus and Claudia looked over their shoulders. Thousands of pink flamingos eclipsed the sky. This cloud of pink coasted down on final approach from a southbound flyway. Sploosh! Formation landings in unison, birds gliding long, pulling back their heads, flaring gently, and landing with hardly a ripple.

These migrants settled into the marshlands, mostly standing on one leg with the other folded under-wing. They busied themselves, preening and gorging on sea snails—free caviar. Supple necks bent in graceful spirals, showing off a color palette of bright fuchsia, salmon, and coral.

The couple wound through the estuary descent till they arrived at lakeside. They sat on the banks of the lake on a small blanket, pulled food out of Jesus' backpack, and witnessed the wonder of a blue-green lake bordered with golden reeds turning porcelain pink.

26

SLOW

We woke up the next morning to a loud braying. Laz deserted his spooning assignment and strapped on his sandals. "Children, let's see what God has brought to us from over there at the edge of Water Drip Canyon."

We all had a wander, except for our elders, who sat by our morning fire fixing breakfast. There around a bend, trapped and frightened, was Hooka's yearling camel, Wisp. She must have bolted off-lead in the flash flood and outrun her mother, Smoke. A scrub oak had fallen on her.

We pitched in to free her. Michael pulled off his shoes and stood on Wisp's back, directing the sun to keep rising in its upward course. He carried on his usual business with a stick he'd made into a Moses' rod, giving orders left and right, "Hope, move that branch over there. Abba, tell Wisp to stand up!"

Eventually, we freed our new answer to unasked prayers. We walked Wisp back to our circle, where Samuel and Sheba waited for us. Laz kept his hand on Michael's foot, steadying him on Wisp's bare back.

Laz said, "Samuel, your ride to Egypt has arrived in the Wisp of time! And we make use of your old burro's saddle. Nothing's wasted."

Sheba's coal-black face, solemn, had ash and dust lodged in the folds of her skin.

I asked, "Do all elders sit so close to the fire?"

Samuel's smile lit up not just his face but his whole body. "In many ways, that's who an elder is. Life withers our bodies, encouraging us to let go and get lighter. That's how elders grow more spacious. The wise among the elders know they gotta get ready for homecoming; the rest of 'em pretend they're still young. Why, the other day, 'fore you all came along, we ran into a northbound group from Egypt. One woman in that group, I'd say, was maybe five hundred years old, but she had enough make-up on to fool folks into thinking she was just three hundred." He hee-hawed at his own black humor.

Sheba played straight woman to his color commentary. "Sam and I sit close to the flame and bear witness. True elders mostly hold souls. You know, being silent witnesses to the young isn't easy. Stayin' close enough, but not too close; reflecting but not interfering."

Sam got back on board. "Yep, that way, young ones like you can make glorious mistakes. Wouldn't want you to feel lonely when you fall or fail. How else will you figure out how to get old?"

Laz helped him up. I took both of Sheba's hands. We helped these feathery elders, made of ash and light, onto Wisp.

Some days passed. Our group journeyed south into sand and more sand. The Negev and Arabah deserts swallowed us, each in turn. We moved deeper down into thin desert air. My throat felt like a gunnysack. I felt like I was inhabiting in-betweens, all my me's scattering and belonging to no one, with the possible exception of God.

I grumbled, "Windy, the air on this planet is too thin to sustain life—borders are too porous. Can't rightly tell between important and trivial, imagination and memory. I snatch light from days behind and see future dread. Clearly, your fault."

Windy blew, inarticulate. Or maybe she was being eloquent, but in a language I didn't know. Where was Jesus when I needed him to walk alongside and interpret the Wind?

I looked at the young camel behind me and said aloud, "Wisp, I know exactly how you feel. Living out your name, I am." Wisp batted her long eyelashes at me, picked up her padded hoofs, and kept moving.

Abby, alongside, overheard my mumblings. She said, "Easy to lose your moorings in all this shifting sand."

I found nutrition inside her smile. My new sister and I were always next to each other, time-sharing Goodness. She walked next to me, or I walked next to her, while the other rode the mule. Either way, the same blowing sand whipped around us.

Abby's new leak seals worked with more than pee and poop. Since Sheba's arrival, her body hadn't let go of goodness, and I don't mean the mule. Jiggle her, and she'd spill smiles like sparkles. Not fair, definitely not fair, for one who felt empty like me.

We pulled into the outskirts of a crossroads, the Saharonim Outpost, complete with a caravanserai, with a tavern and whorehouse. Merchants overnighted in this desert inn, parking their camels all around the northern perimeter of the great box canyon named Makhtesh Ramon. We camped at a distance from the hubbub by a few other travelers who'd pulled into a ragged half-circle.

Nabataean camel trains loaded down with silks, wool, medicines, and spices headed from the east toward Gaza. Merchants from the west, having disembarked from ships in Gaza, headed east with bolts of French clothing, Spanish swords and longbows, gold-mounted jewels, and carved ivory gods from Ethiopia. More merchants back and forth from Damascus to Egypt added to the mix of goods and rough men looking to make their fortune.

Laz looked at the lights of the outpost. He racked out a gob of bloody spit that widened my eyes. Before I could inquire, he distracted me by saying, "Traders look forward to this spot——a wild swirl of life in the middle of empty blow and dead sand."

"Laz, what is this I see on the sand?" I toed the sand next to his wad of blood.

"Probably all the blowing sand. It'll go away."

"It's your thinking that's raspy. That could be a killing cough, Laz."

He pointed skyward, "Life and death, out of our hands. We live or die at God's pleasure."

I said, "I've just allowed myself to start loving you, and what do you do? Get sick. Stop being so spiritual. Mike and Hope need their abba. Let's find a doctor. Better, let's find Jesus."

Evening rambled toward us, straining light from the day like murky waters make sun feeble. We drew our people and animals in a semi-circle, up against the rugged face of the sandstone buttes. Sheba and Samuel once again sat in the center of our circle. We fed them kindling and chunks of dried camel poop for the campfire. They fed Michael and Hope the secrets of fire. Samuel took Michael by the hand, big hand over little, and practiced the use and care of strikers. Sheba showed Hope how to tender a flame.

An older man, adorned with sidelocks and a kippah, spoke to Laz, "I'm Daniel. I came from the central synagogue, Alexandria. We escaped two weeks ago—my family and me. I was warned in a dream to leave town, and quickly. We travel now back home to Jerusalem."

Laz said, "Escaped? What is this 'escaped'?"

"The genocide. You haven't heard? The emperor ordered Alexandria's Jewish quarter to be sealed off. Legionnaires became a living wall and sealed the border. No one knows exactly when the ax will fall, but soon—maybe already done. Orders from Rome, delivered by Consul Caligula."

So, I thought, *we run, thinking we escaped Herod, and what do we do? Crawl into the lion's jaws. Is there no safe place for Jews in the world? And what of Leah and Jesus? Fear juddered through me, drops of water on a red-hot skillet.*

27

WINDY

Cal, like Hitler or Stalin or Mao, didn't start out a genocidist. In fact, they didn't even know what that was. They were all cute baby boys, goo-goo-eying their mommies. And those little choo-choo trains didn't go off the tracks all at one time. It was one loose bolt at a time. And every baby nut took time to loosen. Each loose screw became one of the unseen, the nameless, the unraveled.

In the same way, Cal didn't sit down one day and say to himself, "Yep, I think I'll commit the unpardonable sin."

He didn't know what that was and wouldn't have cared if he did. Just so, little white lies. Natural toddler selfishness. Cute clutching of toys, "mine, mommy. All mine!" That's how it begins. A real chuckle.

And, truth told, Father and I aren't saddened by beginnings. We made all to be free in infancy. The seed of a mustard and the seed of a weed look almost identical. But when loved little ones aren't limited—ah now, that's when the weed roots, breaks homes apart, and my heart begins to grieve.

Love without limits; that's the ticket. Gets you on the milk train to death. The child dies to intimate relationships and faith in One bigger and better than herself. Even if that grown child returned to the place he began, he wouldn't recognize the homecoming. His focus is solely on self. [53] Indeed, she not only doesn't worship Father, but demands to be worshipped. And education doesn't help. The more educated the usurper, the wider and deeper the damage.

Genocide is a journey with many faces and colors—but always one terminal. Death.

28

CLAUDIA

The night before the opening performance of *Antigone*, Jesus and I celebrated my unexpected success with a night on the town. I'd gotten a message from the play's director this morning.

The note read, "Lead actress, sick. You star tomorrow. Shine."

We crowded a small table in a quiet restaurant a few doors down from a noisy bar where we'd ducked inside for a drink before dinner. The heavy backbeat pressed itself on us, with the added bonus that my ears weren't needed. Caligula and another guy danced together at the far side of the dance floor, both in drag, both drunk.

We left after a dance or two, walked down the street for our dinner reservation. Our outdoor table, partly covered by a grape arbor, was covered with a linen table cloth. A tubby, silver candlestick occupied center table. My glass of still water held the full moon, reflected. A string quartet strummed an ancient love song, old as Eden.

I looked at Jesus. "Are you moving on from Leah's death? Seeing her murderer back there, dancing free as a bird... that burned me."

He said, "I'm not moving on. Moving with, that's more like it. I have to use my outrage for good, or it burns me down. That's the point of grief. Make it good grief. Left alone, grief tarnishes into some dark, bitter shade. No. Take that energy and declare, enact, fix, do justice. Whatever Father calls you to do is sacred. For me, that means being Messiah. For you, becoming the actress he made you to be. Both are holy."

I forget whatever it was the waiter brought for appetizers, entrée, and dessert. All that was okay, but Jesus' words were the main course.

The next night, the 15,000-person theater was packed to overflowing. The curtain was about to come up. I had finished applying my make-up and was pouring over Antigone's lines, repeating them under my breath. My feet were both tapping; my heart, racing.

Quiet knock.

"Who's there?"

"Only me, Pontii."

"I don't have time now, Pontii. After the performance, please."

Pontii's voice floated through the door, disembodied, "Orders from Rome, delivered by Caligula, couple of days ago. I've been ordered to take Jesus at intermission; kill him quietly, dump his body in Lake Mareotis. And all of Alexandria's Jews are to be exterminated before dawn."

Creak of floorboards.

"You too, Claudia, have a death warrant on your neck. Your wire harness will fail tonight, and you'll be hung by the neck. I thought you'd like to know."

Silence.

"I'll be off since you don't want to talk to me."

My dressing room door flew open and I yanked Pontii inside.

29

WINDY

John wasn't with Jesus on opening night. He had blown out of town, held within my breath, heading east, under a sky lit by a full moon. He lifted his eyes, and watched while I swirled ragged clouds into a storm. Below his hilltop, the flooded Nile looked like a black snake basking under the watchful moon. A leather belt cinched his camel skin tight to his lean waist. [54] He sat solitary as an eagle on a cliff, brooding.

He said, *Windy, my life has flowed in and around rivers. The beginnings of what would become the Jordan River, at home, near Dan. The river of sewage under Rome's streets where I shoveled poop into the Cloaca Maximus. The River Aeternus that flowed along the Via Tiburtina between Rome and the Adriatic, that place where Jesus spoke his parable of the yeast to Tiberius. Now, swelling and shrinking, this Nile fills wells, irrigates Egypt's fields, and feeds the nations.*

A tiny river of tears flooded John's eyes. A vision came into focus in his inner mind's eye. He saw it clearly, felt his toes squiggle into the mud of Jordan's river banks. Saw a snow-white dove soaring, descending. These rivers of the world were nothing, absolutely nothing—compared to the Messiah. This Jesus, water of life itself, would be a River to all the peoples of this world. His next meeting with this River would be in a muddy brown trickle, the Jordan. There he would baptize My River with a few drops of water, down and up again.

John moved down the hill toward the crossing station. At that dock, a ferry would take him across the Nile. He skipped a rock from the shore out into the river.

Splash to his right. A log rolled over, under the lambent moonlight, snapped its jaws, and disappeared back into the black water. John praised Father, who had made all so transient—that alligator, a skipping stone, the approaching storm, and even himself.

John's wind-blown beard bent east toward home. Fat drops of cool rain spattered his uplifted face. On the horizon, lightning crackled. John unleashed himself, moved down the bank toward his next border crossing. He was determined. Nothing would stop him from crossing over the Sinai, Negev, and Arabah deserts. He would finish what we had begun, preparing the ground for my River to trickle and grow into a torrent, flooding Israel first, and then the world.

Jesus and Julius arrived early for the play. They'd been seated in a designated box seat, courtesy of the lead actress on sick leave. The Prefect's box was immediately to the left of this box seat. Both boxes had a direct view of the stage.

Cornelius and Caligula occupied the Royal's box. Both slugged down expensive wine from golden goblets. Cornelius stood and waved to the many below him, winking, laughing, soaking up their smiles. Caligula squinted long and hard at the guest in the next box. His smooth-shaven, fleshy face creased into something truly unpleasant. He snatched a torch off the wall and wove his way a few steps to the railing that separated the box seats. He lifted his drink and doused the wall torch behind Jesus' chair.

He held his torch out to Jesus. "Need a light?" When Jesus reached for the torch, he yanked it back. Contempt gave teeth to insult. "Your light is overdue for dimming, Jew boy."

Cal huffed the few steps back to Cornelius. He heaved another razored comment over the railing. "Ready, really ready, to take in an excellent tragedy tonight?" Jesus smiled sadly at this lost man and gently shook his head.

He turned his attention to the orchestra pit. The musicians were tuning themselves to the B-flat note that the lead violinist had struck. Jesus felt a whole orchestra of feelings, all discordant, all at once, like those players below him. After a while, the sounds converged, within and without, then grew quiet. The Greek Chorus, all dressed in black, popped up from below the orchestra pit. Their white face paint and startled, painted-on eyes put Jesus in mind of circus mimes.

The Chorus followed a slow backbeat, gathering volume and rhythm, like a reaper moving through a field ripe for harvest. The 20-voice troupe underlined truths embedded in the play at the end of each act. But for this moment, as a preview, the group slam-dance-chanted, in rhythm, a pointy warning:

Antigone,
skip the agony;
"Don't wait. Don't tempt Fate.
Loose the noose, vamoose.

This sophisticated crowd had already seen this 450-year-old play—some, many times. A ripple of alarm skittered across even such a group as this. No Greek Chorus had ever opened the play in this way. Why mess with success? The plot was simple, uncomplicated and everyone knew what would happen—tradition would squash the divine, like a boulder crushes a butterfly—Antigone, buried alive by order of King Creon. In the finale, the king would change his mind and extend mercy—but when he opened the sepulcher, Antigone had hanged herself. Close curtain, *fini.*

Claudia had warned Jesus that this performance was convincing. The wire, buried in her corset and hung from a rafter, would catch her. She had practiced that scene over and over. Her neck would *look* broken, twisted sharply to the right—but that was part of the play. Jesus' nerves jangled anyway—Caligula's threats and the Chorus' warnings had undone him.

The door to the solitary box seat on their right side opened. A veiled woman breezed into the box. She wore a low-cut, form-fitting, silk gown. The color was magenta, smoldering into scarlet. She slid into the velveted wingchair on the other side of the metal railing. A long, braided-silver necklace dangled between her breasts. Marquise-cut diamonds twined along the chain with blood-red rubies, each the size of a small pebble. The woman carried a leather-bound copy of the Septuagint in her right hand.

Jesus took in the wealth, form, and grace with which she moved—the splendor of a cut woman, compressed, and chiseled, gaunt. But what mostly caught his attention? Her Greek copy of the scriptures, so rare, so beautiful. He'd seen her and her book before. He was sure of it, but couldn't place her memory.

Her velveted chair seemed to swallow her and, in turn, was swallowed by deep shade. What he could see of her gown and necklace, from the neck down, sparkled in the solitary torchlight.

He leaned forward in his chair and turned his head to the right. She had removed her veil. Black, glossy hair, parted down the middle, framed a hauntingly beautiful face, narrow and pale.

Sound of a ticking, clicking flickering. As one, both Jesus and the woman looked up to the light of her single torch. A monarch moth had found entry to the theatre, entry to this woman's box seat. The moth flung herself repeatedly at the glass flume around the lit torch—*eager to self-immolate.*

The woman swiveled, reached up her hands, caught and cupped the moth between her palms. She stood, moth in hand, and took a step closer to the railing, closer to Son.

Fragrance of orange honeysuckle wafted in his nostrils.

Her eyes moved to the floor. His eyes followed hers. A key lay on the floor by his foot.

Puffs of sound whispered from her mouth into the air, like a tragedy seeping into his ears. "You will be dead within the hour without my help. And I will be dead within the day, without your help." Jesus tried to sort who she was and when he'd met her. Her face and the Book dangled loose, like a rope hanging in his head.

Her voice, sharp as a stabbing sica, "When the curtain rises, and all eyes are on stage, leave quietly. Number seven, Jewry Row. Side door. Do not fail me... or you." She retreated into the shadows. Jesus watched as she released her moth into the darkened hallway.

30

JESUS

The curtain rose. Claudia stepped into the music as if into a cool stream on a hot day. Julius and I slipped out of our box seat at that moment. We made our way onto the street under overhangs through thick darkness. The moon was caked by thick clouds, sky's light simmered in Windy's stewpot. A reduction of night.

The corner house at the edge of the Jewish Quarter had the numeral "7" nailed over the lintel. The number was painted scarlet, and its building towered three stories over us. I ran my fingers over the varnished cedar. A fine piece of wood with a Lebanon imprint—thick, heavy, flammable. I slipped the woman's key into the lock. The door slid open silently on oiled hinges.

A woman with bright red hair motioned for us to enter. She shut the door quietly and slid shut the bolt. Motioned for us to follow. We climbed three stories up a circular marble stairwell wall, lit with silver candelabras. At the second level, a door to a large receiving room had been left open. A lick of prostitutes lounged, painting each other's toes. Dim light reflected oiled legs beneath slitted lingerie. The room and its occupants conveyed heat but not warmth.

I moved past this lure in a heartbeat and two steps. Julius lingered. I pulled him after me up the steps, past muraled stories of desire and tragedy. We exited onto the roof.

The woman from the theatre sat in a chaise lounge with her back against the wall. She was calm, casual—like she had been created for this moment. She overlooked the city streets below, studying the storm marching directly at us across the waters—also watching a century of legionnaires heading our way.

This woman clicked the rubies on her necklace against the diamonds. She said, "Rubies, diamonds, and bodies bumping in the night. They count for nothing. Before this is over, we'll all be stripped naked, down to our essence."

I said, "I've seen you before tonight. Where?"

"I'm Magdala. I saw you on the street a few weeks ago when you walked by with Claudia. I caught your eye, pointed up. Remember?"

Memory's tumblers clicked into place. I nodded.

She said, "Being a madame for a whorehouse has its perks. Pillow-talk secrets trickle up to me. We don't have much time." She gestured to the streets below.

Julius raised an eyebrow.

She elaborated. "Those soldiers down there? They have been ordered to surround us, sealing the Jewish Quarter. Other soldiers, even now, knock on doors of any registered Jew elsewhere in the city. When occupants answer, they'll be run-through with swords or their throats cut without warning by troops loyal to Caligula. Their bodies will be dumped in covered carts and brought into the Jewish Quarter. Then, just before dawn, "accidental" fires will start. The ghetto and all registered Jews in Alexandria, dead or alive, will burn."

She gazed at me through steady eyes, "This includes me, you, and a few others such as yourself, Julius—though you be Roman."

I answered her not a word.

"You're a special case, Jesus, for some reason. You were to be taken at intermission during the play after you visited Claudia backstage. The Consul's given orders for his henchmen to garrot you with razor wire, then cut you in pieces—scattered in synagogues all over Egypt, an arm here, a hand or foot there."

She raised an eyebrow, "Obviously, Caligula harbors special feelings for you."

I remembered Scodra castle. Cal watching Polyphemus' healing before blinding himself with unbelief. Tiberius refusing Cal's influence in favor of mine on Rhodes. Leah obeying my voice, not his. God's favor resting on me, and not him.

Windy's voice came back to me. *You will feel others' envy and be torn by it.*

I caught up with Magdala. She'd been speaking. "...and Claudia's wire harness will fail at play's end. She will die in front of 15,000 patrons—because of her relationship with you. You, Julius, are to be simply killed without all the fanfare, a simple cut-throat. My fate, as well."

My hands shook, my pulse pounded.

She continued, "That's the plan. Orders of the Prefect, from the Consul, from the Emperor, supposedly. I have my doubts, given what I've heard from three different sources."

Julius asked, "What do you hear?"

"Caligula's aspirations are unbounded. 'Little Boots' wants nothing less than the Emperorship. Anyone who gets in his way is disposable. He plans to kill Cornelius, blaming him for the genocide. If Tiberius fails to appreciate his emperesque qualities, or fails to appoint him as successor, or fails to die soon enough, he'll kill him as well. All in all, a person terrified and terrifying—bad seed married to unbridled envy, unleashed ambition."

I knelt on this whorehouse roof, stretching hands over my head on the floor toward Jerusalem. I called out to Father for him to set the world right, to do what was best. The other two joined me, lying flat, facing the same direction. We prayed a long time. As I recited Psalm one hundred nineteen, Magdala joined me, word for word, speaking in Greek. Julius maintained a respectful silence.

Finally, after reciting the book of Lamentations, other psalms of praise, imprecatory psalms calling for Father to exact vengeance, I murmured aloud, "Keep us safe from ourselves and the Devil. You're in charge, Father. You can do anything you want. You're ablaze in beauty. Yes, yes, yes." [55]

Mail-coated fist rapping against on wood—hard, repeated. Again, insistent thudding on the same door we had entered. Rain began to spatter—the storm's leading edge in what was now the early dawn.

Caligula's voice.

He cried out in a shrill, high-pitched voice, "Open up, Madame Magdala. I know you have Jesus in there. Open the door, or we knock it down."

Magdala's hands shook.

Cornelius' stentorian tones, "Orders of the Prefect, Madame. Forthwith, comply."

Magdala moved Julius and me to the back wall. Ropes hung behind a stack chimney on that wall into an alleyway that led onto the main thoroughfare. Advantages of a corner unit.

She said, "I messaged Claudia to swap another actress into her role for the last half of the play. This actress will act out a less dramatic scene where Antigone doesn't fall before the audience but is found dead in her tomb. Claudia will meet you in the burnt-orange and white-chalk culvert outside the Eastern Gate, the culvert below the lone acacia tree where the wind always blows."

Julius nodded, "I know the place."

Magdala's face was bittersweet. "Get you gone. I'll face the music— better me than you, my Messiah." Her look, unintended, was nonetheless a stab in my side. She, a stranger, sacrificed herself for us.

Windy whispered, *for such a time as this she has been called into the Kingdom.*

Gratitude flashed between Magdala and me—she, for who had been revealed to her; me, for her courage to do the right thing.

I threw a leg over the wall and rappelled down. In my descent, I looked briefly over my shoulder to gauge my landing. In my sideways glance, I caught sight of a flotilla of Roman warships now anchored in the double harbor. They hadn't been there yesterday.

They must have arrived in the night while we prayed. The lead ship reminded me of Tiberius' quinquereme, *Augustia II*, the replacement warship his mother had commissioned for him.

My feet hit the ground running. But not to the Eastern Gate.

I told Julius, "Go find Claudia. Take her to the harbor. I'll meet you there, but I need to visit with Caligula first."

31

WINDY

Caligula stood with his back to the wall alongside the brothel's side door. He waited, impatient, jiggling up and down with excitement. When would Jesus' head pop out? He'd strapped an improvised garrote of razor-wire around both hands—a rough cloth to protect his hands, enough space for the wire to slip over a head, catch a throat.

Cal motioned impatiently to Cornelius. The Prefect pounded the door again at Caligula's insistence. A dozen or so of the Consul's guards surrounded both Cornelius and Caligula.

Sound of feet shush-shushing across the floor. Bolt sliding open. Door opening.

Magdala calmly walked out, head held high—her only garment, the ruby-diamond necklace and the string of pearls I'd shaped as vertebrae down the middle of her back.

She flicked her gaze from Prefect to Consul, saw the stunned look in their eyes and noticed what was in Caligula's hands. "You might want to use my necklace, Consul, since it's quite strong and already in place. That wire might cut your hands."

The emperor aspirant was befuddled. He eyed her with the intensity of a stalker sniffing out his prey. The rising sun's first early rays caught the necklace made of fire and ice. A cut ruby's facet inhaled a sunray and exploded into brilliance, directly into Cal's fragile eyes. He jerked his right hand up to shield his eyes and cut his left hand to the bone with the razor wire.

Blood squirted over his grey tunic. He raised his eyes from torn hands in time to see Jesus coming around the corner from the alleyway. The sun shone from behind him and within him, giving the impression that he was either ablaze or armored in light.

The Lit Man said, "Caligula, you wanted to see me?"

This was too much for Cal. His blood pressure shot up, detaching his retinal wall. Flashers ricocheted along his optic nerve, spreading in a nanosecond to his temporal lobes, unleashing an electrical firestorm. He dropped prostrate, his grand mal seizure twisting and yanking his arms spasmodically, like a child caught in his father's clothing. He sliced his wrists and hands without mercy. He ground his teeth, taking his tongue for breakfast. Swallowed it.

The Prefect was aghast at this falling-down sickness. His stomach rumbled, flaming-red goiter pulsed, and eyes bugged out more than usual. Froggie stared first at the naked woman, then at the glowing man, and now at the writhing man. *What to do?*

Cal's face blued. He thrashed on his back, choking to death, blood spurting from hands and wrists. Tangled razor-wire wrapped him more and more tightly. Arterial blood sprayed a fine shower over his open mouth, filling the space his tongue had once occupied. His platinum toupee had changed colors. He was now a redhead. Cal's bloody nature had matured into full blossom.

Jesus' true nature revealed itself as well. He strode over to Caligula, stripping down to his loincloth. He produced a knife from his side pouch, cutting his tunic into swaddling strips.

Sound of cavalry. Tiberius cantered down the street on his white steed, surrounded by loyalist Imperial Guards. His surprise visit to Alexandria was an administrative stopover on his way back to Rhodes, as well as a booty call for Cal and other lovers. An adjutant pointed out the gathered crowd in front of the Jewish Quarter. Tiberius re-directed his troops. *Let's see what's going on here.*

When he arrived, Jesus had turned Cal's head on its side. He'd stuck his sandal strap into Cal's mouth, keeping his seized jaws open far enough for his forefinger to catch and release Cal's tongue from his throat.

Once his cork was popped, Cal decanted himself. Vomit spewed straight up and then down into his open mouth. Jesus again turned Cal on his side, containing in his own body the violence of the man beside him. He bound Cal's spurting bleeders with strips of his own tunic.

Jesus hadn't yet seen Tiberius and had avoided looking further at Magdala. Over his shoulder he said, "Magdala, could you perhaps first find a dress and then help me unwind this razor wire? We don't want the Consul to further injure himself."

Tiberius took all this in and opened his mouth to speak. As he opened his mouth, he sniffed the wind. Flames shot skywards from several houses in the Quarter.

He shouted, "Fire! Call the *Vigiles Urbani!* The city's on fire!"

Cornelius delegated a messenger. The man galloped off. The Prefect approached and pulled a scroll from his pocket. He held it up to his boss. His hand trembled like a leaf in a strong wind. "My Emperor, the Consul personally delivered your sealed orders to me. You *did* write these orders to kill all the Jews and burn the Jewish Quarter, right?"

Tiberius grabbed the scroll and examined it: the script, signature, broken seal. His hard stare refocused on both Cal and Cornelius. He leaned down in his saddle and enunciated carefully, "Have you also lost your mind? Cal obviously lost his, forging my signature as he did here." He tore the scroll in pieces. I caught the shreds in my wind, lifted them in a swirl, and carried them away.

Tiberius looked behind Cornelius at the flames. "Froggie. I smell the smoke of treason."

Cornelius groveled, not daring eye contact. "I was obedient to *your* orders, delivered by *your* appointed Consul, my Emperor."

Tiberius said, icily, "Orders such as this need confirmation, not impulse. Jews have made this city what it is! Protect them. Delegate your troops, every one of them, to assist *Vigiles* in putting out the fires. If you can't save the Quarter and its occupants, your life will be required of you today, fool!"

Cornelius turned to his adjutant, "Brutus, see to it. Put out the fires. Immediately!" Brutus hurried off. Cornelius stood next to Pontii, dawdled.

The emperor surveyed the scene. He noted the bloody strips binding Cal's limbs, eyed the pooled vomit, and Jesus sitting in the midst of Cal's mess. He pursed his lips in a moue of distaste.

He queried Jesus, "What did you do to my lover?"

Jesus looked up at his friend. "We meet again, Sire. I was assisting Cal in restraining his appetites. He was ravenous for Jewish flesh and blood."

Tiberius asked, "Cal the Cannibal?"

"Well, yes, my emperor. He ended up drinking his blood after he'd feasted on his tongue. Sadly, Sire, he had no hunger for true food and drink. He was blind to me, life's main course."

Claudia's voice suddenly rang out from behind the pair, "Uncle Tibbie! Jesus is waxing metaphoric once again. But his timing is terrible. My theatre coaches say, 'Timing is everything!'"

Tiberius turned and laughed with delight at hearing, and now seeing, his niece. She stood next to Julius. The emperor climbed off his high horse, crossed the distance to his niece in three long steps, and swooped her up in his arms. He whispered in her ear, "Please remind me how to read this mystic. As soon as he starts to speak, my mind goes on strike."

Claudia smiled, demure. "You need no reminders, Uncle. You remember everything perfectly—shreds of gossip, dates, a catalogue of times people have rolled their eyes in your presence. You even remember Cal's birthday when he doesn't. The man specializes in unconsciousness."

Claudia went on, "And please don't let Jesus confuse you, Uncle. Truth and light are his favorite themes. His words appear light as air, but many choke on the truth of such thick fare. His words either clarify or confuse, depending on how bad you want to understand."

Tiberius flashed a thin smile toward Jesus. "You've stretched my mind, God-man. I doubt it will *ever* recover its original shape."

He put finger to mouth. "Your light even pierces amber walls and cobwebbed halls where black widows stalk."

Jesus looked up from Caligula's spent torso, remembering exactly what the emperor had referenced. A glint of understanding passed between them. [56]

Cornelius had not yet run off to administer the *Vigiles*. He decided to risk an offering. "My liege lord, Emperor of the Known World, I've discovered that minds are like head wounds. If one is too open-minded, his brains fall out."

Cornelius's titter cascaded into a symphony of snorts. He cast a glance at Tiberius, hoping to suck up praise. Finding none, he gabbled on. "I've narrowed my mental focus, Sire, to beam, like our great Alexandria Lighthouse, on only one thing—honoring the Empire and her leader! I absolutely stay focused, *absolutely*." He bowed prettily, arms extended, palms up.

Jesus doodled Latin letters in the sand around the circle of Cal's bloody vomit, "Honor only Father."

Julius looked over Jesus' shoulder at his doodling. "It seems like only yesterday, Prefect, when you shunned Honor and Betrayal, choosing Love instead. I suspect a void in your chest where most store their Honor."

Cornelius favored Claudia and Julius with a squinty glare. Claudia turned her eyes upon Jesus. Son sat in the sand, drizzling it over his doodling. She said, "Perhaps we would all do well to attend droppings on honor from the greatest mind of our day—before they vanish."

She suddenly remembered an earlier conversation with the Prefect. She said, "Or is your twice life-size idol of Cupid, adorned with your face in the library's entry hall, where you planned to house your honor?"

Cornelius covered his shame quick as loosed mercury. He knelt and composed his face into a facsimile of rapture. Someone keen indeed to scoop up Jesus-droppings.

Tiberius said, "*Froggie*, did you forget my order to attend the *Vigiles?*" Cornelius sucked in a breath of air, hurried off, patting his chest. Perhaps honor had arrived, unannounced.

Claudia watched him go, knelt next to Jesus, and rubbed his back. "Apart from this confusion, what a lovely surprise! Here you are in Alexandria. Just in time to save your city from fire and mayhem."

"Indeed, Niece. May I assist you two in some other way?"

Jesus roused, looked up, and said, "Perhaps you could arrange my exit from Egypt, in due time? I'd like to return home through the desert, as I did when I was a child. The desert's quiet kills clamor, heightens Father's voice. I long to be cradled in His emptiness."

Claudia weighed in, "Jesus, could *we* wait?" She dropped to one knee, fetchingly. "*Antigone's* current run is finished after a half-dozen weekend nights."

Jesus smiled his wordless 'yes.'

She continued, "I'd love to make it through a whole performance, Uncle Tibbie, without someone trying to kill me. Magdala, there in the shadows, warned me that Cal had arranged for my wire harness to "accidentally" fail at the play's climax. Antigone's death was to become my own, real rather than staged, in front of 15,000 patrons last night."

Tiberius said, "Life and death hinge on moments such as these, times when the assassin's dagger is caught by another's shield, when the poison in the drink is seen by a servant girl, when the angel steps between you and the pride of lions. Such moments have been known to visit earthlings." [57]

Jesus looked up, caught in the emperor's net of memory. Remembering moments. Moments how the emperor's life had been saved. Moments on Father's wheel that had turned him into who he was and would yet become.

"Cal hates me because I love Jesus, Uncle. His envy is sturdy, denies grief or sorrow. Instead, his envy has turned murderous. He's graduated from killing mere goodwill and trust to killing people. He's become a focused beam of hatred, rippling from Jesus to anyone who bears resemblance to him—by birth or faith."

Tiberius paused, raked his eyes over Cal. "I've also been almost smothered by his envy."

In this pregnant moment amongst the world's most potent power players, Jesus still sat in the sand: loving the past emperor's granddaughter, respecting the current emperor, and tending the future one— giving them all yet one more chance to choose another life.

32

SLOW

We arrived at Avdat, a booming trading post on the Incense Route. On the first day, we wandered the lower market, below the jutting hill and fortress. Merchants here trafficked in costly spice, silk, medicines, and perfumes. One tent carried crossbows from Spain; another, gold jewelry from India; a third, wine and olive oil from further north in Palestine. Others specialized in animal parts as aphrodisiacs—beaks, hides, hooves, hair, fins, feathers, antlers, bladders, nostrils, and poo chutes. We smelled that merchant from the other end of the market. Once we'd arrived at his stall, all we could see was a buzzing blanket of flies. The bored vendor waved his feather fan, and a donkey's penis came into view from under the mass of flies.

The walled fortress of Avdat sat high on a hill to the left of our southbound path. We camped at its foot. Once night fell, shadowed figures crawled around the hilltop, heading toward a central building. Wild, pulsing music poured down the hill.

We had a family conference around the oasis campfire that night, including northbound Daniel and his group. A full bushel of beards, bapping up and down, spouted plans with all the substance of moonlight on cooling sand.

All my-me's absented that assembly to play hide 'n seek with my children. I'd fingered into the cliffside behind a wiry ball of tumbleweed, dragging it behind me to cover my tracks. Cutter, Fragile, Bruise, and my grown-up me all hid under an overhang. Harlot was not to be found, but Escape quivered with excitement. We were all quiet, knees drawn to chest—stray tumbleweeds inside a rock.

Michael must have seen my toes sticking out, lit by the full summer moon. He sat right on my toes and yelled for his sister, "Hope! I'm feeling warm. Mama might be close."

He tickled the bottom of my bare foot. I shoved the weed aside, found his ribs, and tickled him back. We rolled in moonlit sand, laughing.

Michael finished a rollover and sat on my stomach next to Hope, who'd found us both. His question stumped me, "Is Jesus real?" He'd never seen Jesus, but he'd heard his name a lot. I could see his little mind working overtime, trying to figure what was real and not real. He grabbed my toe and said, "This is real, huh, mommy? And me, I'm an archangel—real too, along with Hope. Huh?"

I nodded, halfway, not sure how to handle the archangel part.

Mike kept going, "Jesus doesn't *feel* real. He's like the Emperor or Drusilla or the Devil—stuff you make up to get me to be a good boy, yeah?"

I said, "You're such a smart boy. Your abba and I do make up some stuff to get you to obey. But, Jesus? He's real—a friend of mine. He's coming back. He'll get such joy hugging you like I do."

His face searched mine in this mommy inquisition by moonlight. Hope joined in, "I get sad thinking about all the other lives I won't live. They're not real. Like being a princess or fairy or the King of Siam. And I won't ever live on a snowy mountain or the moon or by a swamp's edge. It makes me want to cry sometimes, all the people and places that aren't me or aren't real. Why is that?"

"You're telling your own story by living it," I said. "It's the story God wrapped your body around and said, "Live this one out.""

She said, "I think it was the only story left in his story house. All the good ones were gone."

I had no idea what to say, so I just held on. We three leaned against cooling rock, me in the middle and one child in either arm. We cuddled in the night air that was thick as warm cream, living out the ordinary stories that were our lives.

Hope slept and turned, nestling. In her sleep, she left a trail of snot on my arm, like a snail's trail. I soothed her dark hair back, wiped her nose with my sleeve. I felt the rock behind me, children beside me, my feet nestled into the sand. I pinched my arm to make sure I was real. Decided my walls were strong enough to hold my story inside me.

After I'd carried the children inside the tent and tucked them in, I rejoined the grown-ups around the campfire. They were still spouting doom and gloom. My head was dropping to my chest when two white owls swooped out of the night and landed on Sheba's outstretched arms. Neither raptor drew blood. Instead, they hopped sideways to sit on Sheba's hands.

Sheba had been silent. Now she didn't hesitate, "How in the world can faith grow if what's tidy arrives? God means us to journey with *Him*—not clarity. When mystery weights both hands, or two truths flap off in opposite directions, you're probably on the right trail."

The white owls, as if on cue, took off in opposite directions. Sheba fixed her blind eyes on Laz, me, and Abby. "Where I come from, elders ground themselves in visions and dreams. Inside visions are more real, say, than owl visitations. Here, elders like me are called crazy."

I said, "So were the owls real?"

She smiled, "There's always enough darkness for those not yet ready to see. I think now would be a good time for you to see what's real on that hilltop up there." She motioned with her head toward Avdat. "Samuel and I will babysit while you listen to the sound of that music. No streams to ford, one mountain to climb, and an old friend to be found."

Laz seemed eager. I was not.

I said, "Sure my dreams won't be nightmares?"

Abby's one milky eye rolled into place, and she grinned. "You won't find out if you stay right where you are. Let's go."

Laz took one veiled sister on his left arm; the other, on his right. We walked up a zig-zag trail, past a well, bathhouse, and a burial chamber. We wound past outlying buildings, white limestone arches glinting in the moonlight. I touched a few, so cool, so solid, real.

Harlot moved from background to foreground in my awareness. She said, *you're gonna need my eyes to see what's real in this dive. Keep the kids safe. Let me lead.*

33

WINDY

Four burly guys guarded the compound's gates. Their faces all shared a look of obstinance, anger's bastard child. They looked the trio up and down, particularly the women.

The head guard frisked Laz and then said, "No pimping here. All whores, outside. Weapons, here—with us. You'll get 'em back when you leave."

A table full of weaponry set behind them—daggers, *sicas*, swords, shields, armor—even a tube with blow darts beside it. Violence-on-demand.

While they frisked Laz, Harlot took the time to kneel next to a kindle of kittens playing with a ball of colored yarn. While on one knee, she adjusted each stiletto, one strapped to either of Slow's thighs.

Laz and the two sisters moved into the walled compound. A multi-room Bedouin tent, on the far side, had been constructed of animal skins supported by cut saplings. A square cut in the tent was covered with strips of purple-dyed camel hide, hung from a brass rod. These hanging strips pulsed with blown smoke, outbound, eager to escape noise so loud it throbbed like a hurt thumb. After the void of the desert, the noise beat Slow like a kettle drum.

She thought, *this is the kind of music lunatics hear just before they whack the heads off babies and drop 'em over a neighbor's fence.*

Laz chose a table well away from the dance floor. The trio reclined on Persian carpets. A waiter brought fruit drinks spiked with something that set their throats on fire.

Harlot counseled Slow. *This is the Arabah's big whoop. Tap your toes to the music, girl. Enjoy not-desert. This is the dessert between main courses of nothing.*

Dancing, laughing men in two circles joined arms and swirled, Sufi style. Musicians shaped notes gathered from scattered places around the world. Drunk, high men—Nabataeans, Assyrians, Egyptians, Edomites, and Sodomites danced first one way, then the other, in their circles. A row of darker, shadowed figures at the bar leaned heavily into their drinks and pipes, backs to my travelers.

Smoke wrapped Slow like a shroud. Hairs along her neck rose. She leaned over to Laz, who looked halfway present, head bobbing. She said, "Let's go. This joint makes me beyond nervous."

That was when a man approached Laz from behind. His smooth-shaven smile creased his jowls into something between unpleasant and scary. He was swathed in flowing clothes—turban, broad pants, kirtle. He made nice with Laz, voice honeyed, lilting. Laz rested his head on his closed fist, nodding. He didn't see the other guy. The one holding his dagger by the blade, hand wrapped in cloth. The one who smacked the jeweled haft downwards—hard, precise. One sharp whack to the back of Laz's skull. That's all it took.

Laz was out like a blown candle, and the man dragged him toward a back room. The sisters had no time to cry for help. Hands the size of hams swooped over their mouths, choked screams into whispers. They flew backward like black ravens, dragged into the same back room where Laz had been taken, a place where men did back-room things.

Slow wasn't going to take this lying down. She reached for her right thigh. Her razor missed the man's throat but caught his chest, a superficial slash. He grabbed her arm at the end of its swing, pinned her on a spread alpaca rug, side by side with Abby. His chest squirted blood over her. He worked to free himself from his loincloth, as did the man next to him, the one straddling Abby. The third man who'd robbed Laz waited his turn.

Slow's desperate prayer for deliverance arrived for my disposition. I sent Shade into the room—a silent angel of death. Glints of metal flashed in the torchlight—once, twice, three times. Blinding speed, not size, joined force with precision.

Slow's intended rapist reached both hands for his newly cut-throat, thinking he could undo what had been done. His friend's body also protested being cancelled.

Rabbus shoved both men off Slow and Abby, handed Slow her razor. He threw unconscious Laz over his shoulder and muttered, "Time to leave."

That summed things up. They slid into the night through a side door. Two rugged Bedouins followed them.

Slow asked, "Where's Leah?"

Rabbus ignored her and said to his companions, "Quick now, time to move."

Whoever invented the phrase, 'man of few words' had him in mind. His strength didn't scream, "look at me!" His valor didn't shine. But still, getting information out of him was like talking to a porcupine—a patch of sharp points but hard to get close to.

The wind had picked up while they were inside. Dense, blowing sand surrounded them. Slow thought, *here we are, cocooned in the kind of grit that makes backbone out of mush. Either that or you choke on it.*

Parts of her, Escape and Fragile, believed the better part of what Slow was thinking. Slow trailed her child parts behind her like a pack of spilled breadcrumbs. And not far behind them was a pack of hard men who'd discovered their buddies' bodies—a pack of wolves howling after fresh meat and closing quick.

Slow swooped her forefinger into each nostril and used the grit to grind blood off her face. Harlot looked back at her from a mirror I'd popped in her hand. Slow saw a frightened face staring back at her. Shame, gagged, mirror-bombed her image. I'd stoppered Shame's lethal mouth to keep Slow from crumbling under her attack.

Harlot muttered aloud, "Slow, you do know you are *all* of us—plus that pack of wolves who are after us."

Slow didn't have time to deal with *any* of her-selves and said as much. She turned her focus to the people around her—Rabbus helping Sheba and Sam onto Wisp. Sheba holding Ahud. Hope and Mike holding each other on top of Goodness. Laz, still unconscious, strapped securely to another mule beside her.

Rabbus motioned to that mule. "I liberated Blown from one of those two in the tent."

Slow turned to Sheba. "Did you know what would happen up there?"

Sheba said, "I knew whatever happened would be part of your schooling—night-walking with the Spirit."

Sam said to Rabbus, "We're heading south and west, aiming for Alexandria. Folks here say Jesus is there. You coming too?"

Rabbus fingered the edge of his dagger. He said, "Just might do that. I landed in Gaza, off a ship from Rhodes. Headed down the Incense Route. I wanted to stay lost and drunk. Succeeded for a good, long while. Made some friends in the desert who rescued me from myself."

He stared hard at Slow. "You remember that first journey south from Naz, the one we started at three in the morning with Jesus? That time you wuz beat up, and Laz held *you* on a mule. Now you get to do that for him."

Slow smiled at the irony of their situation. It was true. They'd covered a lot of bad road together. Rabbus turned from her into the desert's blow and led them south from Avdat, deeper under cover of sand. Laz roused. Slow helped him up from his slump.

He said, "What happened? Where are we?"

She yelled in his ear over the howl of the sandstorm, "Rabbus showed up with some Bedouins. Rescued you from being killed and Abby and me from getting raped. We're moving away from Avdat toward who knows where."

Laz coughed up a bloody blob, slumped forward on Blown once again. Slow walked alongside, hand on his head. If she lost touch, for even a minute, he might disappear in the sandstorm.

Toward noon, the wind lulled. Air cleared. An oasis appeared a mile or so ahead of them, off to their right. Once they'd arrived, they staked their burrows and Wisp under a few date palm trees. The two sisters sat together again at another gurgling oasis spring, bottoms buried in shallow water, and neither of them leaking. A stand of blooming cacti was off to their right.

Abby said, "Isn't the light extraordinary? Those two, soaring red-tail hawks circling in the thermals? Ahh, they're so crisp, diamond-bright. And the canary yellow of that cactus blossom. It's like the color could jump off the blossom and root in my eyes—impossibly vivid."

Slow replied, "Waxing poetic, are we?"

Sister smiled. "Seriously, Slow, we needed the whirling dust. We needed it, I tell you, for us to get God's big reveal." She whispered her finger up and down Slow's forearm, raising the fine hairs. "We learn by contrast, you know. Those hairs on your arm wouldn't know the delight of touch without no-touch."

Slow looked at sister's fingers moving up and down her arm. Abby continued talking, "I wish our abba was here to take this all in. He'd mingle his senses, see the silence, hear the colors."

Slow waited just long enough for courtesy to be served. She landed her best stink-eye on Abby. "You're still on a high from Windy light-stitching your pee bag tight."

Abby didn't defend herself but leaned forward, attentive.

Slow said, "Enjoy your sense-tangle with Abba. It'll all be over soon. Murder's waiting for us in Alexandria, sharpening her blade."

"Alexandria is like any woman—she has both excitement and danger on offer. We'll get our chance to birth a new us—or choose death."

Slow got snarky. "Well now, Miss Optimism, I tried to kill off my Harlot-me, but she's done a casket pop-up twice—under force, at Herodium and Avdat. God's hand at work?"

Abby arched an eyebrow, half-surprised.

"Your brothers raped you, tore your guts, and got you pregnant. Again, God's hand?"

Impatience crowded Slow's throat and chopped sister's happiness to bits. "Our married rabbi father had an affair with my mother, not claiming his part in it or me as his daughter. Then he stoned his lover out of jealousy. God's hand, again, huh?"

Abby said, "Here I am loving life, and you're full of dread and anger."

"Yep, Hawk-watcher and Poop-sniffer, balancing each other out."

Abby drifted her hand along Slow's tingling forearm. "God's hand hovers just over our skin, warming us. Her next Reveal is imminent. Like the moment of no return, when you've leaned too far off the ledge and can't recover, cause you're already dropping into deep water."

Slow thought, *mystic nonsense, most of it, but I'm not sure which part.* I stroked Slow's brow, admiring her labor pains. She was on the verge of herself, nowhere she'd ever known, unavoidably herself.

Sheba interrupted my work. She pointed toward a group of Arabs approaching from the south. She said, "I get this tingle about those people coming up here from the south."

Slow squinted. She could barely see a smudge of movement in the sun's glare. Sheba, the blind, kept talking, "Those people are Rabbus' friends, and they'll take us south to Mt. Timna. We're supposed to take extra water from here cause there ain't no water there."

Rabbus heard what she said. "Not sure know how you know my friends. But you're right. Those are the people who found me drunk and almost dead in the desert. They tended me."

His face scrunched up.

Slow looked at him and thought, *oh no, here it comes.*

He said, "Caligula killed Leah out of spite and jealousy. She'd survived the plague, barely, but couldn't survive him. Gabe and the baby she carried didn't survive. I'll join Leah and our children—but not before I take Caligula with me."

Sheba said, "Really? Those with second sight know vengeance as lazy grief. Try saving the life who caused your loss. That is *hard* work and will not only grow you up, but heal you."

Rabbus' spat on the sand. Her words were wise, but premature. His rage filled him, leaving no room for wisdom.

Sheba's words also zoomed over Slow's head. She had crumpled in a quivery heap. Abby sat beside her, cradling her head. Laz sat on her other side. Hope crawled into her lap, and Michael cried under her other arm, only understanding ma was sad. Sheba and Sam linked arms—chanting prayers, faces lifted.

34

JESUS

We'd been traveling east from Alexandria for a month. Every 480 meters, another milestone marked our way along this good Roman-built road. Two full centuries of legionnaires marched in front of our group of camels. Behind us, another two hundred soldiers. All of them marched in military phalanxes— a basic display of might is right. Yet their might was made insignificant by the vast *midbar*, where sand and space were plentiful, and water was not.

Before we'd departed Alexandria, Tiberius called Cal, Claudia, and me into his office—the same elegant corner office Prefect Cornelius no longer needed, having been retired quite recently. I recognized his desk. It was the same ornate antique that Julius' father used when I was a child. Cracks spread across its lacquered top, like crow's feet from the eyes of a ruler too tired of juggling consequences. We stood before him in a row, like penitents seeking favor.

Except Caligula was not penitent. He ranted, "You live in the lap of luxury, Tibbie, and order me around Seth's dusty ass crack. It's not fair." He stomped his foot. A bright patch of purple hives rose on his neck, like an army massing against a brain that had never been easy on its owner.

Tiberius replied, "Dear Cal, I trust no one else to heal your poor vision and general immaturity."

His face sank into itself, running from possible agenda disruption. His eyes remained down on his paperwork. Important emperor stuff.

"Save him from himself, Jesus. God knows, I've tried and failed. The future of our empire rests on you. Heal him, God-man."

Tiberius shot a further comment to his nephew-lover, "Cal, please reel in your impulses and refrain from killing Jesus. Really, now, enough of that. Suffer obedience to *my* rule or remain insufferable."

He kept reading and signing documents, sealing them with his red wax. He commented, still not looking up, "And Cal? You were very naughty to forge my signature. You know, about the Jewish genocide."

He tsked, gazing at the recessed ceiling fresco. Intricate scrollwork, done in light blues and pinks, filled the fresco. Nymphs cavorting with obviously male gods. One small dryad admiring a turquoise dragonfly on her finger.

His tone was embodied beneficence, "Consider yourself fortunate I've allowed you to live, dear boy." He stood up, walked to within a foot or so of his nephew, and pointed his finger in Cal's face. "Lover, please do try to work up a good spate of faith. You *do* remember what the Seer here said, don't you? You know, about miracles happening to believers? And think majestically—this is essential training for Rome's next emperor."

Tiberius turned to his company commander, standing at the door behind us. "Pontii, add two stops on your journey to Jerusalem. Pick up some copper at the Timna mines—a thousand kilos should do. I need ornaments, altars, and pillars for a Temple on Capri."

Pontii furiously scribed his orders.

Tiberius continued, "After that, visit Kadesh Barnea or Petra, whatever that place is called—where the Nabateans hide from me. Get a load of their spices, the ones from India that they store in the cliffs. Five hundred kilos each of myrrh and frankincense, also that gold spice—what's it called? Saffron, curcumin? Ship all that to me in Capri—not to mother in Rome."

Pontii nodded, pen smoking along on the parchment.

Claudia piped up for the first time. "Uncle, these aren't quick trips to the corner rock and spice shop. Aren't they way out of our way?"

Tiberius raised an eyebrow. *Who's emperor here? Play nice, Niece.*

"Claudia, dear. Are you sure you want to go on yet another adventure with Jesus? Who knows, maybe more siege and plague await you. Perhaps I should put you on a boat back to Rome. Your mother could dote on you and also your grandmother. Both could unleash tender care all over you."

His laugh sounded like a dagger's tip being dragged across granite. Claudia shut her mouth and took a step back, holding my arm.

Somewhere in this interview, I'd stopped breathing, or at most, took in little sips of air. My heart raced. I considered my new tasks. Stay alive in the desert with Cal. And heal him not only of homicidal envy but blindness as well. Right.

Why so inscrutable, Father? I wanted to walk alone in silence with you. And now this?

Father's voice breathed into my ear through Windy's breath. *Kindness is harder than obedience. Love your intended murderer.*

I let her words flow through one ear and down my spine, even though I *felt* like having a bit of a meltdown.

Father caught my impatience. *We will not short-change your homecoming, Son, for the sake of those who come behind you and those who came before you. Breathe in our Spirit. You'll need every breath. That, I promise.*

35

CLAUDIA

Fifty days had passed since Jesus and the Jews were "resurrected" from Alexandria's almost-genocide. Those days were gone, like pages of acting script caught in the wind and carried away. We were now hundreds of miles north on our caravan bound for Jerusalem.

Time and sand glided under camels' webbed feet. Mile markers passed in the Sinai desert, each sanded bare by the wild scorch of this heat. One group of Bedouin guides handed us off to the next. Each group of guides wanted payment, in gold, in advance.

Some time ago, I had decided my lonely sedan chair could keep itself company. I'd join Jesus. I told him, "Why be alone? We each need conversation before we get sandblasted into mile markers."

We pulled the shades up, rocked and rolled with the camel's rhythm below us. Jesus read or recited passages from the Torah—prophecies announcing his arrival on Planet Earth. I shaped stage plays from his scripture stories and told him my parables.

Cal rode behind us, secluded in a platform sedan chair, behind a shade. A Bedouin boy, by the name of Amok, rode with him. When my cousin had seen him at the last Bedouin guide hand-off, he'd circled his prey like a wolf might stalk a lamb. Amok was a prize for one such as Cal—astonishing eyes the color of turquoise; oiled, sinewy arms; long legs; and a keen eye for opportunity.

Cal's voice was smooth as silk sheets on naked skin, a thousand years sly. "In this moment, hard wood from my body doth protrude. Come with me, boy; come, with me."

He dropped a few gold coins in the sand between the boy and his keeper, an older Bedouin man—maybe his father or an uncle. I was tempted to lecture Cal on issues of cultural diversity, but Cal was already dragging the young man back to his covered howdah. The boy's keeper turned the gold coins over in his hand briefly before he strode away back to the rest of his family group.

Now, on this day, I lounged next to Jesus. He napped. I felt so intimate with him that when he dozed, my eyes closed. And then a dream roused me—a dark night, wolves howling. First, they were after me, then I was a wolf after Jesus, a very bad wolf, grinding away, gnawing away. I was confused. Was I being thrown to the wolves or turning into one and running with the pack? I tried to twist the dream into me fighting wolves off or taming them—but that didn't take. My dream master refused it.

I shook the dream off and looked out through the side panel of our sedan chair—nothing but sand. Jesus' side-window view was more interesting. Okay, let's be honest. The interesting thing was my side view of Jesus. The inner part of his face, the part toward me, was darker; the other side was lit by a bolt of sun, cheekbones shining over bearded cheeks. I'd trimmed his beard a few days ago, and just before his nap, I'd finger-combed it flat.

My face reflected from the small mirror on the opposite wall. Light and shadow played over me—perfect spot for a mind prone to wandering.

I lounged back against my pillow and checked those lines in the sand I'd drawn between us. In my heart, I smudged one out, moved an inch or so toward Jesus, rearranged myself. He woke up and resumed talking, perhaps not even knowing he'd napped. He talked from his Jewish scriptures, as usual—a story about King David and some hot babe on a rooftop.

The more I listened, the hotter I got. Moved closer. The empty spaces in me grew wanton, wolfish, gnawing away, gnawing away. But still, I drew a mile marker in my sandy soul, chiseled in some kind of porous stone: *I can want, but I will not act.*

I looked up from my inner theatre, looked back at his face. Desire crept back in, pushing me past any lines of honorable intent.

I leaned across Jesus. I said, for lack of something better, or anything remotely honest, "Hey, look out there, more sand."

My breasts pressed against his shoulder—a definite sexual vibe, like knowing hands tuning my body. I checked to see if his hands were moving. They were not. Even the camel's rhythmic movements, up and down, felt sexual. I could tell he was responding to my skin on his. Some kind of purring, panting, restraint losing its grip, in me or him—maybe both. The air buzzed with some kind of wildness.

He untangled himself from beneath my arm, slid out the side door, and dropped to the sand below our camel—heaving deep breaths of dry air. I slipped down next to him. I felt empty as a magician's hat once the rabbit had jumped out. Desire had arm-wrestled with Refusal and lost. I smelled my armpits. My romantic heat sank into stink.

"We had a moment there, now, didn't we?" I said, "Because we've been plagued and starved doesn't mean we can't feel what your Pop's built into us. Desire is normal, if I'm not mistaken. Otherwise, how can this barren planet populate?"

He said, "Fire is good but needs to be kept in a fireplace. Otherwise, we burn with no Vigile to quench our flame. Let Father be the kindle keeper. He'll fan our flame for his glory, in his time."

I surprised myself by busting out crying. "This is *so* humiliating. When I talk with you about us, our needs, desires, you make me feel like I'm waiting to incinerate us."

He remained silent, examined the cliffs to the west. A rush of wind snapped his robe against mine.

I sulked. "Do you know how many men would want me if I opened the door even a crack? And all you want is to crawl in bed with your Father and Windy."

Jesus said, "the man part of this God-man wants you. But marriage isn't Father's plan for me. Your body doesn't belong to me. Let's remain friends, while we wait for your husband to arrive."

A few steps later, Pontii pulled alongside us on his horse. He shouted, "King Solomon's copper mines coming up southeast of Mt. Timna over there. We're headed there now to claim our back-taxes."

He rode off, leaving a dirt cloud in his wake. We were both covered in a thin layer of grime. I stared hard at Jesus and switched my gaze back to Pontii. "Does this mean what I think it means? Pontii proposed years ago to me when I was exiled on Trimerus. He made it into a business deal—I'd get off the rock and pop him into the royal family line. Fair was fair, right? I declined, holding out for you, and he took the occasion to try and kill me."

My eyes kept brimming over in the hot flow of memory. "Even now, he'd break my heart. Don't make me marry that man. He would kill the real me."

We both stood facing each other, holding hands. Jesus said, "I don't *make* people feel anything or do anything. We all get to choose."

I replied, "Yeah, I guess. But you're as thick with your Abba as a vine and its branches, and He's got it all planned out. Your Pop confuses the poop outta me. I want to choose to believe. Belief comforts. Like believing I'm safe because you left a nightlight on for me. But even if that's stupid, flat wrong, it wouldn't matter. You brought heaven to earth. You do the heavy lifting—and I'll coast to heaven on your coattails."

He held my head with both hands, "This Son of Man doesn't have it figured out either. Father only lets me know what I can handle. I stand in the belief gap between Father and people. If you can't believe in Him, you're right to believe in me."

We walked alongside our camel. As we walked, he switched from one scripture story to another. This guy and his stories! This time he told me the story of Joseph and Potiphar's wife—how he'd fled from temptation and suffered the consequences. [58]

I commented, "I hope you don't rot in jail for seventeen years like Joe did. And I resent being compared to that lying harlot, Potty's wife. Even if I did try to seduce you back there. My wanting you is nothing new. I've been trying to get you to love me over fifteen years. You always move the bar higher to a new plateau of painful celibacy. Celibacy that's not me. Might not even be who *you* are today. We've both moved beyond our thirteen-year-old selves to some more grown-up version of sexual desire."

He said, "I've loved you since I first saw you. Remember us in that doorway to your bedroom there in Sepphoris?"

I nodded, "You were sanding the door frame. I was dreaming of boys. A match made in heaven."

He answered, "My desire threatens to drown out Father's voice. In those moments of desire, I run like Joseph. Run to other people, run to Father. Alone, I'm helpless to handle Desire and the Devil."

I released my breath in a spasm. "Just us here, Jesus. You got Desire. Does that make me the Devil?"

"Satan is also here now. He's never far away." Jesus said, "He loves to take something so sweet as sex and sour it. He twists what's best into what's merely very good. Hopes we'll settle."

"And because of incest with my brother, sex will always be my Achilles' heel?"

He said, "I came to make all things *new*—so let's leave '*always*' out of this. But because I've loved you for so long, Satan will use you to tempt me."

I waited a bit, considered his words. I said, "Every bread does have its crust—especially your loaf of truth. But love's been known to soften even the hardest crust."

He smiled at my flirt—but his frustration was clear and spiked mine. We were complementary cuts from a scroll entitled, *Not To Be.* His part and my part of this story, stitched together, formed one whole saga, singeing sad to bittersweet. We stood together, facing the desert.

I looked up, to my right. "Look at that."

A swirl of dust off to our right moved straight toward us—a microburst. Plain to see and scary as hell. I flashbacked to Jesus' abba, Joe, sitting on a swinging crossbeam and Satan using a microburst to kill him. Was this Satan again? The closer it came, the bigger and hotter it looked. Was this a dust-angel from above or a dirt-devil from below? I didn't know.

36
WINDY

I swirled the sand into a tornado of wind, earth, and fire. In today's world, I sounded like a jet taking off. I divided my whirlwind in two as I approached the Roman caravan. I directed all the dirt into one swirl and headed that microburst toward Cal's camel. The remaining half, free of dirt, I lit on fire. I swirled faster, roaring. Before either Jesus or Claudia could move a step, I wrapped them in my blazing whirlwind. They stood in my fire with me. The only thing that burned was the grime that covered them. This dirt popped and sizzled, then fell away.

Out of my hovering presence, brighter than the fire itself, I spoke. "Don't be afraid, child. Be immersed in my purifying fire for the forgiveness of your sins, *all* of them." [59]

Claudia stared at her fingers and toes. None of them were crisping or crumbling to ash. I murmured in her ear, *gold melts, boulders crumble to pebbles, but my Word, standing next to you, lasts forever.*

I shape-shifted from female form to male, grew a black beard with shimmering white tips, and spoke aloud in a voice that reminded Claudia of rocks rolled by a storm tide on a beach, "Here's how to fire truth into your flesh, daughter. Accept all my texts—they're excellent accelerants. Court kind friends with mirrors. They focus my fire where it will do the most good. Take your dreams and visions seriously—and you're already excellent at that. Do those three things, and when you walk out of my furnaces, you'll be bigger than when you walked in."

She asked, "My dream, Windy? The one where I was burning like a deer on the altar?"

I surrounded her, swirling, voice in bass and soprano both, piped in through the flames. "Ah yes, my dear, the dream where you tasted the breast meat closest to your heart, wanting to see if you were done cooking?

I was the deer to your left, and Father lay on your right side. We protected you from too hot a fire, the one that comes from living inside a false story."

Claudia began to murmur praise to Father in a mix of Egyptian, Bedouin, Hebrew, and some African dialect, one language flowing into the next, articulate, seamless. She sat between me and Jesus, taking our hands in hers on either side, raising them up, each "sistering" the other. After she tapered off her multi-lingual praise service, the three of us walked together and burned in peace.

I left, taking my fire with me.

Claudia looked around. Empty desert. Only Jesus and her.

She said, "Was I talking funny in the fire? I couldn't understand myself. Then those ideas and the words all lined up, clear and happy, as I gazed into the kindest face I've ever seen. Reminded me of you."

Jesus replied, "I never can predict Windy. When she arrives, powerful, unpredictable things happen, time and again. Sometimes Windy's fire comes in a dream or conversation, a triumph or a tragedy. Each person, each time, is different. But Father's Word always remains solid, stable, even in the midst of her whirlwinds."

Claudia looked carefully at his face and burned the Word into her memory. She re-focused. "Odd how whirlwinds ambush us."

Jesus said, "Some are burning bushes, not ambushes."

She grabbed his hand. "Does everything have to be part of your scripture? Just agree with me for once. Ambushes aren't ambushes unless they surprise you, right? This surprised even you."

"Ok, you're right. I was wrong. Forgive me, please."

She laughed, "Well now, that wasn't so hard, was it? Practicing those lines will pay off handsomely in our relationship."

Jesus, chagrined, laughed with her.

Claudia looked hard once again at Jesus. "I've got to figure a way to market your radiance in a bottle. Seriously, this is so weird. I've been so frightened for so long about my own fire cremating me before my time. Now I was fired and didn't burn. Instead, I started singing praise."

She was quiet for a while before she said, "I think that might have been your Father I saw. He looked like you—but through a screen of some kind—like I couldn't see him directly, or I'd be ash."

They walked in silence another dozen paces before she resumed speaking. "And another thing from the *Book of Weird and Weirder*. Windy was the only one I could see clearly in the furnace. Now *you're* the only one who comes clear. Everything and everyone else blurs."

Jesus said, "Windy's fire clarifies. We need repeated fillings. Like the one you felt in Alexandria, in that alley? That was good for then, that day. Today we got fresh cleaning, fresh filling."

Claudia said, "We? You needed cleaning too?"

Jesus said, "Things and people creep in, contaminate clarity. Back there, lust-glom hovered, ready to sink into my skin. Then Windy arrived. She burned it all up."

Claudia stopped and put her hands on her hips, stuck one out, and tilted her head. "Thanks a *lot*. So that's what I am to you? Lust-glom?"

Jesus said, "Nope. You're precious and pure in my sight, and Father's eyes. Satan used you to attack me. Don't take it personally. There's not only the two of us in this relationship— spirit armies war all around us."

Claudia walked and murmured, like she was learning lines for a star role in life's play, "Remember—two people. Spirit armies. Don't forget." She pinched herself and Jesus' arm as well. "I just wanted to make sure I didn't make this up—like some kind of myth or wish fulfillment. My fingers say we're real enough."

Jesus took a deep breath. "All this sitting, standing, and walking in fire makes me thirsty. Got water?"

The last water wagon rolled along behind its mules, about a half-mile ahead of them.

Jesus said, "Let's pick up our pace."

They trotted down the rutted track, and Claudia took in their surroundings. The mountains' beauty was unlike any she'd ever seen. Not ten shades of brown. Not like hills in Egypt or Judea. Father and I had done a unique shake and bake here—shook wet rocks out of nothing, mixed them on a color wheel, and left them to dry in the sun.

Jesus looked at Claudia as they walked. "Those Two laugh when they do this, you know. The sheer pleasure of creation."

Saw-toothed, dark ridges of anthracite melted into shadowed foothills of crumpled copper. Jasper outcroppings glowed in the sun, like slabs of gold. Beyond, toward a flat-topped mountain, rounded massifs streaked a glittery granite mix with an orange under-crust. Striated sandstone walls towered above them. The sun moved a bit behind a cloud and the golden hue bronzed. The next cliff face over, magenta-red realgar, had fallen across the wadi floor, leaving crumbles all around.

Son trickled a few colored pebbles through his fingers. He said, "Rocks wrinkle, crack, and crumble. They trickle down cliff faces every night, bowing to sun and rain, hot and cold."

The couple caught up with the water wagon. It stopped, and the quartermaster ladled out cups of cool water with a wooden cask taste. Pontii joined them. He said, "When we enter deeper in this wadi, stay inside the phalanx. These people aren't happy that we're here."

Caligula heard Pontii and ordered his driver to let him down. The driver barked a command. Camel knelt, front legs folding under him, and then his back ones.

Cal and Amok joined Jesus and Claudia. The four of them trailed the legionnaires on foot, passing under four granite arches of triumph, maybe twenty meters in height, the color of old bones. Rome's hubris, past and present, overshadowed them, briefly.

I led this band into a narrowing wash strewn with more color. Timna's top peaked over the scree slopes. Even Cal's near-sighted, astigmatic eyes squinted upwards. He took a step, fell, and skinned his knee. He sat on a waist-high rock the color of Roman red, sparkly. He complained loudly how royals were so much more sensitive to pain than commoners.

"Oh! It is just the plight of the blue blood!" The expedition's physician hurried over to tend him with salves and a bandage.

Jesus and Claudia moved solemnly past Solomon's Pillars. These hundred-meter-tall monoliths loomed over the desert floor. Two gazelles peeked around the corner of a rocky outcropping and scampered to higher climes. Once north of the Pillars, the narrow wadi revealed green and magenta-tinged boulders the size of houses and the color of lettuce or beets.

Claudia said to Jesus, "Your father turned into a grocer, and this is his produce section. That portobello mushroom boulder is balancing so delicately on its stalk."

Pontii offered something more practical. "Amok's father, my senior guide, told me that the miners will likely hide till we go away, then continue business as usual. But, that said, be on guard for archers and slingers on the heights."

Amok's father was right. The miner's village had been abandoned; cliff dwellings, emptied; mines dynamited. Rome was free to claim a graveyard of green copper slag.

Cal fluffed his pompadour. "Tibbie was going to build an equestrian temple for my horse, Incitatus, with this copper! Pontii, produce—or I'll order you to fall on your sword!"

While Cal huffed, Amok sidled up next to Jesus and Claudia. His brilliant blue-green eyes tipped tears down his cheeks.

He whispered to Jesus, "Please, my lord, take me away from that man. He shames me."

He continued, "I might know where the miners are hidden, along with their treasure."

He nodded his head toward the mountains. "But just a few can go, and quietly. Maybe you can strike a deal with them, particularly since they're, uh, family."

Jesus looked at Claudia. Their eyes shifted up, and up again, toward the hills. Jesus looked down and was surprised to see Claudia's right foot, in open-toed sandals, tapping furiously.

She hesitated and then said to him, "Memories of Trimerus flood me now. I longed to climb with you then when I was in exile. You do know from rubbing them—my feet are still callused. I don't even need these sandals to climb those rocks."

Jesus squeezed her arm and drew Pontii to him. He mentioned what the boy had said, what Claudia had requested. Pontii distracted Caligula with another pretty Arab boy. Then he walked over to the quartermaster and got four knapsacks filled with water, bedroll, dried dates, cheese, fish, and bread. Jesus strapped his rolled-up prayer shawl to the bedroll.

The three men and one woman started to climb. It was three in the afternoon.

37
JESUS

Amok led the way. I was on his heels and Claudia right behind me. Pontii served as the rear guard. Waterskins in our backpacks made sloshing sounds. We rock scrambled deeper into the narrow wadi and its lengthening shadows, up through dry, curving water chutes of maroon rock with green stripes. Rainstorms had washed stone white and slick.

I took a break in the middle of grappling with a handhold and looked behind me. Bare-footed Claudia had her sandals tied to her backpack. She looked up at me, positively glowed. I couldn't tell if it was just the sweat of exertion, a post-fire afterglow, or serene memories of climbing hills in exile.

A half-hour further along a steep granite slope, scattered with broken bits of scree, I took the lead. Amok bowed politely and held his hand out, bowing. I bent my knees and head, hunched over close to the ground, to keep my balance. Shortly, we came to an overhang, about three meters up.

Amok motioned a few steps to the right, where the top ledge dipped slightly. He made a stirrup with his laced fingers. "Here, my Lord, let me lift you." I glanced at the bowing Arab boy, this one with worship nestled in his smile.

Each of us helped the other up to the next level, one at a time. We panted hard, climbing into the gathering dusk, as day released its hold to the coming night. Sunset broke slowly, leeched color into the cirrus. Canyons blackened, content to let the heavens steal all their glory.

None of us knew where we were going, not at all, except Amok. We reached a shallow cave that fingered into the cliff and smelled of the wild. Black pellets of scat littered the entrance.

Amok poked into the cave and popped back out—picked up a pellet, sniffed. "A few days old. Coyote. He and his pack have gone elsewhere in search of water. None near here."

We settled into a rough square and took long swallows of warm water from our goat bladders. The water tasted of iron and wood, pungent—but wet and life-giving.

Pontii pulled a wedge of cheese from his shoulder satchel and cut off a chunk for each of us. I passed my loaf of bread around, and Amok shared his dates. A long strip of dried venison in my satchel surprised me. I passed it around, and everyone tore off a chunk with their teeth. We munched, swapped stories, content.

Madame Day bowed to Professor Night.[60] He raised his arm, strewing a spray of stars overhead. The most beautiful, Cassiopeia, kept careful watch over our neighborhood. I got up and rounded a corner out of sight. My stream smelled acrid as it arced over the ledge onto rocks far below.

When I came back, Claudia took her turn and then the others as well. We all brought out our bedrolls. Claudia chose a spot inside the cave's mouth, facing the interior. She pulled her cloak over her. I wrapped my blue prayer shawl around me and laid my head close to Claudia's feet. Pontii and Amok lay down a few feet away, head to foot, on the other side of the cave's entry. After some time, quiet snores.

Claudia whispered, "Jesus, awake?"

I replied with a soft, "mmm."

She rolled around and put her head next to mine. "This reminds me of sleeping with you in Rozafa's infirmary, but a lot better—no plague buboes popping open in our groins."

"Mmm. Go back to sleep."

"Can you hear the cliffs crumble? The scree shower woke me up. I was dreaming of mountains dancing in praise to the Furnace Maker. I had joined in the dance and pulled you there with me, inside the fire, surrounded by rainbow mountains."

Another trickle of rocks clattered down the cliff wall. A percussion band, impersonating a waterfall. The rocks cried out. [61]

I listened with her, praising Father aloud. She turned on her side, facing me. Soon her breath changed to a slow, deep whiffle. Her hand did a little hoppy tremble in the moonlight.

Windy whispered, *enjoy the absence of light. Look. Even the blue-green nebulas, those smudges directly overhead, hang in the leftover smoke from Father's Big Bang.*

I thought, *thanks for the dark*, and I felt Her hug in return. I stayed awake long enough for Cassiopeia to move somewhere else.

The next morning, we made our toilets separately; after, we chewed on bread and dried fish before we continued our climb.

Around noon, Amok ran ahead, scouting for his family of miners. Where Amok disappeared, I followed. A long chute canted up sharply. No handholds. Claudia took the lead but reached back and gave me a hand when I asked for it. This slick, strawberry-vanilla chute could turn into a freefall with one missed step or an unannounced shower.

We were close to the top of Mt. Timna now, the climb steeper and craggier. We talked about each hand and foothold before we executed our moves. I kept my eyes trained on the hold at hand and repeated to myself, *stay on the path.*

Where had Amok gone?

Claudia, one step below me, cried out, 'I'm stuck. Everything's off-kilter. My feet feel out of place, like they're not on a flat ledge. I think I might be fear frozen. This seems *way* steeper than anything I climbed on Trimerus."

Pontii, below her, said, "Remember the ledge where the fish yanked you into the blue? The climb to *that* point was no harder than this."

She said, "Thanks for the memory. I remember how I lost my grip and fell a very long way."

He said, "Come back here. Feel my hand on your ankle. Keep hold of the ledge above you with both hands. Grab hold of the crack in the rock with the toes of your left foot and release your right foot. I'll plant it on the next rock up. Keep your eyes on Jesus."

The last sentence was the best advice he ever gave her. In spite of that, she looked down. "Pontii, I've turned to stone. I'm no longer worth my salt as a rock scrambler."

He held tight to her ankles, "You're the same woman I knew on Trimerus. Still brave. Close your eyes."

She did that. She muttered her thoughts loud enough so I could barely hear her. "I'm pressing into the rock. Sun's heat is on my back, Pontii's hands are on my feet, Jesus is above me. But how is it, God, that my world keeps folding over, pieces of past meeting chunks of present, all stirred by Windy's hand?"

Pontii interrupted her. "Okay, open your eyes. Look on the man's feet above you." She did what he said.

I prayed praise, *Father, you use oracles of all sorts—rocks, fire, fish. Sometimes, even people. People like Pontii.*

Those words had barely gone through my mind when I reached the next ledge. Claudia pulled up next to me, panting. We stood there, recovering from our struggle up to Mt. Timna's flat top. Claudia and I stood, poking our heads up and over the sharply angled rock.

God had delivered us here to this moment, delivered us into an about-face I never saw coming. Blood trickled over the maroon rock in a stream, heading straight for us. My mouth gaped open, slack-jawed at what I saw.

38

WINDY

My southbound group of journeyers was in trouble. They had misjudged how much water would be needed, and were fast running out. Cacti pockmarked desert between them and the towering limestone cliffs to the west. The odd patch of tumbleweed blew into branches of upended acacia trees. A few brave tamarix trees clawed into patches of shade at cliffs' edge.

This collective wheeze was all that remained of life in the Arabah desert— along with my appointed travelers. I'd dried up the last few oases. Just three days ago, Laz had told Rabbus that he spent a lot of time daydreaming of swimming in Galilee's springs, waterfalls, and rivers. Rabbus wished him luck and turned away to study the mountain steeps.

That very night, two days ago, stillness had settled. Cooing noises caught Rabbus' attention. A peregrine falcon nesting on red-brick-colored eggs was up there, fluffing her feathers over future predators, hunters still— in oval form.

Rabbus abandoned the caravan while his friends slept. He slipped into the desert with his business partners. They both needed one another to accomplish their revenge. Neither had fully learned that truthful words, mixed with compassion, were a better way than weaponized words or weapons. They hadn't yet realized that my Word, even when he whispered, would be heard over the clamor of armies.

Rabbus' meeting with these Bedouins had been accidental—but then again, in his way of thinking, 'accidents' like this weren't enemies. They were weapons. Rabbus and his weapons arrived by Father's design at Mt. Timna from the north, even as the Roman legionnaires arrived from the south. They all crossed, more or less at the same time, into desert space these nomads controlled.

No one in these tribes wore color in their clothes. Nothing shiny. No beads or mirrors sewn into their kirtles or shoulder bags, like citified people might wear. Nothing that might reflect the sun, making them visible from a distance. This particular landscape shaded into variations of cream and brown. These Bedouins blended in—dun camels, dirty harnesses, worn saddles, leathery people—all dust in different stages of falling apart.

They, the decomposing, sat on crumbling mountains, watching Rome's soldiers and wagons creak and groan over dry knolls and rocky ravines. They watched Rome break its axles and then repair them. Watched soldiers taking frequent hits from the water wagons. Saw them run eagerly, run and check the well there at the southern mouth of Wadi Nadal. Laughed as the Romans cursed that dry well. Sat and swilled water from their own skins.

Rabbus sat with this group, cross-legged on the hilltops. He adjusted his cowl, shaded his eyes. Saw Caligula jump down from his camel, fluffing his blond hairpiece, primping in a hand-mirror that flashed in the sun.

Rabbus' rage woke up. Inside monsters stretched, rising from their uneasy nap. They flexed their muscles and started to howl like a clutch of coyotes in the desert night, their voices rising almost to his skin. Vengeance pickpocketed his moral compass, and he was glad for the theft. Lightened his load of all he had yet to do.

Rabbus saw Jesus slide down from his sedan chair, followed by a gaunt woman. Claudia? Would Jesus allow her to sit secluded with him in that howdah? Huh. The stuff of scandals, up north in Galilee. Even pagan Rozafa, in Dalmatia, kept men's and women's balconies separate. What *was* this? Was he kicking tradition under the wagon wheels? Wait and see.

He waited and saw. What he saw from the clifftop stretched his vision into the realm of the mystic. I swirled fire and dust together with my pinkie. Rabbus' eyes—and the eyes of all his Bedouin warrior friends—squinted hard at the two tornadoes I'd split off from each other, one darker than the other. Fire surrounded Jesus and Claudia. The dirt tornado surrounded Cal's camel and its occupants.

After some time, fire and earth whirled away, back from whence I'd brought them. Two figures remained, shining like angels.

Curiosity filled Rabbus chock-full. I swirled his curiosity with imagination and memory. He sat, stropping his knives, remembering lessons in skinning and stuffing that Bado-the-taxidermist had taught him long ago.

Night fell. The first watch, darkest hour. Rabbus crept into the Roman encampment. Casually side-swiped a sentry with his blade. Laid that mother's son, twitching, in a dry gulch beneath a loose overhang. Took the dead man's uniform and attached his own officer's epaulets from the Imperial Guard, the ones he'd saved from Rhodes. Stomped hard on the overhang. The loose bluff collapsed—a quick burial. He strode into the camp and aimed himself toward the water wagons.

The other sentries, sleepy, roused briefly when they saw his form and heard him filling his goatskin. Went back to sleep. They didn't hear when he turned all six water taps on. A steady, silent flow disappeared in cracked ground—life drizzling out and down. The earth was still parched, even when all the water wagons had been emptied.

I planted thoughts in Rabbus' mind. *Noisy presence can kill—the clatter of sword punching through armor, the battering ram on castle gates, the raging tantrum, the banging fist. But what can be said for affection growing cold by inches, friendship withering from disuse? Quiet absences trickle into dry ground. Are they not more lethal than noisy presence?*

Rabbus headed toward Cal's camel, resuming the look and manner of the Imperial bodyguard to Emperor Tiberius himself. Soldiers saluted. Such was the weight of quiet authority passing in the night.

Caligula cuddled next to Amok's cousin, snoring. The boy had done as he'd been told—put a sleeping potion in Cal's wine. The two men, Samaritan and Bedouin, lifted the Roman from his bed. Rabbus stuffed Cal's wig in his pocket, slung him over his shoulder, and slipped into the night, quiet as a cat.

Rabbus thought, *let Jesus handle light. Half of every day is night.*

39
RABBUS

I carried Caligula to the waiting camel. Friends strapped him down. We set off for a mountain top experience.

I said to Amok's father, "I'd make short work of Little Boots, but I want to make sure the job's done right, and that's gonna take longer."

His laughter ground like glass being crunched under my sandals.

A few hours later, my trotting camel arrived at the limits of where camels can go. I switched my package to a mule for the steeper trail. We walked up. The restive royal didn't appreciate the gag in his mouth for that last part of our trip up the backside of Mt. Timna.

Now, at midday, Caligula broiled upright on the scaffold's big X-shaped crosspieces—spread-eagled, naked. I sat on a stool beside him, stropping a carving knife already sharp enough to split hairs.

I talked loud enough for Little Boots to hear—even with the wind whipping my words, ripping, slicing, and stripping my words into sharp sound bites.

"Cal. They say love's the only cure for rage. Whadda ya think?"

Cal gurgled, "Ugghhh."

"Oh, sorry, Cal! Forgot to take out your gag."

I unplugged his foul hole, filthy as only an atheist's mouth can be. Cal's bright red face screamed a blue streak, threatening crucifixion for me and my descendants 'in perpetuity.' Whatever *that* means probably ain't good.

I ignored his rudeness. "My opinion? Love is way overrated. Maybe it comes in different stripes, though. For example, I *love* my work as a carver."

I stood up and turned around, dropped my mantle so he could see my back, full of scars. "Learned from the best, Badu the Bedouin, when I was a kid. Started my love affair with these Bedouins way back then."

Cal's eyes widened.

"Back to Badu, Cal. Now listen up. Want you to appreciate what a fancy school I went to. Yep, that man knew his way around a knife. Lots of book-learnin' inside a blade. Badu didn't need no words. You know those country hicks, don't cha? Real big on doing, not yakking."

I nodded to my friends, coming and going, doing life on the mountain top. "Badu wuz the first to show me how to skin a whole animal and not wreck the pelt. You know, keep it all together in one piece, like a complete suit, stretch it out so it wouldn't shrivel. Then sew it all together, suitable for framing."

I favored him with a quick grin. Motioned to the wooden gibbet that framed him in the sun, "A crude wooden frame like this wouldn't do for such a one as you. No, gotta pack you up, send you back to your main squeeze, the one scribbling fiction an' calling it history. Won't he be surprised when he unwraps you! You two always did have a skin-deep love, so no loss."

Cal's head flailed back and forth. More profanity, in Italian, his mother tongue. Saved the delicate ears of my Bedouin friends—but they probably got the idea he was upset.

"Practiced tannery and taxidermy in my younger days, but lately, got rusty. That's why I'm stropping Badu's old gift here. Getting ready for our special, intimate touch 'n tickle time. Together, tomorrow, you and me, bud."

I called to the turquoise-eyed kid. "Turnover time."

I looked back at Cal. "Wouldn't want you to get overdone on one side and not the other. Torah is death on half-baked cakes, you know." [62]

The next morning, everyone enjoyed a grand breakfast buffet—nothing lacking on this mountain top restaurant. Ladies sat at two tables by themselves, men at another. Everyone was chattering about the upcoming entertainment. I'd stoked up on sticky breakfast rolls with dates, nuts, and honey from the hive, all rolled in flour and baked on both sides.

I wandered over to my work. Everyone followed. The ladies bleachers were a little off to the side, but they still had a good view. Sippin' on their tiny cups of expresso, loaded with cardamom. Stuff was so thick it would stand up when you took away the cup.

This morning, Cal's head had flopped down to his chest. I tapped his face. "Woo-hoo, sugar cakes. Time to rise and shine." I turned him over.

He opened his eyes and immediately shut them again. But his head stayed up.

"My apologies, Little Boots. Bedouins are the world's most hospitable people. I probably had a bad influence on 'em, being trained in Rome 'n all. Don't know what got into me, leaving you hung out to dry like this, with no refreshment. And Amok here tells me you royals are so much more sensitive to discomfort than the rest of us. Is that true, now?"

I threw a bucket of warm water over his head, sloshed a little in his open mouth. I called for two of the women. The pair came over with two tubs of pig grease. Slathered it all over him, top to bottom, then re-joined their lady friends.

I said, "Need to make sure your skin's supple. Not all dried out. So, what do you say? Let's get to work, shall we?"

I started at the nape of his neck, giving instruction to Amok, my junior carver, as I worked. Giggles mixed with sharp intakes of air from under the ladies' veils.

I spoke to my apprentice, "Ears are the trickiest part. Skin's thin here. Might lose a piece if you're not careful. So, grab his head and hold tight. He's bein' frisky."

Amok put him in a headlock.

"That helps. Cal's always been hyperactive. But never really used his ears, so I'm expecting thick and thicker— right here. See? I was right. That one came off real nice."

Cal kept keening. I waited for Cal to inhale. "Now, now, Cal. Don't forget, I'm only a working man. I've got a wife and child to support."

He stared at me, confusion joining pain.

"Whoops. I forgot. It was you who killed my wife, now weren't it? Suffocated her, by the look of the husk you left behind. And my son? Died of dehydration before he went on your dinner plate. Lucky you. He didn't have plague. You royals got the little ones. Meat was so tender, so they tell me. Did you fricassee or bake that night? What sauce did you use to baste him?"

Cal's eyes widened even more.

"You were a real bud, Cal. Loosened my bindings to this world, you did. Let me tell you a skinner's secret. Don't get out of binds till the bind's got your lessons into you."

I pulled the skull cap forward over his eyes. "Sorry 'bout blocking your eyesight. Hang on. Won't be long. Want to make sure you can see the consequences of what you've done."

I loosened his face bindings a little at a time, caught a bleeder, and used the white-hot iron beside me to cauterize the flow.

I said, "I want you to appreciate my little poker here. I call her Truth. Helps me out, since I lean toward the over-emotional end of things."

Cal didn't seem to be given to rational discussion. Mr. Talk-a-Doodle was all scream and slosh. Wasn't makin' a bit of sense. I stripped the last few bits of muscle, and Cal's whole skull cap dropped off in one tidy piece around his neck.

"There we go. You can see again, now, can't you?" I motioned to one of the pig-grease ladies, and she brought over a mirror. I wanted him to see himself bare of all that pretense.

I lowered my voice to a confidential whisper. Only Cal and Amok could hear, "Frankly, Cal, I'm concerned about your soul, not just your skin. You thought I'd judge you by the color of your hair and not the content of your soul? Well, well. Too late now. It's clear that part's a little rotten. Needs ventilating."

Cal looked a little lost for the moment.

"But let's look at the bright side, Cal. You wuz never real good at holding yourself in—think something, say it; want something, get it. Now your soul and body's just alike! The good Lord gives and the good Lord takes away.

"Some of you squinty sort don't like things getting taken away—including face. Look at it my way. All straight-edge, no chaser. Without all that skin to confuse yer soul, humility's in sight. And only the humble see past the skin of things. One big circle of life. Ain't it grand?"

Cal closed his eyes.

"Oh my, my, Cal. You still don't want to see? Got to admire your dedication. Let me help you out."

I cut off his eyelids with two quick swipes of my blade. "You notice I didn't even knick your eyeballs? Nope, that wouldn't do at all."

He stared at me, for lack of anything better to do. One eye watered. I mopped it up with my sleeve, just to show my compassion for a tearful man.

"Now, there we are. Obviously need all the help you can get with this clear seeing thing—and that's the truth. Don't be fooled by this righteous pablum goin' around. Truth don't set you free. Truth fries your ass."

I coughed up a wolfish smile from somewhere deep, close to my heart, before I put his eyelids next to the brazier. I said to Amok's father, "These eyelids are the exception. Everything else stays together. When I'm done, I'll paste them back on. Cute little Cal pasties."

Immediately Cal vomited. Spewed all over my front. Eyes rolled back then. He seized and went unconscious. Started chewing his tongue. I jammed a wedge in his mouth and used the firebrand on his tongue to keep him from drowning in his own blood.

I turned to Amok. "Truth will purify his tongue, like, uh, who *was* that Jewish prophet? You know, the one who got his tongue seared when his king died." [63]

I wiped Cal's vomit off my face and chest. "Full of tricks, aren't we, Cal? Never seen anyone *refuse* not to see good as you do."

I kept working and coaching Amok. He wanted to join my art project, but I refused. "Just watch this time. You're too personally involved with this man. Might make your hand a little edgy. Me? I always stay clear of personal involvements."

I felt wonderfully detached as I sliced down his torso, zipped off his chest and back skin, then headed down his legs, past his knees, and finished with those tricky little toes.

I said to no one in particular, "I've been remembering while I work. My memory's so sharp it cuts things together, not apart. For example, I cut past into present, and I join both of them with the future. All that with my memory blade. Wonderful sharp."

I finished stretching and sewing Cal's skin together on netting I'd hung within another scaffold. This gibbet was painted bright Roman red and provided a lovely re-frame for a skin-deep man.

I'd filled the skin with swaddling and straw from a mountaintop manger. I'd even pasted his eyelids back on, half-open over blue marbles glued to his sockets, giving the *appearance* of sight—some things don't change, you know.

Little threads connected skin to frame, supporting and shaping my sculpture in strategic spots for drying in the desert sun. I positioned his hairpiece just so, at a jaunty angle on top his head. Some of the women had brushed it out, stroking and curling it. Didn't want anything unsightly. No, indeedy. The new and improved Cal was ready for curing. Hadn't happened in his first life. Now he had another chance. After, we'd box him up, ship him home to Tibbie.

All my friends milled about, admiring the new member of their community and ignoring the dripping, trembling chunk of meat behind them.

I looked his way. He turned his head toward me, squinting. That was when four hands appeared on the top of Timna's southern edge.

Claudia and Jesus' heads pulled into view.

40

CLAUDIA

What we saw on Mt. Timna's flat-top was a crowd in dust-colored thawabs and abayas. They all milled around a pulsing piece of meat stretched on a scaffold. Blood from that meat drizzled around my hands. A wake of buzzards circled overhead.

Amok came over and pulled us up on Mt. Timna's tabletop. "Welcome! We succeeded in our journey. My father will speak with you. Let's go find him." He motioned with his head toward the crowd behind us.

A man's skinned body was spread-eagled on a wooden gibbet. Next to him, on netting inside another X-shaped gibbet, the hull of this victim, all one piece. The women examined the stitchery—*oh's and ah's. What lovely work.*

Amok's father, a weathered man with a white turban, stood next to the skinner. He asked questions about technique and taxidermy. Examined the stretched skin. He reminded me of a museum visitor listening to a docent explain an artifact. Skinner was also dressed head to toe in traditional Bedouin garb. He carried himself with surety. His form was familiar, but the cowl shadowed his features.

I wanted to look elsewhere, anywhere other than these two gibbets. But my eyes had a will of their own. They crept back, riveted on these twin tragedies.

Skinned man twitched. Tears rolled where cheek skin had been. Skinner stood, hand to chin, studying Meatchunk. When Skinner spoke next, he said, "Ah, now, Leah would enjoy your hairpiece over there. Notice how the ladies combed it all out, just like you used to like it."

Then I knew *both* Skinner and Skinned for who they were.

Amok sidled up next to Jesus and murmured loud enough for me to overhear, "This man's a great teacher. Very highly recommended. He didn't make a mess of the job. Others have tried, mainly with our enemies from Assyria, but they always make a bad job of it. End up with pile of flaky pieces. A real tragedy."

Amok turned back to the chief skinner. I retched on the ground behind me. Amok stopped in his tracks when he heard me vomit. He returned and handed me a clean cloth to wipe my mouth. "Oh, Claudia! Are you ill? Perhaps you should take a rest in our tent? Have a nice cup of tea?"

I demurred.

He continued, "I particularly like Poker Truth. She's setting in the brasier over there. A clever touch we've not used before. That rapist should last longer, and this will help too." He threw a bucket of water over Meatchunk.

Jesus steadied himself by grabbing my left arm. Then he used both hands to cover his mouth, gagging, eyes flooding. We'd often spoken of what he called his "curse" of compassion. He'd said, more than once, "Father made me with thin skin. I can't *not* take in what others refuse to feel." Now he took in Caligula's terror, mine as well, and Rabbus' disowned grief as a chaser.

Jesus whispered, "I can't stand this any longer. I'm asking Father what to do. Maybe He will allow me to release him from this life."

Jesus' compassion must have been rubbing off on me. I had no love for cousin Cal, but this calm barbarism was beyond anything I'd ever seen. Terror was being burned or skinned alive, but horror was watching another go through it, even someone I didn't like.

The skinner turned. His cowl dropped away, and Rabbus gazed calmly at the two of us. This was our first meet since Rozafa. He stood before us, skinning knife in hand, looking quite cool, remote.

He said, "I saw you two walking in that fiery furnace down there. You gotta tell me about that one. But let's wait and do that over lunch in the open-air tent, the one with the buffet tables over there." He head-nodded to a large tent behind him.

I opened my mouth to speak a word of reply. Before I could say anything, Jesus whispered one word, "Sleep."

Everyone obeyed. Executioner, assistant skinner, gawkers, and a condemned prisoner were transformed into dreamers. His one Word gently laid us down, his Father cradling all his cranky ex-babies down for an afternoon nap.

And then, this even more peculiar thing. Everyone dropped into their own dream, or was it my dream of them or their dream within mine? I don't know. What I do remember is that I walked amongst the sleepers and entered their dreams with them, but once removed. Some dreamt nightmares; others, wet dreams; and still others, ecstatic visions. As I walked amongst them, each person's dream became a sound and light show. When I moved on, the next sleeper provided me their own special effects.

Jesus walked beside me. He said, "El Abba, You put me in charge of everything human so I could give life to all in my charge.[64] Help me give life."

He then lapsed into silence and touched each person on the forehead. After his touch, a whisper. I hovered and heard what he said, giving them words of life that only the sleeper could bear. Life was in that Word.

We walked together, and he touched me too, whispering, "Bear witness to the Dream-Weaver." I cannot say what was real to the touch or only real to the mind, or even which reality was more reliable. After all, I am by nature a wonderful liar. My mind conjures variations that aren't *really* lies, just alternate versions of the facts. But keep in mind that this revelation was given to a still glowing woman, burned from a desert furnace. So maybe my lying self was burned to a crisp. Let's hope. And even if what I remembered is true, my memory goes all fuzzy beyond these few people.

First, Caligula. He was a few years older now. The golden leaf-crown rested on his brow, but uneasily. On this day, this other nightmare of a day, he walked through a tunnel beneath Palatine Hill with a crowd of actors to the stadium beyond. I trailed on the margins of that crowd.

At labyrinth's bottom, in a snaky place within that tunnel, they turned on him. Slipped their knives into him, more than thirty times. [65] The last thing he saw in his dream was someone leading him to a side door from a Hall of Judgment. The Presence ushered him out the door into a void. No boundaries, no light in that darkness. The door snicked shut behind him.

Rabbus, next. He dreamt as he slept. Dreamt of being transformed from a lone wolf to a real person—trading four legs for two and walking upright. He still was covered in hair, and wild—but pardoned, exchanged.

He dreamed of a crowd roaring approval that his life be exchanged for that of a worm. [66] He dream-puzzled and couldn't sort it out.

His dream shifted to a cemetery. He'd found Leah, Gabe, and his unborn babe in a grave outside the walls of Jerusalem. He lay next to their grave in the dirt, trying to cover himself, trying to join them.

And then, in his dream, quite suddenly, sadness unrolled itself. Leah, Gabe, and the babe's grave busted open. They popped out of their ashcan and were reassembled by the Wind, whole, complete. Together the family held hands, wandering the streets of Jerusalem, giving witness to the resurrection. [67]

Amok, third. He dreamed of his people in Egypt flowing freely back and forth from there to Assyria. No need to kill each other. All had been drawn to Jerusalem. Together, all bent their knees to Messiah.[68]

And fourth—me and Pontii. A worm wound us together. I saw through a glass darkly, a smeared vision. A worm of a man caressed my head and whispered in my ear. Pontii stood and looked at this squashed worm. There was no beauty in him, none at all. [69]

Pontii and I were connected indeed, but in pieces, porous, and separated by a veil. I sat at an ornate writing table in an inner room of a big palace, floaty, detached, watching him as from a great distance.

Solemn Pontii stood over Worm, thoughtful. I yelled a warning to him, but the words caught in my throat; my tongue, furred like a caterpillar, wiggled inarticulate. I wrote my warning to Pontii on a white linen towel. *I've been warned in a dream. Leave this man alone. Send him on his way.*

My maidservant took the towel, bowed her knee, gave it to Pontii, both hands extended. He turned the towel over carefully but saw nothing. [70]

I desperately wanted to hold his feet on this slippery slope, hold them with both hands from below, out of sight from the public's view, planting his feet on solid rock. I wanted to protect him from being remembered as a consummate coward—*the man who caved to the clamor of a crowd, the man Caligula ordered to kill himself, and he did.* [71]

I failed to protect anyone. Pontii washed his hands and dried them with the clean, white towel I'd used to write my warning. He disappeared from view, as did my warning, and the bleeding worm.

There's more, much more, locked inside me. Visions like these change people, create havoc, harbor hope. The words are there, but I can't reach them now. I must wait. Windy will make my cryptic scribble clear. All will be made plain in that day.[72]

41
JESUS

Claudia slept-walked next to me, gradually waking as we walked. We stood before the chunk of raw, pulsing meat on the scaffold. I whispered in his ear after I touched his forehead. Windy taught my hands; Father empowered them. Together we undid the works of darkness. My eyes widened as We worked, Father's fingers under mine, Windy's over mine. We soothed new eyelids over his eyeballs, re-joined cut blood vessels, touched healing into ravaged tongue. I brought him down from the gibbet, shaken but whole in body. Skinful but still not mindful.

I raised Pontii from the dead of sleep. When he roused, his hands shook. He asked for water to get blood off them. Claudia said, "Pontii, there is no blood. You're okay. Do what Jesus tells you."

All the others still slept while Pontii came along with Claudia, me, and Caligula. The future emperor of Rome slumped between Pontii and me, one arm hoisted over each of our shoulders. We all stopped in front of the second gibbet. Looked at Rabbus' artwork, sizzling Cal's old skin into our memories. Night fog rolled in wispy tumbles across Mt. Timna's tabletop, moving between statues frozen upright, sitting, or curled on their side, all skinned of wakefulness and skimming death's tiny sleep.

Caligula said, "Do you think we could get my hairpiece off that atrocity? What will my public think when they see me like this?"

Claudia sliced a sharp glance his way, and we all kept moving. We passed sleeping Rabbus, standing glassy-eyed beside the fiery brazier, skinning knife in hand.

Cal eyed his glittering blade and Truth, white-hot in the fire. He spoke once again. "Let me loose for a moment. I need to plant something in that dirt over there."

Pontii and I tugged forward. Cal was weak-kneed, little boots flopping behind him, neither leg on civil terms with the other, and both losing to gravity.

Four travelers, one Jew and three Romans, aimed ourselves off the mountain's tabletop by another path. This path down was littered with donkey droppings.

We walked single file in the narrow places, dazed Caligula in a daisy chain between Pontii and me, Claudia following closely. More than once, Cal spasmed, out of control, ready to pitch off the mountain. Either Pontii or I caught him in time, settling him down to rest.

There were many hidden sinkholes and dry stream beds in this mix of karst, sandstone, and volcanic cinder—all kinds of dangers for anyone less than sure-footed. About a third of the way down the mountain, we arrived at an overlook.

Behind us, a collapsed cave entrance looked like I felt. Rainbow rubble cluttered the mouth of this particular cave, like so many others—magenta, pink, violet, yellows, flaming reds, and greens. Dusk leeched them all of color before my watching eyes.

A few acacia trees and one dead tamarix hung off the mountainside in front of the cave's entrance. All in front of this collapsed cave's entry had the look of a giant's hand at play, boulders strewn from Father's mix-master.

A voice called to me from within the cave. *Secrets rest within me. Come. Follow.*

I said, "Let's stop here for the night. Help me unblock this cave."

Pontii had already started chopping up the tamarix for firewood. He joined us, and we three cleared what rocks we could. Caligula sat and dozed. Dry froth stuck to his lips. His re-seeded scalp, always patchy, looked like a blown cobweb.

We opened a hole big enough for one person at a time to crawl through. The cave opened up after a few feet. Cave's ceiling was high enough for us to stand. Gnarled roots clawed their way down into thin air, like they'd taken a wrong turn but couldn't go back.

Two old oil lamps and a sealed amphora of oil leaned together in a tumble by the entry. Pontii struck a flint, lit the lamps. He carried one, and Claudia the other. I walked between them, grateful for the light Father had provided. The tunnel followed a gradual gradient upwards, curving first left and then right, but always up.

Silence lived here, but not a drop of water. This tunnel had been worn smooth from those who had gone before us. After a hundred paces or so, twisting and turning, a small cavern with the look of a routed burial cave. Shattered shards of clay jars were strewn about.

I asked, "Claudia, bring your lamp over here." Pontii joined me with his light, one on either side of me. We looked in a recessed niche back of two chipped amphorae. A thin crack in the wall, like dried plaster, ran vertically along the niche, back of the sealed jars. I tapped on the plaster, tentative.

Claudia took a different approach. She handed me her light and borrowed my blue prayer shawl. She wrapped her fist with the shawl and punched the wall, hard. Hm. Praying with your fists—perhaps the most practical prayer that shawl had ever seen.

Plaster crumbled and another smaller space opened up. A purple amphorae sat alone in that hidden niche within a niche. Ornate Egyptian script etched its neck. A date had been inscribed in the sealing wax—a date 1,500 years earlier.

Before I could say or do anything, Pontii stripped off the seal but left the jar intact. He pulled a scroll and a tiny, glazed pot from within the larger vase. This pot was also sealed. He cracked open the pot, upended it. One seed dropped in his hand. Not gold, or copper, or precious stones. One 1,500-year-old seed.

Disgusted, he threw it on the floor and headed for the door. "I'm in trouble with Caesar."

Claudia said, "leaving so soon?"

I thought, *how could he know he was leaving? He didn't even know he'd arrived.*

We watched his light get smaller and disappear around a corner. I gave Claudia back her lamp. It was bright enough for me to find Pontii's spilled seed in the thick dust.

We both examined the larger jar more carefully. Two etched lions pawed the air on either side of the seal. The lioness on the left stared at us, open-eyed. The lion's eyes on the right were closed. [73]

I turned the jar and scraped away the grime. A faded inscription:

Zaphnath-Paaneah.[74]
Only one true Seed is worthy.
All other seal-breakers be cursed.

My skin crawled with excitement. "Claudia, this seed and scroll are from my ancestor, Joseph. This is the name Pharaoh gave him, Zaphnath-Paaneah. I am the one of whom he speaks, Father's true Seed." [75] We clasped hands, mine over my seed, hers over mine. We stood alone together in the dim cave, holding Joseph's seed between our bellies.

The sealed scroll, from the outside, appeared to be in perfect condition. Who knew what treasures it might hold? I carefully placed the scroll back in its vase and held it tight, cradled in my left arm. I pocketed Joseph's seed in my singlet's sole pocket. Buttoned it.

Our torch flickered out, and darkness swallowed us. Claudia and I felt our way back to the entrance, hands trailing along the dry inner walls.

Pontii and Caligula sat outside the entrance, chewing bits of dried venison. Both had run out of water. The two men ratcheted their jaws, working up enough spit to swallow.

We told them about the scroll. Pontii shrugged, gagging down a piece of venison. "Big whoop about your dry seed and that old rag. I'd give a whole library of scrolls for a long drink of water."

I plopped down. A sharp stone bruised my tailbone. I cried out and rubbed my butt with the heel of my hand. Claudia saw me wince and reached over to rub my low back. Her touch comforted me.

Claudia sat and shivered beside me, her eyes dancing. Her excitement was for me, not her. "Your hidden seed is so much better treasure than bars of copper or gold. What we found could feed thousands."

Caligula sniffed. "One old seed? Face it, life inside that pip's long gone."[76]

Claudia picked up a handful of soil and drizzled it from her fingers. "We have plenty of dirt. Ancestor slung that seed straight down the halls of time at God-man. All we need is water."

I picked up her flask and mine. We both had about a mouthful of water left in each flask. I prayed over her water and asked Father to bless it. Claudia sipped her last swallow. She let the water and blessing soak in.

Caligula stared hard at my flask. I felt his longing.

He said, "I lost a lot of blood up there. Sacrificial Lamb, me. You can tell a lot about people by the scapegoats they choose. I could order my cavalry up their little mountain. Crucify them. Instead, I soaked that small hill with my blood. But now, me, a royal, could die of thirst. Gimme your last swallow. That's an order."

His eyes glittered in the flickering flame. I was exhausted, and my discernment weak. I prayed, *Father, watch over us. Watch within us.*

I said, "Ok, it's yours."

I gave Cal my last swallow. He squeezed the last drop of water from my flask. Flipped on his side, turning away from me—but not before he'd turned his heart from me.

Pontii shrugged, laid his head down on his empty goatskin. Soon, sounds of snoring from both men.

Claudia also laid on her side, spooning around me for warmth and comfort. I sat cross-legged, my hand on her shoulder, rubbing her back. She made soft, happy noises, murmurs of contentment.

That simple act of her warm body wrapped around mine slammed me. A surprise attack—this thrumming, throbbing wanting. I longed for her to be my wife, even more than I wanted Joseph's scroll. Like Esau wanted a bowl of stew and was willing to sell his birthright.

I felt a cracking in my chest, like the chambers of my heart pulling apart—a thread teasing apart inside a dry sigh.

I whined, "Why, Father, why can't I have her?"

No answer, no nothing.

I stoked the fire with the remaining brush Pontii had gathered. Empty, desiccating Drought appeared, dancing inside the crackling firelight. Lust danced with Drought. Two life-sucking demons, swaying in their furnace, waved at me and the woman I could not have.

I prayed, "Father, post a night watch. Protect me, and these you've given me, from the Evil One—except for that rebel bent on destruction, the exception that proves the rule of scripture." [77]

Father's voice came to me through Windy's breath. *Choose the path you want. We won't stop you. But that other path, the one you see waving at you? That path leads to the end of another man's life.*

The fire died. Demons went elsewhere to conduct their seductions. I faced east, a watchman waiting for morning.[78] I waited for an easier answer to my complaint, one I *wanted* to hear. But why would Father answer this Son of Man any differently he answered Job? [79]

A moan escaped from someone's mouth, maybe mine. A newer, deeper layer of awareness: Claudia would never carry my seed. I'd been letting go of her for so long I couldn't remember when I'd not wanted her. I felt her breath behind me—even and deep, body twitching in her sleep.

I cracked open my left eye. No light in the eastern sky, not yet. My closed right eye opened inside. I saw a single seed spinning in space.

Windy breezed into my hearing. *Joseph's seed will spring forth from your dry root.*

I felt dryness, for sure—but that was all. My seed spun in space, looking to root, but with nothing or no one to root into. My tongue, a strip of sandpaper, lay alone in its cave.

Hours passed. I sat still as a sphynx. Pontii snored, and Caligula lay quiet as a tomb. Claudia faced the cliff, whiffled softly, dreaming her dreams.

Father came to me wrapped in mystery. I knew he was present, but my feeling self barely budged off zero. Father likes to encourage faith in dry places.

Windy also arrived. She misted onto my open hands, moist. Or maybe that was just my sweat.

My closed eye, the knowing eye of faith, saw Father and Windy create a drop of water from nothing. They dripped it on my seed. One drip, one seed.

Nothing now. Nothing happened for the longest hour, the darkest hour before dawn. Seed sat still in mind's eye. Then, in slow motion, seed crumbled. Glistening, golden microfilament crept out into Windy's one drop of mist. Curled around me, rooting in Father and Windy.

Suck in Father's kindness, little seed. Root into Windy's wellsprings.

Seed's shoot inched up from dry ground. Almost invisible filament rooted down.[80] Praise limped up from my lips, spread over Claudia, Pontii, and even Caligula.

I closed both eyes now, and this is what I saw. Father held my seed in his hands. Seed grew vine. Vine grew branches. Branches wrapped the world, heavy with fruit that would never spoil. [81]

This vision, me-as-a-vine, began on the Night of Drought.

42

WINDY

My small group was having a long, lost wander. They'd hit some dry holes. Banged their bucket down dark shafts hoping for a sploosh. Nothing but a bang at the bottom.

Since she'd discovered her rabbi father, Slow had staked a claim to full Jewishness. She had honed her complaining into an art form, practicing kinship with her forebearers who'd circled Grumbleville with Moses for forty years in this very wasteland.

Laz walked next to Slow, praying out loud, reciting cheerful promises of Father's provision. Slow imagined them turning into a pile of bones—rib cage here, bleached skull there. She *was* glad he wasn't coughing up blood, but for the most part, her believing part, Fragile, had taken off with Escape.

She complained, "Sheba, you're taking us further and further into the middle of nowhere."

Sheba said, "You grew up in the middle of nowhere. What's the difference? I'm obeying God's voice. I might be blind, but I can still hear. We gotta go this way."

That shut Slow up. They walked in silence for a while until Abby piped up. "I felt a splash of cool water on my face when you spoke just now, Sheba. I reached up to see if my mouth was wet, and my lips felt cool."

Slow smiled at her 'new' sister's cool lips. She thought Abby was cool, but since she personally felt un-cool, she suspected her impact on public opinion might be limited.

Abby wouldn't let it drop. "I know you can't see any water, Slow. But we need to re-define water."

Slow said, "Redefine water? It's the wet stuff that keeps us kicking."

Abby started to explain, but Slow cut her off. "We can't go much further without real, un-redefined water—whatever *that* is. We've got a half-full goatskin for the lot of us. Two senior citizens, two children, one nursing infant, three adults, one camel, and a mule named Goodness—who we may need to eat—after we drink her blood. Eleven living beings, half a goatskin of water. Not good."

Abby remained silent, plodding along on Wisp. Kept nursing Ahud. She motioned Slow over. "Look at him. Isn't he adorable?"

Slow grumped, "He might be cute, but a thirsty kind of cute." She took the goatskin and made the rounds again. Hope and Mike had a long drink, then Sam and Sheba. Abby took a long swill.

Slow said, "Take enough for two, milk factory." Abby took another drink for her child's sake.

Laz looked at the goatskin quick-like, then away. Slow gave in. "Oh, go ahead. But a short one."

He gave a quick glug and stayed in step with the children on their mule, holding their halter. She stoppered the goatskin quick-like, so she wouldn't drain what little was left.

She fell back a few yards, walked next to Abby, who came out with a thought she'd been nursing for who knows how long, "Sis, when my brother, Zayan, was "playing doctor" with me as a kid, he would joke that I could win the Itty-Bitty-Titty contest in Flatville any day. He hurt me."

Slow answered nothing, studied her feet. Picked 'em up, put 'em down.

Abby fell quiet, then gathered her courage and told Slow what she'd dared not ask. "Even later, last year, when he was, you know, doing me—even when Abba was in the next room and I begged him not to be so loud—he said the same sort of thing. Now, I'm torn. Part of me wants him to see how cute his kid is and how plump my breasts are. Another part of me wants to kick him in the nuts."

Slow said, "I vote with the nuts part. He got what he deserved."

"I guess," Abby said, "But if God gave any of us what we deserved, we'd all be a pile of dry bones."

Slow said, "Look around. What we deserve isn't far off."

They all dragged along for another hour, surrounded by sweat-stealing sun. Slow looked at a drop of sweat pop out on her hand and disappear just as fast. She made the rounds again, giving everyone another drink. Laz only got half-a-glug this time, but it was the last.

Goatskin was dead empty. Dead. Empty.

Abby had been watching Slow as she doled out the water. She got down from Wisp and motioned her sister over. Ahud was sleeping.

She said, "That streak of white in your hair is so beautiful, milk-white. I was just thinking, can you do me a favor? Ahud's been draining my right breast. My left one is still full to the point of sore. Could you take some of my milk?"

Slow said, "That's sweet, but not for me." She got Michael, who was listless, groggy. "Here, feed him." She did, and Slow was satisfied in a strange sort of way.

I planted a memory in her mind. She said, "Abby, I just remembered a time before I met you. I'd dreamed I died and had sifted down into a grave with the man I thought was my father at the time, a man named Ach. This was the man who sexed me regular-like, taught me my trade as a whore. In my dream, the only part of me showing above ground was this one piece of white hair."

Slow fingered that shock of hair I'd turned white. "The wind blew hard. Jesus was dancing over me in the dream, dressed up like a combat soldier, lifting his hands, raising me from the grave. When I woke up, this streak of hair had turned white."

Abby raised an eyebrow, "I took a long drink from that story. Redefined water in yet another way."

Slow moved on, struggled to get words up and out of her bone-dry throat. "Another memory from right before we met you. We were traveling south with your brothers and their spice caravan, not quite to Moab. We'd run out of water. No oasis, no date palms, no signs with a big red arrow pointing down, 'Dig here.'"

"Emil told Laz to look down. Directly under his feet was a piece of tan shale, like a round dinner plate. Mike circled, mouth open like it was a giant hairball. Zayan helped him pick it up. Under the rock, a hidden shaft went down maybe fifty or sixty feet to water. A bucket sat there, conveniently located on a shelf under the rock, beside the shaft."

Sister said, "Isn't that just like God? He comes sneaking up on you when you're out of divining rods. Like the Holy poking his ghosty-head around a corner and shouting, 'Boo!' Wants to wake us up."

Slow said, "I guess. But you gotta remember, I'm a devout sleepwalker. Dreams feel safer and more real than the nightmare of outside life. I walk through life expecting bad things to happen."

Abby grinned. "Huh. I've always called that being afraid. But, tell me, isn't outside life cluttered with more miracles than you can divine?"

Sister shook her head. "I wouldn't know. I'm not too different from my half-sister, Leah. She liked to say she'd lived all her life on the skinny side of miracles."

Abby was silent, holding her thoughts inside of herself, as you do when there's nowhere else to put them.

Slow zapped Me with a pouty accusation. *Well, well, well—and all are dry. I could use a good miracle, but your miracle shelves are barren. Must have been a rush order on miracles, this place being so full of people.*

She tried to hawk up a gob of something solid that had stuck in her throat but was too dry to get anything out. She tried to cry, desperation tears—but none of those came either. Too dry.

She continued her winsome, snarky, silent mix of cajoling and whining that she called prayer. *God, since you're short of water, I don't want to put you out. Let me die of thirst. I don't mind. After all, mother was an adulteress. And that sperm donor rabbi? He never showed up to father me, 'cause he was so busy running Your house.*

She squeezed out one mad tear that disappeared in the ether.

Slow kept praying. *The oldsters, Abby, and the kids—keep 'em going, would you? Not for my sake, but for their sake, or maybe even for my friend, Jesus? Yeah, yeah, do it for Jesus' sake, even though he's nowhere to be seen. Well... ok, bye.*

I said nothing but blew my hot desert wind around her. Father's sun beat straight down.

She said, *oh yeah, I forgot. Laz? I'd just as soon take Laz with me. Heaven might be less lonely, and he's frail. Golden streets gotta have water fountains here and there, ones where even ex-whores can get a drink.*

She snagged all her selves back on track. *Don't know about all that heaven stuff, but here's the real deal. Take little Fragile and Escape soon. Harlot and me can wait till they've gone. But this thirst is killing all of us.*

An afterthought. *And get some water for the others before it's too late. I'm serious, like pronto.*

She looked up from her righteous bitch session and thought, *I'm just like Michael, ordering God around.*

While she was praying, I'd changed the scenery. The flat desert had more sharp-edged bumps and lumps in it. Some were even colorful.

Slow heard my whisper in my head, even as Cutter reached for the razor strapped to her right thigh. I said, *you're powerful, child, not because any of your-you's are strong, but because you've all kept on keeping on. You haven't opened a vein and let life drain from you.*

Slow took Cutter's hand off her blade. Got dizzy. Held onto Laz's arm as he walked along next to her. She thought, *not going to fall over. When the time comes, I'll rest my head against a rock for a while. That's all.*

43
SLOW

We rounded a maroon-and-olive marbled bluff. A bunch of red uniforms lay scattered in the sand. Very still uniforms. Suits and brass glinting in the sun. Ok, maybe not a whole army of them, but a few hundred redcoats, camping out sideways. All of 'em napping in front of tall-columned cliffs, twining reds, creams, and purples—limestone and granite by the looks of them. Dry wadis fingered behind these cliffs.

Those men in the redcoats looked like I felt—maybe they were better off. They'd passed on already, by the looks of 'em. Laz walked directly past those bodies toward a circled group of six or so water wagons. Put our goatskin under the spigot. Turned it on. Nothing. Repeated for all six water wagons. Same result. Bone dry.

Laz returned with his empty goatskin and held onto me with one arm and Goodness with the other. I looked around for a patch of shade to pull over me. Maybe a rock to lean against. My legs trembled, looking to give out. Treasonous legs. I fell to my knees and sat back on my heels, graceful as I could manage. I lowered my head, dug my fingernails into the dry earth.

It was then that Samuel and Sheba pulled up alongside me on Wisp. Sam pointed up into the hills with one hand. Shaded his eyes with the other. "People up there! Maybe they know where to find water!"

There in the distance, on the top one pillar, two men and one woman. They stood, looking our way. Samuel saw me looking up at them.

He said, "Locals call them towers Solomon's Pillars. Gateway to the copper mines."

Opposite the trio, on an opposing cliff with a deep wadi in between, another group of people had gathered. Sun baked both of those groups, and us, each in our own space. Equal opportunity ovens.

Sheba's nose was a-twitching. She cried in a loud voice, "I smell the sound of water. Fresh, loud. Slow, do ya hear it comin'?"

I immediately occupied the corner where Mirage meets Making-Things-Up. Will someone stop mixing senses, please? Smelling sounds, sniffing colors. I'm an ordinary ex-whore. I saw nothing but wavy heat rays, scattered men lying sideways on sand with tomato-red faces turning to black.

Hope slipped off her mule. Mike joined her. They started running, making a beeline for a crack in the hills, shrieking with laughter. Those children were running toward what looked like a finger of water, maybe 20 or 30 yards wide, water rippling out of the hills.

I couldn't rightly move to the water, but that was okay. It moved toward me. Colorful streams flowing out of earth's dust—red and yellow, black and white—all were strange to my sight. Earth's blood—sifting, purifying, dropping its color, swirling toward a very confused me.

Hope reached the water first. Lay down in it. Wherever it came from, still more came, but not in a flash-floody sort of way. Somewhere between a trickle and a gush.

Ankle-deepening now. Slow stream swirled around the red bodies, filling gulches, making high places low. Deadheads took heed and bobbed up. Attached bodies sat up. A bleached-out wash of dry bones had come to life. [82]

One soldier stood up, poking his head and shoulders out from under a collapsed sand dune. Touched his neck, felt a puckered, angry scar that extended across his whole throat. He lowered his face into the water and drank. The water didn't spill out his neck; instead, it piped down to his innards.

The water reached us. We all knelt. Drank sweet water flowing around our ankles. Wisp gulped it down, and Goodness too.

Fragile swore to me, *that mule looked right at me and brayed, in donkey talk, 'why did you ever doubt Bright?'*

Harlot said back to her, *we've all got heatstroke.*

I said, *you're right, whore of mine. We're inside a fold in time. This is nothing more than me getting my wishes filled. Spray without substance.*

Shame weighed in. *I hate to thieve laughter outta your joy, but this water's not real. We'll wake up dead any time now.*

I didn't know who of my-me's to believe.

Abby's voice broke into Doubting-Self-Central. She handed off Ahud to Sheba. "Here, take the kid." She knelt next to me, put her arm around my shoulder, and dunked both our heads underwater. Pulled us back up. She threw her jet-black hair over her head and shoulders. Sun slow-motioned fractals of light through her hair that was so black it was almost purple. Rainbow sparkled. Looked real to me.

I said to her, "So, is this water, redefined?" Her face was half-submerged again, gulping water, but her head was nodding.

We all waded into the wadi, heading upstream. I looked up to my left as I waded and saw those cliff-top people. Two men and a woman started to climb down, angling toward water's source.

I splashed and floated in the stream, joined Laz and the children in a song we'd learned long ago in Sabbath school, a song I'd forgotten I knew. Something about God's weapon being a melody.

Hope led us. Her clear soprano lilted over the water's sounds—bubbling, laughing, splashing—a chorus of many voices, untold tongues.

Abby had been right. Water had become a living thing with parts, like me. Part rainbow, part people groups—Romans and Arabs, Africans, climbing down from our left and right sides along Z-paths. No walls between those parts.

One young man with brilliant turquoise eyes led his pack of Arab-looking people. His face glowed. He called out, "Father, come to the water! Rabbus, come to the water!"

Ah, so it was. The warrior-protector had appeared again. He'd found us, or we found him. Or the Water found us all.

A thought popped into my head, and it felt like a Windy offering: *People of the Desert, come to the Water.*

We all converged into the now waist-deep, gently flowing river. Rounded a few bends, splashing each other with the crystal-clear water, strangers joined by a common execution reprieve.

The three people on the left had been winnowed down to two, a man and a woman I didn't recognize. The woman's thin, pock-marked face was stretched tight around her skull. Her hair streamed behind her—auburn glinting gold, her colors flowing together and making up a new color. Solemn man wore his torn Roman uniform with his officer's insignia. Pock-marked led Solemn, each steadying the other, pulling toward water's source.

The third person that had been with these two strangers, where was he? I looked up. He'd perched a quarter-way up Solomon's lowest pillar. He lay on ledge, watching us out of squinty eyes under a patchy crop of sparse hair. His chin tilted down toward us and then up, eyeing the other group. Why did he hold back? Why not move toward life?

He sat on his overlook and appeared to shrink. Cutter said, *looks like that guy's skin is shrinking.*

I wondered if I was losing it big time—like, uh, more than usual. Were his insides shrinking away from his skin or his outside wrapper shriveling? I couldn't tell, but the man was dwindling to the size of a thimble.

Thimble tantrumed. "Get back up here! Right away, Pontii, or you'll have to fall on my sword!" Thimble's sword shrank with him, shrinking to the size of a needle. Thimble grew more and more insignificant.

We'd rounded a last turn, past an overhang. There in front of us were two enormous trees at canyon's end, different from the usual acacia trees we'd seen all along. A slight man sat between them, sheltering in their shade.

Water gushed from his chest. [83] He sat placid as you please, inside the cascade that came from within him. Or was the river pouring from the rock behind him? Sun played off ripples in the water, off and on his skin, confusing my eye.

Sitting Man had stationed himself between these two fruited trees in front of a towering massif. I squinted, re-focused, willing my eyes to see clearly. I asked myself again, was the water coming from within him or behind him? My eyes couldn't make out truth from lie, but my guts knew what my eyes could not—he was journey's end and river's beginning.

Our group moved toward him. Sheba and Samuel waded in the middle, arm in arm, water lifting lame Samuel. Laz bobbed those two buoyant elders forward. Abby and I fanned out on either side of them, holding the children's heads above the waist-high water.

We met Pock-marked and Solemn in the stream. She looked sanded clean of knots inside her heartwood, like she'd come off a carpenter's worktable.

I felt certain we'd both seen hard times. Felt we were more alike than different. I hugged her. And then, no longer strangers, we resumed our upstream journey toward the cliff, the trees, and the Man-in-the-Middle.

As we moved, Solemn spoke. His voice sounded the way their rocky path had looked, all gravel and scree. "Claudia, I'm back on duty. My legionnaires need me. Also, Caligula. He's in danger from these Bedouins and that man in particular."

He pointed toward Rabbus on the far side of the river. Rabbus' one foot seemed caught between a rock and a hard place. His other foot stood in the river. His outside feet didn't move. I got the sense inside feet were making tracks to faraway places, and he didn't even know it.

Solemn Pontii kept his head high, hawk eyes lighting briefly—here, there, then flicking to another spot. He said, "He does cool tricks, but he's not rock solid—like me, like Rome. He'll float you into fantasy, magic seed, scrolled enchantments. And that's the truth."

"Rock-solid truth, huh, Pontii? All Rome's legionnaires just died in the desert, and Mr. Fantasy brought them back, including the flayed Prince of Rome up there. None of you protected him unless I'm missing something."

Claudia was no longer as I remembered from Sepphoris—a sassy, entitled royal.

I bumped into a purple boulder with green marbling that stuck up above the water. I stood on it with both feet, solid. I closed my eyes, resting them, inside pieces coming home to me. The last I'd seen of Escape and Fragile, wolves were chasing them. Now they swam toward me. Harlot too. My arms were big enough now to hold them, along with Hope and Michael and Shame, who'd morphed into a kind of she-wolf, but with a muzzle over her mouth.

Cutter also came, shy-like, moving our hand to my thigh. She unstrapped my stiletto. Used it to pare off a hangnail and dig red dirt from under my fingernails. She took my shock of white hair, a patch hanging in my eyes. Took it in our left hand and gave me a quick trim, right there on the rock.

We may not have been sparkly or shiny. But we were together.

Pontii stepped out of the river, put one foot on a rocky path up, the other foot remained in water. He turned his head up to examine Thimble Man, then down toward Claudia. I imagined him being split in two with indecision—half of him peeling off toward rock-hard duty, the other swimming toward love. He stayed stuck for a long while between rock and river, with the look of someone who'd made true words empty by unbelief.

I imagined what he must be going through. *What was faith-water or drinking-water, dream or wakefulness, intention or action, prayer or whining, living or dying?*

In that moment of doubtful wonder, the Man-in-the-Middle called out in a loud voice to all who had ears to hear—calling each person by all their names. The sound bounced off the canyon walls and became a rushing river, mixing, flowing, rising and falling, a cataract of color, loving all us river people.

He dove off the ledge and swam toward me. He gathered all the river people into a circle—Claudia, Laz, and all my-me's; Sheba and Samuel, our children, Turquoise Eyes, and those people who'd followed him into the drink. He looked at Rabbus-on-edge and waved a beckoning arm toward him, "Jump in, friend. Take the leap."

Rabbus looked longingly at Jesus and then up at Caligula. His eyes grew black with something not nice. He looked at Pontii climbing toward his charge. Back and forth, caught in a vice or two that clamped his skin white. Then Rabbus moved back up the hill away from us— away, away, and yet further away.

Jesus took all who were given to him, all who came of their own will. Danced with all who had jumped in, Mike in one arm and Hope in the other. He danced with no brakes. Danced in that impossible river gush. Joy flowed from him to me, letting all my-me's add our little trickle to his river.

Yes, Jesus had come home. He'd come for everyone in the river, true. But in this moment, that didn't matter. He'd come for me. [84]

44
MARY

We'd been staying with family in Bethlehem and Bethany for the past few months. I wanted Deborah to know her father's family in Bethlehem. Joe's younger sister said, "We've all swept that nasty piece of business under the rug, Mary. We've agreed to bear up under the shame—you know, with your *mamzer* child, Jesus. But we don't need to bring him up now, do we?"

Simeon's words rang in my mind. [85] Jesus always would be a source of contradiction for all peoples, a forcing bed for honesty.

Deborah and I left Bethlehem soon after that. We made our way to Bethany, where Mary and Martha begged us to move in with them and make a new life.

Martha said, "Our children would all love to have another grandma and a new playmate in Debbie! We've got a little apartment on the side of our compound. Just help with the rent, time to time. All will be good."

This welcome felt more genuine. John, my nephew, had arrived a few months earlier from Egypt. Now he too lived with them in a back room. Kept to himself, an eccentric uncle. He told us Jesus would come home one day soon. 'One day' had never come, nor had any word come from Egypt.

All the rest of my family were living busy lives. I hardly ever saw Miriam since she had married; she and her husband lived in Nazareth with his family. The other boys were scattered into Yeshiva schools, or the trades. My only child still at home, Deborah, was a lonely, moody child. She didn't want to be touched or talked to. Kept her eyes down and held friends at arm's length.

I felt my age and stage of life—a 42-year-old widow. My body receded from me like it had other things to do. Legs became dry sticks; knees turned swollen and painful. Veins in my thighs ached; teeth began falling out. My body left me indignant, affronted. I felt like an old woman, waking with the birds, and not able to hear them sing.

I dressed in black, scanned street corners for the one familiar face I could never find. Maybe my one remaining daughter was sucking up my lonely and living it out with me. Debbie's time and energy were spent waiting with me. We wanted news from afar but got only snippets of Spirit-soothing.

John, in his stilted monotone, kept me up with the local news. "Herod Antipas finally ditched Phasaelis, that Nabataean ice queen. Got himself a new wife—his brother's wife, but before her divorce was final."

He delivered his news with indignation—maybe because he passed Herodias, the new wife, in the hallways in his job as a palace plumber. He fixed their reservoirs, water closets, mikvehs, and kitchen sinks. He worked in *all* their palaces—Jerusalem, Herodium, and Masada—circulating where needed.

One night at dinner, a new moon lay on her back, letting go her scant light between snatches of cloud. After his usual diatribe about Herodias and Salome, John muttered, "Jerusalem is stinky as Rome was. Poop smells the same no matter where you go."

That was last night. Today, early, as was my habit, I walked to the village well for water. On my way back, a shadow slipped up alongside me. The man beneath the cowl said, "Let me help you with that, woman."

I dropped the pitcher. Jesus caught it before it hit ground. He let it down easy and then wrapped me in his arms. I felt safe for the first time in years—safe, while my heart thumped wild in my chest. I couldn't stop sobbing. I took his face in my hands and studied his features. He'd lost weight. He'd been branded, and the number on his arm seemed like it was fading. He'd gained a few pockmarks here and there, on his temples, and one on his chin. Kindness flowed from his eyes.

Behind him stood a few other folks. Laz and Slow, along with another, thin woman. Her face was pockmarked like Jesus' face. The thin woman seemed familiar.

Jesus said, "Mother, you remember Claudia, don't you?"

I took her hands in mine. "Of course, Claudia, how could I forget our ocean voyage from Caesarea to Rome. You were *so* brave to jump from so high into that stormy sea."

She nodded, "my main memory was Jesus on the cargo doors, bobbing in that wild sea. If he hadn't dived so deep for me, I'd be on the ocean floor with Claud, my twin."

I remembered the shipwreck like it was yesterday. Remembered that shaft of light on my face as I clutched the handles on those blown-off doors, that make-shift raft.

"Mama, who is this lady?"

I looked down. Two children, a small boy and his older sister, peeked from behind Slow's skirt. Slow popped the littlest one into my arms, saying, "This is Auntie Mary, Michael. You'll love her!" He played with a gray strand of my hair, a shy look on his face.

Another shapely woman, with a nursing infant, stood behind them. She smiled at me, bouncing her baby back and forth, soothing him. All the while, her right pupil slipped its way up and in toward her nose, disappearing from view.

Behind these folks stood a train of people—an older African couple, a young man with turquoise eyes, some of Laz's friends from Jericho that he introduced me to—El Roi and Lydia, Maltesa and Rastus, the blind double-Cy's, Zacchaeus and Esmerelda, Cornelia, and others.

I said, "We're going to kill the fatted calf tonight! My son was lost to me, and now he's found! Oh yes, Father, you've sent him home with the people he loves. We feast tonight!"

And feast we did. That night in the courtyard around a low banquet table, we had a full house. James gave Jesus a brittle, side-by-side hug. Took his food to the edge of the courtyard, where he could sit against the wall and watch. Jude and Justus clamored closer, crowding Deborah, who shyly filled Jesus' glass with wine whenever it got two sips short of full. She seemed happier than I'd seen her in a very long while. Maybe Jesus could help with her moody blues.

I sat close on Jesus' left side while Claudia reclined on his right. Mary and Martha served us. Martha went barefoot tonight, in honor of Jesus' talk with her at Laz and Slow's wedding. Simon the Cyrene and his wife, Penelope, reclined toward the foot of the table.

I absorbed Jesus' presence at a reserve, though he sat within touching distance. He and the others told stories and more stories of their lives on the road. Each listened and interrupted, often at the same time, one texturing the other's point of view.

Jesus would laugh and say, 'no, no, no—here's how it *really* happened.' Claudia would shake her head, waggling her finger in his face, disagreeing with a laugh.

John sat opposite Jesus, half in and out of the torchlight. He quietly rocked back and forth, taking Son in. His eyes stayed on Jesus while he tucked in matza bread, loaded with hummus. Conversation lulled.

John stopped ripping skin off a drumstick long enough to pop into the conversation. "So, Jesus, did Rabbus ever get his blade on Caligula again after you healed him? I've never even seen a stuffed animal wrapper. Can that even be done? And what's a museum, anyway, and what's in it? Never even heard of that."

Claudia answered for Jesus, "John, you're so *curious*. You'd love a museum. It means, 'a place to think.' Rabbus didn't re-skin my cousin, Cal. Pontii hi-tailed him out of Timna for Gaza, and they were all on the first boat west to Capri."

John didn't look at her. His teeth set in again, ripping chicken skin off a drumstick. thought, *Get over her, John. There's enough love in Jesus to go around. You won't miss out. Father has this one.*

Claudia calmly rattled on, "They're probably still in Capri. That's as close as Uncle wants to get to Grandmother. Uncle burps out the occasional decree. Mostly, he tries to feel younger than he is, surrounding himself with young flesh of both sexes."

I remembered Crispus murdering Claudia's father, her grandfather's assisted suicide, Julie starving herself to death soon after Claudia left Trimerus. This woman had been surrounded by death.

I asked, "And your mother? The last I heard, she was supporting young Luke with his medical studies in Rome."

Claudia said, "Luke's a doctor now, practicing in Greece. Mother looks on the whole family circus from her villa on the other side of Rome. Stays out of Augusta's way. Fills her time feeding feral cats, wandering in the hills, talking to herself. Her servants take turns rescuing her from herself. I think she's gone whacky with loss. All the death and dying's done her in. Weirdest family ever, and I don't want to get close to any of them."

Son touched her arm. She looked at him and saw her grief in his eyes. Tears sprang unbidden to her own eyes. "I keep forgetting, Jesus, that I can walk in the fire with you, breathe, and not get burnt. You did say life would get complicated after the desert, didn't you?"

Jesus nodded. "I tell you everything Father tells me." [86]

Claudia abruptly switched to a new topic. She said, "That night in front of Seed Cave, I remember going to sleep beside Pontii, Cal, and you. I was half-in the cave, and you were on cliff's ledge. When I woke up, you were gone. What happened?"

Son smiled. "I wondered when you'd ask. I climbed down the cliff face by moonlight. Windy's breath blew me. He angled my steps toward wadi's end between those two trees growing from the rock. I knelt between the trees, facing the cliff, made myself small and still, meditating.

"I didn't empty myself of thoughts, like they do in the east when meditating. No. Instead, I filled my mind. Filled my thoughts with Father and his Torah, meditating on one passage after another. *Mind full.*"

Son took a sip of new wine, eyes closed, remembering. "Father's promise came to me—that he'd supply our needs, be a wellspring, a river of life, a sheltering Rock. Verses bubbled up from within me, where I'd stored them as a child. Father's promises flowed from Windy's currents. I stayed and prayed what He'd made clear to me. Father's words became my words back to him. When I looked up, dawn had streaked the sky purple."

Son's face broke into a smile. He poured butterscotch light from his face, it seemed—sweetness that lit my world. "Father struck me with a new thought—thirst is at the root of things. We're all fruit-bearing trees that need water."

"The thirst of those two trees cracked the mountain. They'd driven their roots in deep. The mountain's stony face split into tiny fissures. Other roots had done earlier work—decades of work. All those roots, growing in the dark, became underground passages for water.

"I was Father's Root, a team player. My faith in his goodness worked with other roots. Together we moved a mountain."

Jesus laughed out loud. "That stone cracked up with laughter, first a giggle-trickle out the crack between my fingers, down the palms of my hands and over into the wadi. But then rock had too hard a time holding it all in and busted out a gusher."

I felt something swelling in my breast. Was that pride or gratitude? Didn't matter. Whatever it was came out of my eyes.

Jesus flashed a smile at Slow, "Somewhere in my prayers, I spoke to the mountain, 'Go slow, please.' The Wailing Wall kept laughing happy, sad, and mad tears into its current of life—all the stuff that threatens to bust out from everyone all the time. You all came around the corner after that, just in time."

Slow said, "God answered my whine with your laughter."

Son looked down at his lap. "I did something small as if it were big. Father then did something big, like-giving, as if it were small."

45

WINDY

The following week, Jesus, Mary, and Deborah waved goodbye to the Jericho crowd of friends. They stood in front of Mary and Martha's compound waving till their friends were all out of sight around the next bend on the steep, twisting cobblestoned lane. Father and I made roads—and the earth itself—curvy. Best not for folks to see too far ahead. Sure knowledge grows pride, not faith in Father.

Shortly after they'd gone, and Deborah left for school, Jesus said, "Ma, let's go for a walk."

Mother and Son walked. Jesus slowed to her pace. They went to the other side of Jerusalem, on the main road out of town, passing by Skull Hill. Today, it was empty of bodies hanging on cut trees. Often as not, naked men and a few women, in varying stages of dying, stared at you eye to eye. Roman legionnaires stood by the living signposts, making sure that Rome's message was clear, "Don't mess with might, or this will be you."

Jesus and Mary sat on top of a cave in sight of the Skull. A lonely shepherd boy led his flock of fat-tailed Awassi sheep through the grove of olive trees. He herded his lambs, all trembly with youth, into the cave. Lambs sheltered in the shade while the young shepherd napped in the cave's entrance. Hirelings herded their lambs into a stockade and left. This young shepherd became a door, as do all good shepherds, staying to protect his sheep from wolves and other wildened, wanton predators.

Mary scanned the city skyline. Seamlessly, she prayed, *all those synagogues, closed right now—chained front and back, tight as a tick. Cages to keep You, Husband, so You don't stick Your nose in people's business. We don't want You wandering loose on the streets, putting light in our locked places, now do we?*

Stretching on either side of her, closer, much closer than the city walls, limestone wrinkles riddled the ridgeline. Open caves, all different shapes and sizes, bought up by the rich to tuck away their bones when the time came.

Jesus interrupted her reverie. "I was in the temple yesterday when one of the Pharisees pulled me aside. He asked if I did construction. I told him I wasn't as good with wood as my father had been. He stroked his beard, gave me a commission anyway."

Mary felt a tingle go through her. She thought, *we could use the cash.*

Jesus said, "Know what he's hiring me to do, ma?"

Mary shook her head.

"He wants me to cut and tool a custom door for his grave—the cave below us where the boy and his sheep sleep. That's why I brought you here. We're sitting on top of the work Windy will do through me."

He went silent. Then, he spoke, "I don't know what I just prophesied, but as I spoke, my whole body trembled. Whatever will happen will be good, very good. But not before it will be painful, very painful."

I gave her a thought, a preview for the Son who sat beside her—*the walk to the Skull is short, but the loneliness in-between stretches for an eternity.*

She shivered, throwing off that thought like an old shroud. Instead, she studied his face, deepening empathy with our Son. "What is this, Son, this 'very good, very painful?'"

He replied, "Don't know, ma. That's too far down the road for me to see. All I know is that Joe wants a grave door recessed into the stone. Shaped exactly to fit the opening, hinged with sturdy iron hinges on the left side, and he wants it finished with a hefty iron bolt and secure lock, with a small skeleton key." He smiled at his mother. "Small keys open big doors, ma—and some are even made of iron."

Mary admired his gift for speaking in parables.

He shrugged, "Just that bit about small keys and big doors—that was metaphor. The rest was about actual wood for the door, an actual millstone that Joe wants shaped and rolled in front of the cave. The metal key. The stone benches. All real and ready for actual bodies to be wrapped in graveclothes with real spices to distract the nose from all that stink."

Mary was full of unspoken questions, practical things like the kind of wood, and how thick, and how would he ever make it fit since the opening wasn't smooth, and….

Jesus interrupted, "The cave's not that deep. Joe wanted me to chisel deeper into the hill—making stone niches in the walls for him and his family. I'll get James and Jude to help me. They're better masons than me, good with stone chisels. They'll carve the niches and shape the millstone. I'll be the Door."

Mary looked at his face and considered his words. "Didn't you mean, *make* the door, Son?"

He laughed, "I started out saying that, but Windy changed my words in mid-air. Meant to be, I guess. I'll start work on it next week." He laughed and stretched out his arms on either side. "Your Door will form that door."[87]

At the time, all Mary thought was, *maybe this will pay my rent.* Martha and her husband, Mordi, hadn't mentioned her being late again with the rent. Her younger three sons were stretched tight, each with their money issues and mouths to feed. Mary made a few coins by taking in sewing from neighbors, but it was a pauper's wage.

Jesus had mentioned a guy named Joe. Moments like this made for Joe longings. Her husband had been gone so long, almost a decade. It was the rare moment when she'd loosen the screws from her floorboards long enough to let those longings out. This was one of those times. Memories of her earth husband splashed out, flooded her heart.

She'd calmed herself by praying, *Husband of Heaven, help.* Father had answered her prayer and sent Jesus.

She re-focused. She asked Son how much he would bring home after taxes. When he told her the number of shekels, minus what he'd pay his brothers and the tax collector, she smiled. The money would catch up her back rent and pay for a few more months. James, Justus, and Jude would help with groceries till she left for home in Galilee. Once Sukkoth was finished and Jesus had celebrated his thirtieth birthday, they'd travel back to Nazareth. [88]

Jesus said, "Got a surprise for you, ma." He pulled out a tiny, ancient flask from his pocket and held it up for her to see. It was full of hieroglyphics.

He pointed his finger, word by word, across the ancient Egyptian lettering and spoke words she'd never learned. He told her the story of Joseph's seed.

He said, "Once the others had gone to sleep the Night of Drought, I popped the seed back in its home for the past millennium and a half. It had already begun to sprout, so I'd added some soil inside the flask. Windy then whispered that we, you and me, should plant it at a place she would show me. Today, she prompted me."

He pointed at the loamy spot between them. "Right here, ma. We're to plant my seed at this exact spot, over Joe's sepulcher, facing that Skull."

He stared at Golgotha. "Doesn't look a bit like Caligula's skinned skull. It might look a little like me. Joe's seed, now my seed, should get plenty of sun here." Mary caught the catch in his voice.

He said, eyes flooding with tears, "This will be the world's biggest grapevine, ma."

A drumbeat of terror rose up out of the ground and grabbed Mary by the heart. A murder of crows cawed in the wind. The sky's blue folded into her mood. She drifted out of time for a moment, saw Jesus' lips moving, but could not hear him call her name. She eyed the empty crosses along Skull's base. She gazed at them the way a nursing ewe eyes the empty brush where once a wolf had waited and would yet return again. In her heart of hearts, she felt tangled in woven threads of grief, and that tapestry wrapped round and round Golgotha.

She blinked, and Husband's kind face appeared. She said, *too soon, our son will be gone. But you let me sit on this grave top, at this moment, with our only Son. You did your best to get me ready, Husband, for something very good, very painful.*

She snapped back into the moment from her reverie and found her body shaking, tears dripping on her lap. Jesus cuddled her head on his shoulder. They sat like that, side by side, while the sun crept across the sky toward mid-afternoon.

Finally, he said, "This Pharisee I mentioned? He purchased his cave a long time ago. Joe's a man of integrity, ma. Hails from a small town in Judea, Arimathea."

Jesus would one day have a nighttime conversation with Joe's cave neighbor. The neighbor's cave was two over in this row of graves. This other

Pharisee, Nicodemus, would walk and talk with Son over these graves one night while I blew round both of them. [89]

Jesus and Mary planted the sprouted seed into soil over the sepulcher in the shadow of the Skull. They fanned out the tendrils an inch deep into the warm dirt, patted the earth down all around and over Son's broken seed. The seed pushed out its tiny roots and shoots, readying itself for that day when it would push through the dark into and around the empty cave below.

Jesus took a flask of water from his other pocket and held his mother's hand under his. Together, they prayed for what would grow from this one seed. They prayed for everyone who would one day look over their shoulders and see a line of faith-filled seeds connecting each to the other, and to Father, through Son, by My breath.

Mary wasn't privy to Our thoughts and plans. We left her wondering, not knowing, having to grow her own tiny seed of faith. She had no clue why Jesus would ever choose this place to put his seed. She didn't understand until later—after many tears, and a very few years.

46

JESUS

We all settled into a new normal. I went to the temple daily, arguing Torah with friends from my yeshiva group. Father was getting me ready for my 30th birthday, and so were my friends. On that day, I would take on the role of rabbi.

After hours in the temple, I would work on Joe's project at the Bethany compound. Evenings, I would most often meet Claudia at a local restaurant in Jerusalem, close to her theatre arts studio. We'd share stories and a few drinks with friends from her group of actors and actresses. Salome, Herodias' daughter, had become Claudia's best friend, but she kept me at a distance.

One night Claudia said, "Jesus, what do I do with my mother? She keeps messaging me. A horseman lathers into town every few weeks with a sealed letter in his pouch. Always the same hysteria from mother, "Come home! I've lost my husband and son in that scummy armpit of Palestine. Come home. I need you."

I gave her the eye. "You're quite the actress. But this is a perfect time to work out issues with your mother. Set sail with Windy. Perhaps you've done all the running away you have time for in this life."

She said, "Your mother is great, and mine is bat-crap nuts. The other day, at theatre, Salome said, 'We should write a play about our crazy families. But that might get us both exiled if we hack off my new step-father or your grandmother in Rome.'"

Claudia smiled at me and shook her head sadly. "Both Herod and Grandma make me understand why tiger tamers feel safer working in the cage—at least they're protected from the people outside. Salome hasn't made up her mind whether she loves or resents her mother more."

I said, "Meanwhile, she pays for her refusals—as do you. The miracle of compound interest applies to more than the temple's money changers. It also hits the heart's purse strings. Act loving, feelings follow. Refuse loving action, hate roots and ruins you."

Claudia gave me a wink, motioning with one hand to her feet, the other to her head. "Your furnace burns both ends. I can't endure my nights. But ah, my love, we are such lovely lights." [90]

She stood and twirled, beaming. Who, I wondered, could resist such a wonder? I hugged her.

Encouraged, she continued, "Salome is immersed in theatre—writing, staging, and acting out our loves and hates. We two talk about how, at one level, our craft is like getting to play make-believe or dress-up.

"But on another level, you get to be god. For example, your Father says Ka-ZAM! and life or death happens on a grand scale. Same for a playwright, but tiny. We create something from nothing. But then, after, the tough part is letting go. Creation has a mind of its own—in the reader or the listener."

I said, "Or, in the creator."

She rode over my comment. "For example, Jesus, I've written a tragedy. Salome's part includes a dance with a lot of sexy, see-through veils and slinky hip movements. An Electra thing she does for her father, the king— complete with a murder at the end. [91] She serves up his enemy's head on a silver platter. Her character is sexy and evil, full of hubris. She kisses like a sacrificial nymphomaniac on a death cruise to the Underworld."

Claudia was on a roll. She said, "I told her, 'Salome, don't become our creation. As it is, you remind me of a tornado stuffed in an evening gown.'"

I smiled, "and what's *your* role in the play?"

"Me? I'm a pauper who sits at the gate of her castle, scraping my sores. A wandering rabbi teaches me what's real and what's illusion. Together, with clear eyes, the two of us watch Salome. She moves stiff-kneed into the castle courtyard, in a daze, holding her enemy's head before her on straight arms."

I commented, "Such grief is the gold of great theatre, and real-life as well."

Claudia smiled, "I work out my stuff on stage. You do it in the temple. We each have our platforms. We each work the crowds."

I was quiet for a while. "I listen to your plays and tell them back to you as parables, swapping Roman characters out for Galilean Jews—but life's lessons stay the same. And the two of us? We're parables in progress. Walking words. What we *do* counts more than clever, staged words."

She chewed on that, quietly digesting the meal I'd plated.

The next night, Shabbat, Claudia ate dinner with our family in Bethany, like she did every Shabbat. We Jews did our rituals, cups of wine, all that— and included her. After, she and I walked the streets of our little village. We sat overlooking Jerusalem to the east, fireflies dancing between the tips of twig-sedged grass across the rolling hills.

She said, "When good things happen—like tonight around your table—good turns to great only because I share it with you. And when we're separate, a cold, clammy ick settles in my guts. Hurt, grief, being human. All the same, I suspect, but tolerable only because I share it with you."

I squeezed her hand, lingering my touch over her ring finger, not wanting to overburden the air with words. We strolled back to the compound where her driver and carriage awaited. Before she climbed up in her buggy, I slipped her some leftovers, pasta and meatballs, that ma had made for her lunch the next day.

We went along for months in this way. I finished Joe's door. My brothers finished his niches and the millstone. Joe's grave was ready for business.

My vine grew. Ma and I took turns keeping it fertilized and pruned back.

During these halcyon days, I would sometimes wake up with the same dream—a huge wave, gathering force and size, moved me along on its crest. I guided my skiff with a small rudder—but had no sails, no oars. Just one big, clunky anchor. I knew no destination, no tomorrow.

A silky voice wove 'round my rowboat, *you'd never dare love or be loved if you knew where I was taking you. You wouldn't eat or drink or get out of bed in the morning. You wouldn't dare.*

I shook off that evil voice. *Satan, I'm in Father's care. Beat it.*

Calm returned to me, with effort. I would shake off night's terror and steer into

the day. By the time I reached temple, I would feel more anchored in the Word. As usual, my friends and I would argue Torah.

On this particular day, Laz's birthday, Claudia came to get me around noon. I'd forgotten about Laz, her, or anyone else. I was preoccupied with discussing a particularly vexing passage with my friends, one that previewed Father's here-but-not-yet Kingdom.

She said, "Ah, excuse me, Mr. Kingdom. Let's blow this joint for Jericho. Get your party clothes on."

Maltesa had sent her carriage up from Jericho— a mini-palace on wheels. Her souped-up, six-seater sported creamy leather seats, gilt-edging, and fast horses. Salome, Debbie, and my mother waited within. John stood outside, waiting. He'd planned to sit inside with us, but when he stepped up and saw Salome inside, he turned as if on a coin, choosing to sit on the carriage roof with the baggage.

Our driver lathered those horses straight down to sweatbox Jericho. Rastus and his cronies cantered alongside, keeping us safe from other men like themselves. Once we arrived at Rahab's, we partied—a blow-out 29th birthday celebration for Laz. The best wine, food, games, dancing, and storytelling. Debbie filled my glass; served me my favorite, spicy chicken wings. Then she sat on the edge of things, under the portico.

Michael, Laz's son, was now almost five years old. He was a curious joy-boy, still fond of crickets, stray dogs, and questions his mother couldn't answer. She dropped him off on my lap and said, "Here, you have a go while I dance with the birthday guy. He's better, you know since you came home. Every time he sees you, Laz lightens up and doesn't throw up. Some kind of magic healing in your presence, I suspect."

I jiggled Mike up and down, scratched behind his dog's ears, and listened to his stories. He stopped telling me about talking donkeys and gully-washer baby deliveries. Stopped full-on and asked me, "Jesus, where will today go when I wake up tomorrow?"

I told him, "Great question, Mike, and I don't rightly know. I'll talk to Father and tell you on our next visit."

He said, "but you're a grown-up. Ma said you were the smartest man she knew, even smarter than *abba*!"

I told him, "I'm grown up enough to know when I don't know." I kissed him on the forehead, and he held on, content in my lap. Soon he fell asleep and I put him, and his sister, Hope, to bed.

When I returned from putting them to bed, complete with a long, rambling bedtime story, Sheba did something very interesting. She left her husband, Samuel, and walked toward Debbie without having anyone lead her. She walked like a ballerina, gracefully stepping around small tables and small talk to sit beside my youngest sister, quiet-like—no demands for meaningful conversation. Even a casual observer would think she understood the language of the vulnerable.

In between dances, I laughed at Laz's jokes and Abby's sly humor. Whenever the band struck up a favorite tune, I pulled Claudia up, and we spun around the floor in a larger hora circle. Even John cracked up at my jokes. Waves of food and drink came from the kitchen, one after another, like tiny tidal waves. Dances and toasts and speeches whirled around and around till almost dawn. What could be better?

Then, toward sunrise—a more sober note. The Double-Cy's called Claudia and me outside Rahab's back gate. They said someone had asked for us. The blind couple led us to a recessed wooden door near their two-room apartment. Cy's lined face grew even longer. Claudia leaned over and whispered, "those vertical lines in his cheeks are deep enough to have a chariot race in there."

I looked around and saw Debbie and Sheba, a few steps behind us. The two of them held hands, the blind leading the sighted.

Cy said, "On the other side of this door is a storage room, no bigger than a closet."

Cyrena groped around, found my hand, took it. "Lord, Crispus is in there. He's dying. He never did recover from Sarah thin-slicing his throat using his own cane's poison tip. The venom's been eatin' him up, even after all this time."

Cyrena continued, "No one else wanted a used-up, sick terrorist, so we took him in—trying to act nice to a not-nice guy. Doing for him what you did for us. Anyhow, he's lingered for a long time, maybe waiting for you. He weakens, recovers some, but keeps ratcheting downhill."

She said in a quiet voice, "He'll not make it through the night."

Debbie took a step forward, eyes terrified, trembling like a twig shakes under the weight of a sparrow. She took my hand.

Cy finished, "Here's the thing. He has nightmares about what he did to your sister, Jesus, and your father, Claudia. He cries out—choking and crying. Wants to make his peace, somehow, but hain't figured it out yet."

I said, "Let's all pay him a visit."

47

CLAUDIA

Split in two. Anger rolled through me like a tsunami—but another part, probably the Jesus-part, felt still, watchful, on edge—like on the ledge outside Joseph's Seed Cave. Not compassionate exactly, but not rageful either.

The right side of my neck and my right eye flashed pain. Watchful-anger pain, off and on. Like Alexandria's Pharos Lighthouse, blinking in the night, but now re-housed in my body. Felt like when my father was killed.

I got conscious enough to watch more than just me. Debbie's fist balled up. Fist speaking for brain, "Yes!"

Jesus looked back and forth. Looked at the one who had been murdered by that man. Looked at the one his love had resurrected from a living death of selfishness. Studied each of us, back and forth.

Something shifted in me, an earthquake tremor re-arranging my furniture. Anger gave way to something softer, sadder. My Jesus-part popped up and out. Tears dribbled down my cheeks.

I wiped them away, took charge. "Okay, this will be a role rehearsal for my next play."

Jesus looked at me, head tilted to one side, curious.

I grinned at him. "Not done yet. I'm busy creating, as I speak. I'll call the production, *Mercy We*. Act One, father's murder. Act Two, mother's abandonment. Act Three, you mercy us."

I proceeded to compose myself. After all, I'd just acquired a starring role.

A thunderclap shook the house. Clouds had blown in while I was posturing. They were taking a dump on us. No warning. Rain so thick it looked like columns of water connecting heaven and earth. Solomon's Rain Pillars here in this bone-dry desert.

Windy murmured, *I'm taking the pen from your hand and writing My play. Jesus is the only star.*

I stood under the eaves, bowed forward, submitting. Rain drenched my head.

Sheba stood next to me under the eaves, rain also slamming down half a foot in front of her face. She held both hands out, catching rain in her cupped hands, bringing water to her mouth, drinking.

Jesus held his empty cup up and out, filling it slosh-full.

Debbie stood behind him, dry.

Sheba said, "I'll stand watch."

We remaining three walked into a stinky room with a creepy deathbed vibe going on. Gray-green guy on a cot, dome bald as a boiled peacock egg left too long on the rocks. Two or three greasy strands of white hair flopped over each ear, bouncing up and down while he hacked out a goober-slobbering, rib-cracking cough. A rope of yellow-green gook hung over his lower lip. Looked like he had one foot in the grave, the other on a snot gob.

Jesus took a half-step forward, arm around his sister. Debbie gagged, stomach heaving. Jesus kept his one arm around sister.

He said, "Crispus."

Called his name. What could be simpler?

The neighborhood murderer-rapist woke up, sat up, focused both eyes on the Name Caller. No eye-rolling, decoy nonsense, like in the past—fully alert, now.

Jesus took a knee beside his cot. "The two Cy's say you want to make your peace with God. That so?"

Crispus hesitated, then nodded. Flicked his gaze from Debbie to me. Sucked in green snot rope, swallowed.

Debbie deposited a puddle of vomit on the floor next to his bed. Jesus wiped her mouth with his wet sleeve. Gave her to drink from his cup of water.

I thought, *how can this kid be helped by burrowing through filth? But if Jesus loved her and let her come in? Hmm. Must be the right time. He might even see something growing in Crispus. Like the plague.*

I said, straight-faced, monotone. "Hi. I'm Claudia. You cut my father's head off and ate his brains. Pleased to meet you."

Wan smile paled his green color into a shade of plumber's putty. "If you wuzn't truthin', might be funny. Your pa the centurion?"

I narrowed my eyes, watchful. Stone-walled him.

He switched his gaze to Debbie, smiled. "Hey there, purdy girl. You done grown. Remember me?"

Debbie hid her head in Jesus' shirt, stood behind him.

I whispered to her, "you'll know when it's your time to trust Jesus with your life. You'll be terrified. That's how you know."

She flashed saucer eyes my way, nodded.

We waited. Crispus collected what was left of himself. While he passed the collection plate, my less-than-best-self took center stage, used my inside-voice. *Die, scum-turd. Your sympathy? Sadism with its make-up on.*

Not a sound escaped my mouth. A new part of me arriving?

Jesus sat on the dirt floor and wrapped his arms around his knees, making a little wall between Crispus and his sister. Motioned for Debbie to sit behind him to the left. I squatted on my haunches by his right side. Crispus lay on his bed a couple of feet in front of us.

Jesus said, "Remember throwing my sister over the cliff off your fishing pole? Remember that, Crispus?"

Green Gob's eyes glazed over. He nodded.

"And before that, remember abusing her sexually?"

Crispus swallowed hard. Looked at Debbie hiding back of Jesus. "Just twiddled with yer knobs a bit. You didn't say no. Fact was, you liked it. Fun and games we had, girly-girl."

Jesus swallowed hard, lines on his forehead all pushed up together. Right hand had a stranglehold on his opposite knee, fingertips white. Left hand reached back and touched his sister's twitching foot, took a deep breath, modeling that act for her and me—grounding us in him, Windy, and the earth.

Jesus said, "Liza and Ben mentioned your aunt's body was all rigid and purple when she died. You were the only one around, a boy of ten. Got an early start with the whole murder thing, huh?"

"She wuz goanna rat me out to the Romans. That did her in."

Jesus commented, "You mean, that was the time you *chose* to poison her?"

Crispus' eyes closed. Head tipped forward.

"And then there's Rabbus. Remember knifing him in the back and cutting his throat?"

Nod. Grin flickered.

"And that landslide you triggered, killing all those legionnaires?"

Hack-a-rack cough, shoulders moving up and down.

"And Centurion Gaius, cutting his throat, spitting in his mouth?"

Distant gaze, as through a grist of memory. Eyes blinked, up and down.

"Remember sinking *Ouroborus* and all those other ships? Throwing even your best friend to the sharks?"

Crispus squinted his eyes—like he was thinking, *how did he know that? Coughing fit.* "Yes, yes, yes. Despicable me."

Querulous tone. "So what? *Yer* God *made* me the way I is. *He* put me smack in the arsehole of the world. Ain't no surprise I'm full-a crap."

Sucked a snot gob straight up his schnozz, but then it flopped back out.

When you're unhinged, Crispus, true things come out when you're not looking.

I imagined maggots crawling around back of his eyes, eating his mind and heart. But, I wondered, was this about him, Maggot Man, or me?

I asked for help. Windy's whisper was right there, close as my breath. *I gave you a sneak peek behind his curtain. Let you see the strings and pulleys in his chest, the petting zoo in his head.*

I answered the Him inside me, *thanks, Windy*—and said to Crispus, all in one breath, "You terrorists, whining about others while calling yourself Freedom Fighters. How noble!"

I might have imagined Crispus flinching, but then again, maybe not.

I kept ranting, "You complain about what others do to you. Others' injustices. Never you—always them.

"You know what I think? *Shame on you*, not them. Pedophiles and murderers like you don't claim rightful shame. It's your right to shame those who don't agree with you."

Crispus started to say something between hacking fits.

I interrupted. "Go to hell, Crispus. Sooner's better than later."

Jesus moved his left hand from Debbie's foot to my forearm, shushing me gentle-like. Laid his right hand on Crispus' forehead. "I went over a few of your sins with you, so you'd know how much Father could forgive through me. I'm Father's amnesty program. He's *way* more merciful than you are bad, Crispus—and you're plenty bad. *Believe me.*"

Crispus' chest collapsed like a crushed paper cup. He whispered, eyelids twitching, "Mercy for me? Even one like me?"

Jesus was coopting my theatre production. Felt like kicking him in the shins but didn't—him being the Messiah.

Crispus whined, "Now I believe ya, finally. The good Lord hisself sent ya here. Death bed confession better than none, don't cha know? Lean closer, I pray, my lord. I wanna kiss you, 'fore I pass—be holied up when I go."

Uh-oh. Something stinks in Jericho.

Jesus leaned toward him.

I yelled, "No!" Lurched between Jesus and him, grabbed Crispus' right hand with both of mine, this hand that had snaked from under the covers with a dagger flashing toward Jesus' heart.

I didn't think. I acted. The huntress in me grabbed his clenched hand with both of mine, used his energy to turn his knife around, and plant it in his foul mouth—all in one split-second.

I stared down at him, breathing hard. His head was pinned to the mattress beneath him, like I'd pinned Postie's chest to another mattress a lifetime ago.

Satan's silky voice, *gotcha. Guaranteed your place in hell, bitch. This way, we can do each other like we did that once at Sepphoris. That was the place you lost your soul to me, remember?*

Crispus gurgled out his last breath, blood pumping in gouts over my hands. I could feel Satan's creepy presence, escorting Crispus home.

Jesus stretched between Debbie and me, astonished anguish on his face.

I still had my hands on Crispus' dagger, sticking out his mouth over eyes gone blank. "Thought he'd changed?"

Jesus nodded. "I so wanted him to believe, receive forgiveness, so Father could reclaim one more from the Evil One."

I said, "You keep getting surprised. Hope runs like a river outta your guts. But my opinion? Dig deep for pessimism. Postie was like Crispus. Caligula too. Jury's still out on Rabbus and me."

Jesus said, "Those others, maybe. But you? No. You've been made pure, consecrated—like you, little sister. Whole and holy in Father's eyes, because you love me. Remember, remember, remember, lessons from *our* desert furnace. Don't take in Satan's lies, by any means, at any time, Hunter Woman.

"And you, Debbie, remember Father using Claudia here and now to exact justice for you. She did it in the same way your namesake, Deborah the Prophet, executed justice in her day. Did it just like Jael with Sisera."[92]

I sat back on the floor, held his face in my hands. So glad he was alive.

I put my hands down and sat on them, just as Slow and Laz busted in the door, with the Cys behind them. Laz saw the dagger haft sticking out of Crispus' mouth. He didn't see the blood on my hands—just the blood I'd left on Jesus' face.

Laz said, "Crisp musta provoked you mighty bad, Jeez."

I brought both my hands out from under my bum, palms up. "Nope. Jesus' hands are clean. I did the deed. Jesus was showing mercy to him, and me."

Slow stared at the dagger in Crispus' mouth. "If that's his blade, don't touch the edge. For sure, poisoned."

We all left his room, walked through the pouring rain to Rahab's guest rooms for what was left of the night. Salome was sitting by a candle, reading, when I came into our room. In a sort of daze, I told her the story of what had happened. She sat silent once I'd finished my story, cross-legged on her bed. She reached over to her bedside table, took the birthday present for Laz in hand, the one she'd not yet given him. Bent over that polished, silver platter.

I planted my feet on the floor and swiveled my butt across the narrow space between our beds. Sat beside her. We both leaned over, examining the plattered heads staring back at us.

Salome patted a stray hair in place, laid down, and went to sleep. I couldn't. Too riled up. I had to *do* something. I left our room, walked around the inner courtyard in the early morning dark, doing laps. Only one wall sconce blazed away on each side of the quad.

The candle to the right of the synagogue entry door dimly lit a few table sculptures on the acacia tabletop directly beneath the light. One sculpture caught my attention. It was a woman, arms out to either side, stretched, head and body half-split in two, a daub of red dabbed over her heart. The plaque read, *Splittina.*

A puff of wind blew out the light, leaving its afterglow in my mind's eye. Must have been Windy. Why waste Light when no one's paying attention?

I agreed with Windy and became her instrument of darkness. I went around the courtyard blowing out candles, learning dark-walking skills. Then I walked up the stairs to the second floor, blowing out the solitary candle on the stairway, practicing my new craft. I walked our hallway, blowing out the lights. Snores back of doors, up and down the hall. The whole house slept.

Nothing happened here tonight, now did it? No, nothing at all.

Windy blew open a window at the end of the hall by way of reply. I heard a vague sort of whisper in the dark.

Plenty happened, Warrior Woman. I'm training you. Keep practicing. Keep my Light inside, without splitting. Son's light will soon be gone.

48

CLAUDIA

Crispus' covered body went out with the morning pee 'n poop. El Roi tapped me on the shoulder. He said, "I want you and Slow to take Crispus to the dump before you head back to Jerusalem. This'll be a training ground for royalty."

We harnessed up together and trudged Rahab's garbage cart toward the burnings. On the way down the path, I told Slow what I had done in the night. She shared with me about the table sculptures El Roi and she had made.

I said, "I can't figure out what Windy meant when she said, 'keep My light inside you without splitting.'"

Slow shrugged. "Not sure. But there are lots of ways to split, and most of them suck, believe me—I'm the queen of splitting myself into pieces. But here's the way I see it—Splittina, Lot's wife, divided between loyalties to love and faith. She chose love for her friends and faith in God at the same time. Split her studs and took her to ground."

She put her shovel down, eye-measuring our shallow grave to see if Crispus' body would fit. A strong gust of wind took her corn-silk hair, flyaway thin, and flung it straight out behind her.

She said, "I figure Hope, Faith, and Love are the big three. But if push comes to shove, choose love. After all, Jesus is more about love than anything else. Follow him."

Together we put Crispus' body in the trash on the edge of where the fires were burning, smoke in our eyes.

We pulled our cart back into Rahab's and ditched it in the stables. I washed up. Before getting on Maltesa's coach for Bethany, Slow and I hugged goodbye, each squeezing the other's pieces into place.

A few days later, I stayed with Jesus' family during the Feast of Booths. We all camped in lean-to's, getting a taste for temporary. About that time, another thing happened. Jesus celebrated his thirtieth birthday. He took pleasure in all his family and close friends. Even so, his eyes had that far-away look part-timers get. Heaven and earth scrabbled for his attention. Earth got the lesser part of that split.

The longer the birthday party went on, the more I felt like a joyless cow who moo'd melancholy over everything. Mt. Timna's dreams coiled through the mist, some clear and crisp; others, not. I shucked my dreams and let my cow-self out to pasture. I grabbed Jesus' hand and pried him away from the others. I wanted the last dance and wanted it to last. I got one of those two.

A few days after he'd taken on the mantle of rabbi, I sat at my study desk, chewing the end of a quill, going over a new play. An Imperial messenger knocked on my door. This guy was no different than the other couriers. His mouth was open wide enough to jam a return letter into it. I thought, *another mother-missive*.

It wasn't. This one came from Uncle Tibbie in Capri. I didn't dare open it alone. My parents, I'd realized, hadn't raised me to be strong. They'd raised me not to show weakness and called that strength. I went to the temple, to the man who showed strength through his weakness.

Jesus the Rabbi was going for it—debating Torah with the elders, listening and asking imponderable questions that left them scratching their heads. I stood in the shadow of a column, admiring his style. Caught his eye. He dragged himself away from the fun of a good knock-down, drag-out Torah squabble.

He walked with me through drizzle to the backside of Skull Hill, the place where we Romans crucified Jews, Samaritans, and anyone else who got on our nerves. We walked, hand in hand, beside a latticed fence that separated The Skull from Grave-Cave Row. Jesus showed me what he and his brothers had done. Oak door with iron hinges and a brass keyhole—sanded, lacquered, labeled.

We climbed up and over the top of that cave. The tall cypress trees swayed in the cool breeze. The leaves on a young grapevine fluttered in the wind, whispering.

Jesus said, "Remember Joe's seed?"

I raised my eyebrow.

He nodded. "Ma and I have been pruning, watering, weeding."

The grapevine's branches grew among blue agapanthus and wild wisteria, spreading between graves and The Skull, twining over the misty wattle wall. That young vine twined around the trellis, strong and vibrant, like it could grow and go forever.

Jesus noticed a pile of sheep poo a few yards away. Tucked some of it around the roots of that vine. A huge earthworm crawled between his fingers. I thought he'd smush it, like I would have. He carefully tucked it down in the poo and dirt, where it could feel at home. Then Worm Guy pulled snippers out of his backpack and pruned the vine a little here and there.

I did not want to love this earth or its keeper too deep. I couldn't let my heart be moved too much in his presence. No. That would split me down the middle with no hope of faith or love. So, I guarded myself from ruin—shook off what I couldn't say and wouldn't feel. Pulled out Tibbie's sealed missive from my shoulder satchel. Told Jesus to be careful. I'd been scorched by that letter, but could he get his oven mitts on and read it for me?

He prayed over it, asking Father for His will to be done. I wanted to plug my ears since I wanted *my* will to be done. That's why I brought it to Jesus. He was the only one worthy to open the scroll.

He took it in his hands and was not burnt by that fire. He studied it silently, then put it down on the grave top. Took me in his arms. Told me what was in the letter. His words pruned me down to a stub, barely above ground level.

Uncle Tibbie had arranged my marriage to Pontii at mother's request. We were to be married on Capri, at his estate. A destination wedding. Everyone who was anyone in Rome had been invited and would attend if they knew what was good for them. A ship would arrive within the month and take me from this man I loved to a man I barely tolerated.

Mother's little controlling fingers had reached me in Palestine. She was making all things ready, according to her will. All that remained was to present myself a living sacrifice on her altar. I shook with angry tears. Mother pulled me to Italy; love for Jesus pulled me to Israel. Split.

Jesus held my face with both hands, beleaguered love leaking from his eyes. I laid my head on his shoulder. Inhaled his earthy odor of sweat and sadness, sealing him into my memory, letting his touch and smell soothe me once again. I wanted to take him with me, tuck him in my heart, seal him, steal him. That part didn't work out.

Instead, I wept; Jesus wept. He said, "You've come home to yourself. Instead of putting your tears in a dream or play, you feel them now, in your body, while with me."

We rocked back and forth over an empty, rich man's grave. God-man held my grief. He took my grief personally and made it his own.

49
WINDY

Son perched once again on Judgment Cliff, staring at the horizon. Claudia's ship disappeared over that horizon. Father had arranged her homecoming, what promised to be a hard one with her mother, in Italy. He'd closed the door for her as a single woman in Palestine but opened another one to marry the future Roman Pilate—a man she would struggle to love. Jesus grieved her loss deeply but also accepted Father's judgment as better than his own.

Mary, Deborah, and Jesus had walked from Bethany to Judgment Cliff. Jesus had asked Father to jiggle loose more of Debbie's memory cobwebs. He prayed, *help her feel, help her heal.*

He said to his sister, "the last experience with Crispus was a hard one. This also will be hard. We don't know what will happen, but we'll walk through it together."

Once they entered the place where Crispus molested her, Debbie collapsed to her knees. She faced out to sea from the cave's entry and stared for the longest time, lost inside. And then, as if in slow motion, she bent her head to the ground and began to bang it on the cave's dirt floor. Jesus, on one side, held her. Mary also held her littlest child, but from the darker side of the cave. The tempest rolled through this young woman. The storm raged for most of the morning and afternoon in waves.

When the grief subsided, toward night, Jesus was hopeful. But even then, even with the ground of abuse under her feet, her memories were shrouded under the cape of childhood's amnesia. Shadowy body memories were all that remained for her.

I held those memories for her, trickled grief into her awareness now and again, through different doors. Dreams, visions, books, theatre, social media—all provide back doors, front doors, and side doors.

But here's the thing about doors, then and now. What I open, can't be sealed. What I seal, cannot be opened. [93] Doors into good judgment, memory, patience, what is real and not real; doors to an opportunity of a lifetime and the lifetime of any opportunity.

I let my three children wear themselves out. And then, the next morning, just as they climbed up, they climbed down—slowly, carefully, holding hands on the scree-riddled path. They walked home through the woods, single file.

Debbie said, "I don't know what to do with my sad and mad feelings. I come to a door and get scared, turn away. My feelings sit upfront in my wagon, steer it places I don't want to go, saying 'giddy-up.' All the while, I feel hog-tied in the back under a wet blanket."

Her older brother knelt next to her on the path. "After my rape in Rome, I had to fail, fall, get up again and again before I could let Windy work Father's healing into me.

"Your story will be different than mine, but I'll walk alongside you. Tonight, when you sleep, I'll be your night watchman. And one day, when I've gone home, each chosen breath can be a Windy-breath. If you don't know what to pray or do, it doesn't matter. Windy will take your needs to Father, and He acts on your behalf. He'll maybe not answer prayer *your* way, but He'll answer them *anyway*." [94]

Her face saddened, even more than it had been, at the mention of his going. "But I don't know how to follow you. I don't know the way."

Jesus said, "I'm only a step or two ahead of you. Put your feet where mine have been. When I go, Windy will gather up the pieces of your mind and give them back to you, whole, but only a step at a time. She'll comfort and befriend you, just as He's done with me."

Debbie looked confused. "Windy's a he, then a she—make up your mind."

Jesus blew a little truth in her ear. "Remember, Windy's he and she— and neither—but all you need in any moment. All you need."

Jesus took them down the King's Highway. The road dwindled to lesser ones, fainter trails, and then goat trails. Debbie put her feet where Jesus' feet had been.

Jesus found a familiar cave beside a stream. A fire still smoked. The entire skin of a lone wolf had been stretched out over a wooden frame next to the fire. A light skin of ash covered the stretched-out wolf. An unblemished, live lamb lay tethered to the wolf's frame. The skinned wolf's eyes glittered. The lamb shook itself, and ash flew all around.

A parchment from an animal skin had been cured and nailed on the crossbeam of a stake connecting wolf and lamb. Whether it was cut from a wolf or sheep was not clear.

A bold scrawl, in Hebrew—

Who would have guessed a Lamb could shepherd a wolf?

Jesus read the parchment out loud, and Mary teared up. Jesus spoke loudly enough for shadows to hear, "This place looks lived in. The fire still burns."

I blew some ash into the creases of Jesus' face. He spoke again loudly, prophetically, cryptically— "Some of this ash will be un-done one day, Barabbas."

Mother and sister and Jesus had no idea that Son spoke of his resurrection day, when Leah and their children would be raised to walk the earth again with Rabbus. Mary didn't understand, but she listened well to My voice, and harbored Father's peace.

Father reminded her, through my whisper, of the ear inside a heart. *You do so well, daughter, listening with your heart's ear.*

She replied, *Husband, you chose me, an insignificant girl from a no-name family in a nothing village. Let it be to me according to your Word.*

Jesus took them down to the Jordan where he'd walked with his mother to Passover so long ago, the time when he'd first seen how the tapestry of grief wound through light to dark, and back again.

They caught up to a young shepherd, all ruddy of face, leading his fat-tailed flock to pasture. He looked long at my Son with curious eyes. I prompted him. He offered Jesus his staff.

Son smiled at the boy and blessed him. He took the staff, leaned on it. The boy led his sheep off along a side trail toward a brook.

Jesus looked left, up in the hills, toward Samaria. Mt. Gerizim hovered under blue mist in the distance. A single man sat high on a foothill's outcropping. Son could hardly tell shadow from rock or rock from man—

until the man lifted his chin, and howled at the full moon rising over Gerizim.

Son raised his staff in greeting to Rabbus.

The man raised his arm back in greeting before he pulled back into the shadow of the cliff. He dozed, warmed by his sheepskin. I let him sleep, and then, I jolted him awake by sounding a bell in his ear that tolled the hour. Son's voice came to him on my wind, "lay 'em down, Rabbus—skinning knives, throwing knives. They're all too heavy. Lay 'em down. Don't study war no more."

Rabbus kept sharpening his blades. His stropping movements were swift, frugal, exact—a marriage of wolf and tanner. Yet still, still, something inside him soaked in Jesus' words, like a dry bean in river water. He reached into his pocket, felt Leah's small birthing stone. Rolled it around in his passing currents.

Below, the Jordan rushed on. Jesus led his small flock of two 'round a bend in that river. A white dove floated over the branch of an olive tree. Thunder rolled. Sun shimmered behind a dark cloud. One golden ray broke open on Son. Father and I sang our pleasure in Son.

Beyond the tree and below our sun, a crowd gathered around a rough-cut man standing waist-deep in the Jordan. He wore a leather girdle over coarse camel hair. He stood in the Jordan, baptizing anyone wanting to make public their private faith, one person at a time.

Jesus took a step toward him. John met his eyes. The cousins smiled at each other, right before Jesus stepped in the river.

End of Book Four

Beginning of the Gospels

DISCUSSION QUESTIONS FOR GROUPS

1. **Homecoming.** What does home mean to you? Getting clear on this will help with the whole homecoming theme. Some comings-home are a lot less than what they're cracked up to be. Rabbus came home to a dead wife (chapter 20), Crispus came home to hell, Claudia came home to claim her own body, and her unfinished mother issues. Slow's part-selves came home to a non-dissociated sense of self (chapter 43).

   Home. has been famously defined as the place people will take you when no one else will. Others think of it as a resting place in the heart. Contrast what home is, and isn't, from your way of thinking.

2. **Abuse.** Some abuse, like what Jesus experienced, is vivid in one's mind. Other such memories of abuse, like what Deborah experienced as a small child, may be fuzzy, or even absent. Body memories alone mark the grief by *that* roadside.

   Such early abuse may confound and perplex. Devilish feelings and false memories may evolve. Other times, a pervasive sense of disorientation or loss of reality might follow a person. Still other times, somatic illness or psychoses or dissociative disorders plague a person. Windy comments that there are many doors to recovery (chapter 49). What open or closed doors to recovery from abuse have you experienced, past or present?

3. **Vengeance.** Sheba describes vengeance as lazy grief. Rabbus relishes it. Crispus gets sliced with his own poison blade and knifed with his own dagger as he seeks revenge. Jesus takes a higher road, compassionately aiding his enemy. What's your experience with retaliation and revenge? How is this working out for you? Would you like to make any changes in your response to vengeful thoughts and feelings? Did this book open any hopeful doors for you in the process of dealing justly in an unjust world?

4. **Water.** Abby pressed to redefine water, after Windy lasered tight her pee bag. Slow just wanted a drink of the wet stuff. Jesus pressed into hard rock with both hands and asked for help. Water's absence kills. Water also can flood or come in cup-sized drinks. What "tells" alert you to thirst? How do you sate dry places inside you?

5. **Animals.** Goodness was a mule who acted smarter than most people (chapter 14). How do pets, farm animals, or your body instruct your mind with clear seeing?

6. **Memory.** Eggie and Ehud dance with Slow on this issue (chapter 6). We often invent our memories even as they invent us. Personal memories have different streams: photo albums, what relatives have told you, actual recollection, the pressure of current narratives or future hopes that sculpt past into future.

    Windy teaches that memory and truth do not play nicely with each other. Using a financial metaphor, discuss your own memory "bank"— deposits, withdrawals, and accrued compound interest. Start with one or two specific "memories" from one or more streams listed above.

7. **Clarity.** Clear-sightedness is storied variously: blind leading the sighted, night-walkers in canyons or courtyards, parables of illusion and reality, children playing hide and seek in desert moonlight with mommy while they wonder what's real and what's not real. In many ways, *Jesus' Silent Years* is a primer in listening, seeing, and obeying the Holy Spirit. Ask Windy for help in discerning what's the next step you need to take in your journey.

8. **Footing.** Standing on thin air or sitting on Jesus' shoulders as he air-walks, short drops off stacks of spice, walking on slippy scree, standing on status—all are metaphors that focus on footing. What is your preferred grounding, the place you feel most secure in your standing?

9. **Splitting.** Splittina is an image for division within the self. Lot's wife divided before she turned into a pillar of Salt. Slow was fissured by abuse and learned to cope with a house divided. Debbie felt life just happened to her, and split choice from fate. Claudia split theater and dreams from real life. How were you prompted to integrate split-off chunks of your brilliant and plodding or despicable part-selves?

10. **Faith.** Fate fuels indolence. Faith struggles. Shoulder-shrug fate contrasts with brawny, mysterious faith (end of chapter 10). What's your *lived-out* belief as you struggle for footing on this slippy slide bar between fate and faith?

     Jesus often stood on the cusp of not knowing his next step. When you stand at the intersection of fate and faith, not knowing what to do next, what insights did you gain from these imagined Jesus' stories?

11. **Friends.** Sheba advises Slow not to blab her stuff on the street corner, but only to a handful. These stories were about Jesus and his handful of friends. They helped him learn to receive help as well as give it, learn to be unoffendable, learn that right relationship is more important than being right. Name and claim, if you can, those you trust, have trusted, and are yet learning to trust with your vulnerability and character flaws. In other words, how are *you* fixed for close friends?

Dear Reader,

Thanks for reading *Jesus' Silent Years*. This story has ended, but yours and mine continue. Practical life skills, such as breathing and inquiring of Windy, emerged as I imagined Jesus' life as a young man. His Spirit twined with mine, and I grew up more. How were you influenced? I'd like to hear from you. Write me your comments or questions at vance@vanceshepperson.com or visit me at www.vanceshepperson.com.

Reviews are hard to come by in our world. You have power to influence others.

If you've been helped through these "exercises in holy imagination," would you post a review on Amazon's product page? Your post might help another follow in Jesus' footsteps more closely—maybe even save a life.

Inquire of God what your next step might be, as Jesus did. See what happens. Listen well. Perhaps no review, but a prayer for your day and those you love. Perhaps a call to action.

Go to my product page on Amazon.com and leave your comments.

Thank you so much for reading *Jesus' Silent Years*, and for spending time with me.

Grateful,
Vance

ENDNOTES

[1] This Latin phrase describes death, suffering, and loss as necessary suffering. https://dailystoic.com/amor-fati-love of fate/

[2] This story happened some 45 years later, but with Romans against Jews. According to Josephus, the siege of Masada by Roman troops at the end of the First Jewish–Roman War, about 72 AD, ended in the mass suicide of 960 people. *The Wars of the Jews*, by Flavius Josephus, translated by William Whiston, Project Gutenberg, Book IV, Chapter 7.

[3] John 18: 37-38, *Everyone who cares for truth, who has any feeling for the truth, recognizes my voice. Pilate said, "What is truth?"* MSG

[4] Albania: The state of a nation". *ICG Balkans Report N°111.* p. 15. The coastal Chimara region of Southern Albania has always had a predominantly ethnic Greek population.

[5] Deuteronomy 29:29, *GOD, our God, will take care of the hidden things but the revealed things are our business-MSG*

[6] Reference to I Samuel 3:10, God was trying to wake up his prophet, so He could speak to a wide-awake person.

[7] 2 Kings 6:16-22 tells the story of Elisha in a similar situation.

[8] Esther 6:1-2 recounts a similar story of a king's interrupted night's sleep, and the results of a late-night history reading.

[9] The seat of long-term memory, the hippocampi, are shaped like sea horses, one each in right and left hemispheres of the brain, in the medial-temporal lobes.

[10] See *Adventures in Memory: The Science and Secrets of Remembering and Forgetting*, Hilde and Ylva Ostby, Greystone Publishers, Vancouver, BC, Canada, 2018, p 2.

[11] Judges 3:22, a counterbalance for the scripture, where Ehud couldn't get his sword out of the Moabite King, Eglon the first, because the king's fat sank over the haft of the blade.

[12] Matthew 19:24, Jesus humorously says it's easier for a rich man to enter heaven than for a camel to pass through the eye of the needle.

[13] Reference here is a shadow of Slow's dream of her mother approaching heaven's gates in *Jesus' Silent Years, Foundations*. In her dream, Gabriel meets Ester and slams shut the gate.

[14] Relic discovered by archeologists from ancient Moab, André Lemaire The Mesha Stele and the Omri Dynasty in *Ahab Agonistes: The Rise and Fall of the Omri Dynasty*, Edited by Lester L. Grabbe. Continuum International Publishing Group. 2007

[15] A quote from the White Queen to Alice, in Wonderland— "It's a poor sort of memory that only works backwards," Lewis Carroll, *Through the Looking-Glass, 1871.*

[16] Romans 8:1, *Those who enter into Christ's being-here-for-us no longer have to live under a continuous, low-lying black cloud. A new power is in operation. MSG*

[17] Matthew 5:8, *You are blessed when you can show people how to cooperate instead of compete or fight; that's when you discover who you really are, and your place in God's family. MSG*

[18] Galatians 5:1, "It is for freedom that Christ has set us free. Stand firm, then, and do not let yourselves be burdened by a yoke of slavery." *NIV*

[19] Romans 8:2, *The Spirit of life in Christ, like a strong wind, has magnificently cleared the air, freeing you from a fated lifetime of brutal tyranny at the hands of sin and death. MSG*

[20] Proverbs 6:16-19, *Here are six things that God hates, and one more that he loathes with a passion: eyes that are arrogant, a tongue that lies, hands that murder the innocent, a heart that hatches evil plots, feet that race down a wicked track, a mouth that lies under oath, a troublemaker in the family. MSG*

[21] Esther 4:16, *Esther said, 'I will go to the king, even though it is against the law. And if I perish, I perish.' NIV*

[22] Ephesians 4:16, *Jesus keeps us in step with each other. His very breath and blood flow through us. MSG*

[23] Romans 8:5, *Those who think they can do it on their own end up obsessed with measuring their own moral muscle but never get around to exercising it in real life. Those who trust God's action in them find that God's Spirit is in them—living and breathing God! MSG*

[24] John 21:17, story here is reminiscent of Jesus asking Peter three times if he loved him, to balance out Peter's three public denials of Jesus.

[25] Tobianah, Vicky. "Pianist explores Hatikva's origins". *Canadian Jewish News*. 16 May 2017

[26] Cytowic, Richard E. (2002). *Synesthesia: A Union of the Senses* (2nd ed.). Cambridge, Massachusetts: MIT Press.

[27] Reminiscent of Portia's speech, "The quality of mercy is not strained. It droppeth as the gentle rain from heaven upon the place beneath. It is twice blest: It blesseth him that gives and him that takes. 'Tis mightiest in the mightiest; it becomes the throned monarch better than his crown."—William Shakespeare, *Merchant of Venice*, Act 4, Scene 1.

[28] Personal communication, Major Ian Thomas, founder of Capernwray Hall, Torchbearers Association, UK,1970.

[29] Hebrews 11:6, *Each one of these people of faith died not yet having in hand what was promised, but still believing. How did they do it? They saw it way off in the distance, waved their greeting, and accepted the fact that they were transients in this world. People who live this way make it plain that they are looking for their true home. MSG*

[30] Romans 8:26, *God's Spirit is right alongside, helping us along. If we don't know how or what to pray, it doesn't matter. He does our praying in and for us, making prayer out of our wordless sighs, our aching moans. MSG*

[31] Romans 8:24, *waiting doesn't diminish us any more than waiting diminishes a pregnant mother. We are enlarged in the waiting.... The longer we wait, the larger we become, and the more joyful our expectancy. MSG*

[32] John 14: 23, *A loveless world, said Jesus, is a sightless world. MSG*

33 1 Samuel 15:2 mentions the Amalekite's battle tactics—picking off the strays from passing travelers.

34 See Numbers 22:21-34 for the story of this talking donkey and how he was given the gift of speech. God spoke to the stubborn Jew through the mouth of his mule and an angel. Both ass and angel gave the man new eyes to see, new ears to hear.

35 Reference is to an earlier volume in this series, *Jesus' Silent Years: Journey*—Goodness responded to spiritual energies that Slow couldn't see, broke Rastus' willful spirit, and his legs.

36 Higgins, Reynold (1988) "The Colossus of Rhodes," in *The Seven Wonders of the Ancient World*, Peter A. Clayton and Martin Jessop Price (eds.). Psychology Press.

37 Incest was reported between Caligula and his three younger sisters, Agrippina the Younger, Drusilla, and Livilla. After he got bored with them, he pimped them out to other men. Cassius Dio, *Roman History*, LIX.11, LIX.22; Suetonius, *The Lives of Twelve Caesars*, Life of Caligula, 24.

38 Matthew 6:14-15, *In prayer there is a connection between what God does and what you do. You can't get forgiveness from God, for instance, without also forgiving others. If you refuse to do your part, you cut yourself off from God's part. MSG*

39 John 14:28, *If you loved me, you would be glad I'm on my way to the Father, because the Father is the goal and purpose of my life. MSG*

40 Philippians 2:9-10, *Because of that obedience, God lifted him high and honored him far beyond anyone or anything, ever, so that all created beings in heaven and on earth—even those long ago dead and buried—will bow in worship before this Jesus Christ. MSG*

41 Historical reports vary, but many agree that Caligula smothered Tiberius in bed with his own pillow when the older man was age 77, in AD 37. Caligula was assassinated at age 28, four years later, on January 22, AD 41, after he had ruled as emperor only four years. A group of men stabbed Caligula 30 times. He was betrayed by his own blind refusal to see what was happening, within and around him. Suetonius, *The Lives of Twelve Caesars*, Life of Caligula, 45–47.

[42] Matthew 7:13, *Enter through the narrow gate. For wide is the gate and broad is the road that leads to destruction, and many enter through it. But small is the gate and narrow the road that leads to life, and only a few find it. NIV*

[43] Dio, Cassius, *Roman History*, volume 59, p 28; C. Suetonius Tranquillus, *The Lives of the Twelve Caesars*, Life of Caligula, pp.14, 55.

[44] Genesis 33:13-14, *But Jacob said, "My master [Esau], see that the children are frail. And the flocks and herds are nursing, making for slow going. If I push them too hard, even for a day, I'd lose them all. So, master, you go on ahead of your servant, while I take it easy at the pace of my flocks and children. MSG*

[45] Luke 9:33-34, *Peter said to Jesus, 'Master, this is a great moment! Let's build three memorials: one for you, one for Moses, and one for Elijah.' He blurted this out without thinking. While he was babbling on like this, a light-radiant cloud enveloped them. MSG*

[46] For this story, see Genesis 21:15-19.

[47] http://www.unmuseum.org/pharos.htm

[48] Sophocles (1991). *Sophocles: Oedipus the King, Oedipus at Colonus, Antigone*. Translated by David Grene. University of Chicago Publishers. p. Line 48.

[49] To learn more of Apollos, check out Acts 18:24-25, *MSG*

[50] John 20:22, *Then he took a deep breath and breathed into them. "Receive the Holy Spirit. MSG*

[51] Matthew 11:29, *Walk with me and work with me—watch how I do it. Learn the unforced rhythms of grace. I won't lay anything heavy or ill-fitting on you. MSG*

[52] Matthew 11:29, This identity statement from Windy to Jesus is the only self-description given by him in all the Bible, same verse as last note, but different version, different connotations: *Take my yoke upon you and learn of me; for I am meek and lowly in heart: and you shall find rest unto your souls. KJV*

[53] Romans 8:7, *Focusing on the self is the opposite of focusing on God. Anyone completely absorbed in self ignores God, ends up thinking more about self than*

God. That person ignores who God is and what he is doing. And God isn't pleased at being ignored. MSG

[54] John the Baptist's clothing was carefully chosen to convey a message. [His] leather belt is a symbol not seen for many years, *many years* in the land of Israel. *Mothers would tell their children of the days long past of men who entered towns wearing a leather belt, men who spoke from the heart of God, who prophesied of a coming day when justice would be meted out and the faithful to God would enter a new golden age.* That leather belt was the symbol of a true prophet of God. Clothing made of camel's hair was course, itchy, stingy. He wore this garment, which no normal person would wear because it was visibly uncomfortable. He was showing his rebellion against the corrupt governmental and religious leaders who made their fortunes off the back of the common people causing them to live in poverty and suffering as if they were living in clothing covered with camel's hair. He ate locust and honey not because he was a wild man but because it was kosher (Leviticus 11:21-23) and to show he followed religious law. There is a small bird in the desert that flock together in such swarms that Bedouins call them locusts. They are a food source for desert dwellers as they are easily caught." https://www.chaimbentorah.com/2020/02/aramaic-word-study-vipers/?inf_contact_key=47eed7764ad734f7abbbd08de04e71d0680f8914173f9191b-1c0223e68310bb1

[55] Matthew 6:13. *MSG*

[56] Reference here is to a waking nightmare Tiberius had experienced in Rome, under Palatine Hill, when his mother had summoned Jesus, in order to assassinate him. *Jesus' Silent Years, volume II, Parable.*

[57] Tiberius refers to various experiences in which Jesus had saved his life. See volumes I, II, and III in *Jesus' Silent Years* for those stories.

[58] Genesis 39 tells the story of Joseph and Potiphar's wife.

[59] Acts 2:38, *each of you be immersed on the authority of Yeshua the Messiah into forgiveness of your sins, and you will receive the gift of the Ruach HaKodesh! CJB*

[60] Psalm 19:2,3, *Madame Day holds classes every morning, Professor Night lectures each evening. Their words aren't heard, their voices aren't recorded, but their silence fills the earth. Unspoken truth is spoken everywhere. MSG*

[61] Luke 19:40, *I tell you," Jesus replied, "if they keep quiet, the stones will cry out. MSG*

[62] Hosea 7:8-10, *Ephraim is half-baked. Strangers suck him dry, but he doesn't even notice. His hair has turned gray— he doesn't notice. Bloated by arrogance, big as a house, Israel's a public disgrace. Israel lumbers along oblivious to GOD, despite all the signs, ignoring GOD. MSG*

[63] Isaiah 6:6, *one of the angel-seraphs flew to me. He held a live coal that he had taken with tongs from the altar. He touched my mouth with the coal—MSG*

[64] John 17: 2, *MSG*

[65] Suetonius, *The Lives of Twelve Caesars*, Life of Caligula

[66] Matthew 27:26, *Then he (Pilate) pardoned Barabbas. But he had Jesus whipped, and then handed over for crucifixion. MSG*

[67] Matthew 27:51-53, *Tombs opened up, and many bodies of believers asleep in their graves were raised. After Jesus' resurrection, they left the tombs, entered the holy city, and appeared to many. MSG*

[68] Isaiah 19:19-25 prophesies this union of long-time enemies who will one day join around the Messiah, worshipping him in Jerusalem.

[69] Psalm 22:6, a Messianic prophecy: *And here I am, a nothing—an earthworm, something to step on, to squash. MSG*

[70] Matthew 27:19, *While court was still in session, Pilate's wife sent him a message: "Don't get mixed up in judging this noble man. I've just been through a long and troubled night because of a dream about him. MSG*

[71] Pontii, by one reputable account, was forced by Emperor Caligula to commit suicide by falling on his own sword, in the year 39 AD. Maier, Paul L. (1971). "The Fate of Pontius Pilate". *Hermes*. 99 (H. 3): 362–371.

[72] John 14:26, *The Friend, the Holy Spirit whom the Father will send at my request, will make everything plain to you. He will remind you of all the things I have told you. MSG.*

73 An ancient symbol of being watchful from within and without by both feminine and masculine energies.

74 Egyptian for "Revealer of Secrets;" Hebrew interpretation is "Savior of the World." In English, Joseph, son of Jacob, the Vizar of all Egypt under Pharaoh Ahmose, founder of the 18th Dynasty of Egypt (1550-1525 BC).

75 The following reference details seventy-five similarities between Joseph and Jesus, some more reasonable than others. Regardless of any individual comparison's validity, Joseph is widely accepted as a foreshadowing, or type of Christ, by biblical scholars. http://www.bible.ca/d-bible-archeology-maps-timeline-chronology-Joseph-types-Christ-Shadows-Antitypes-similarities-comparisons-2166-1876BC.htm#full

76 See this reference for how long seeds last. http://timeline.com/methuselah-judean-date-palm-b3782ff1d731

77 John 17:12, *As long as I was with them, I guarded them in the pursuit of the life you gave through me; I even posted a night watch, and not one of them got away, except for the rebel bent on destruction. MSG*

78 Psalm 130: 5-6, *I pray to GOD—my life a prayer—and wait for what he'll say and do. My life's on the line before God, my Lord, waiting and watching till morning, waiting and watching till morning. MSG*

79 See Job 38, God's reply to Job's misery.

80 Isaiah 53:2, *He grew up before him like a tender shoot, and like a root out of dry ground. NIV*

81 John 15:1-16

82 This is a foreshadowing of Ezekiel's vision of dry bones coming to life; people from all walks and streams of life coming together. See Ezekiel 37.

83 Revelation 22:1-2. These images foreshadow John's apocalyptic phantasma, the end of all our journeys: *Then the Angel showed me Water-of-Life River, crystal bright.... The Tree of Life was planted on each side of the River, producing twelve kinds of fruit, a ripe fruit each month. MSG*

84 John 7:37-38, *On the final and climactic day of the Feast, Jesus took his stand. He cried out, "If anyone thirsts, let him come to me and drink. Rivers*

of living water will brim and spill out of the depths of anyone who believes in me. MSG

[85] Luke 2:33-35

[86] John 15:15, *I've named you friends because I've let you in on everything I've heard from the Father. MSG*

[87] John 10: 7-9, *Then Jesus said to them again, "Most assuredly, I say to you, I am the door of the sheep. All who ever came before Me are thieves and robbers, but the sheep did not hear them. I am the door. If anyone enters by Me, he will be saved, and will go in and out and find pasture. NKJV*

[88] This article makes a case for Jesus being born in the fall, not in December. Whatever. Worth a read, but only for the seriously studious: "...Not everything is as it seems. For instance, that sheep only give birth in the spring is true for most sheep in the world. However, the Awassi, a fat-tailed sheep, is a local breed found only in southeastern Turkey, Syria, Lebanon, Jordan, Iraq, Cyprus, and Israel. It has been found that when rams are introduced to the ewe Awassi flock while the lambs were weaning from spring birth, the sheep give birth in autumn - indicating that they had become pregnant while the lambs were still weaning. So, given the fertility of the Awassi sheep, the number of lambs required for Temple sacrifices and the skill of the Temple Priests in managing sheep found locally; it is entirely plausible for the Messiah to have been born in the autumn as the scriptural account indicates: Yeshua was born earlier in the year, in the fall, during the festival of Sukkoth, "the Feast of Tabernacles." Yeshua was 33 1/2 years old at the time of his death. His ministry begins at age 30 (Luke 3: 23) with his baptism by John the Immerser approximately six months *prior* to the first Passover of His ministry (John 1:33, 2:13, 23). The second Passover is recorded in John 5:1. If the "feast" mentioned here is not the Passover Feast, then it would be one of the other two major feasts, either the Feast of Weeks (seven weeks after the second Passover) or the Feast of Tabernacles (six months after the second Passover) - but, still occurring *within the same year.* The third Passover, at the feeding of the 5,000, is mentioned in John 6:4 with the fourth and final Passover, coming when he is crucified, mentioned in John 11:55. Using this chronological information, it appears that Yeshua's ministry lasted around 3 1/2 years. He was crucified at the

Hebrew feast of *Pesach* (Passover) which occurs in the spring (John 19:13-15). So, dialing back six months to the beginning of his public ministry at age 30 would place it into early fall (September or October as there are six months between Passover and the Feast of Tabernacles) which would also be when Yeshua was born 30 years earlier - not in December. *Sukkoth* (the feast of Tabernacles) is also marked in late September to early October (depending on the lunar cycle.... It would be so like the Father to arrange it this way." http://hethathasanear.com/Birth.html

[89] John 3: 1-21 tells the story of Jesus' talk with Nicodemus.

[90] "My candle burns at both ends; it will not last the night; but ah, my foes, and oh, my friends—it gives a lovely light!" Edna St. Vincent Millay, *Figs from Thistles: First Fig*

[91] Electra, a play by the ancient, Sophocles, refers to a daughter's complex, tragic relationship with her father.

[92] See Judges 4:17-22 for the story.

[93] Isaiah 22:22, Revelation 3:7

[94] John 17: 10-12, *Holy Father, guard them.... As long as I was with them, I guarded them in the pursuit of the life you gave through me. I even posted a night watch and not one of them got away, except for the rebel bent on destruction. MSG*